Priv

Maybe I was meant to be the one to discover Christopher's diary. All of us knew the legend of Foxworth, but no one really knew the whole truth. It wouldn't be long before I would.

I picked up the book and continued reading like someone starving for news from the outside world, like someone locked in an attic . . .

> I have to be as honest as I can about what I saw, what I heard, and especially what I felt. I think it's important that more people know what really happened to us before and afterward. Cathy used to call us flowers in the attic, withering away. It helped her to think of us that way. But we weren't flowers. We were young, beautiful children who trusted that those who loved us would always protect us even better than we could protect ourselves.
>
> We weren't the creations of someone's imagination. We were real flesh and blood. We were locked away by selfish greed and by cruel hearts. How that happened and what became of us is too important to just let it disappear in the dying memories of those who lived it.

V.C. ANDREWS®

CHRISTOPHER'S DIARY: SECRETS OF FOXWORTH

V.C. Andrews® Books

V.C. ANDREWS®

Christopher's Diary:
SECRETS of
FOXWORTH

POCKET BOOKS

New York   London   Toronto   Sydney   New Delhi

Pocket Books
A Division of Simon & Schuster, Inc.
1230 Avenue of the Americas
New York, NY 10020

Following the death of Virginia Andrews, the Andrews family worked with a carefully selected writer to organize and complete Virginia Andrews's stories and to create additional novels, of which this is one, inspired by her storytelling genius.

This book is a work of fiction. Any references to historical events, real people, or real places are used fictitiously. Other names, characters, places, and events are products of the author's imagination, and any resemblance to actual events or places or persons, living or dead, is entirely coincidental.

Copyright © 2014 by Vanda Productions, LLC

All rights reserved, including the right to reproduce this book or portions thereof in any form whatsoever. For information address Pocket Books Subsidiary Rights Department, 1230 Avenue of the Americas, New York, NY 10020.

First Pocket Books mass market edition November 2014

V.C. ANDREWS® and VIRGINIA ANDREWS® are registered trademarks of the Vanda General Partnership

POCKET and colophon are registered trademarks of Simon & Schuster, Inc.

For information about special discounts for bulk purchases, please contact Simon & Schuster Special Sales at 1-866-506-1949 or business@simonandschuster.com.

The Simon & Schuster Speakers Bureau can bring authors to your live event. For more information or to book an event, contact the Simon & Schuster Speakers Bureau at 1-866-248-3049 or visit our website at www.simonspeakers.com.

Cover design by Anna Dorfman
Cover photographs © Jane Mammey/Stock4B/Getty Images (Boy); Lowe/Vetta/Getty Images (House & Trees)

Manufactured in the United States of America

10 9 8 7 6 5 4 3 2 1

ISBN 978-1-4767-9058-9
ISBN 978-1-4767-9061-9 (ebook)

Christopher's Diary:
SECRETS of
FOXWORTH

Early Days

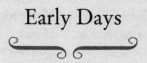

"Where are you going today, Dad?" I asked.

It was Saturday, and he hadn't mentioned any new construction job. I had come out of the kitchen, where I had just finished the breakfast dishes, and I saw him in the entryway pulling on his reluctant knee-high rubber boots, the muscles in his neck and face looking like rubber bands ready to snap. He already had his khaki "aged like wine" leather coat and faded U.S. Navy cap on. His tool belt lay beside him on the oak wood bench he had built, its heavy leather belt curled on itself like some sleeping snake. It had been a birthday present from my mother nearly ten years ago, but with the tender loving care he gave it, it looked like it had been bought yesterday.

I wasn't surprised to see him dressing like this. It was October, and we were having weird weather. Some days were cooler than usual, and then suddenly, some days were much warmer, and we also had more rainy ones in Charlottesville for this time of the year. Whenever anyone complained about the unusual changes in the weather, Dad loved to resurrect an old '50s expression, "Blame it on the Russians," rather than just saying "Climate change." Most people had no idea what "Blame it on the Russians" meant, least of all any of my friends, and few had the patience to listen to any explanation he might have. Dad wasn't old enough to personally remember, of course, but he told me his father had said it so often that it became second nature for him, too.

"Oh. Didn't I say anything about it at breakfast?"

"You didn't say much about anything this morning, Dad. You had your nose in the newspaper most of the time, sniffing the words instead of reading them," I reminded him. He said that was something my mother would complain about, too. She used the exact same expression. She told him that eating breakfast with him was like sleepwalking through a meal.

My reliance on any of my mother's expressions, whether vaguely remembered or coming from my dad's descriptions, always brought a broad smile to his face. As if he had tiny dimmer switches behind them, his hazel eyes would brighten. Perhaps because of his constant time in the sun or his worry and sorrow, the lines in his forehead deepened and darkened more each year. His closely trimmed reddish-brown full-face beard had been showing a little premature gray in it lately, too. Dad was only forty-six, and ironically, there was no gray in his full head of thick hair, which he kept long but neatly trimmed. He wore it the same way he had when my mother was alive. He said she was jealous of how naturally rich and thick it was and forbade him to return to the military-style cut he had when they first met.

"Got to go inspect this mansion that burned down a second time in 2003. Herm Cromwell called me at the office just before I left yesterday, and I promised to do it today and get back to him even though it's the weekend. Bank's open half a day today. He's been working hard on taking the property off the bank's liabilities since that nutcase abandoned it and went off to preach the gospel. Herm wants me to estimate the removal and see if the basement is still intact. The bank has a live one."

"A live one?"

"A client considering buying and building on the property, which, after two fires and all that bizarre history, hasn't been easy to sell. Why? What are you doing today? What did I forget? Was I supposed to do something with you, go somewhere with you?" He pulled his lips back like someone who was anticipating a gust of bad news or criticism.

"No. I'm not doing anything special. I was going to pick up Lana and hang out at the mall."

Lately, Lana and I had become inseparable. I was close with many of my girlfriends, but Lana's parents were divorced, and sometimes her problems seemed close to mine, even if divorce wasn't what made my father a single parent.

He relaxed, smiled, and shook his head gently. "'Hang out?' You make me think of Mrs. Wheeler's laundry. She still doesn't have a dryer in her house.

Don'tcha know they call you kids 'mall rats' these days? I hear they're coming up with a spray or something."

I laughed but nodded. Ever since I got my driver's license last year, I looked for places to go, if for nothing else but the drive. As I watched Dad continue getting ready to leave, I thought about what he had said for a moment. And then it hit me: inspect the foundation of a mansion that had burned down a second time?

"This property you're going to, it's not Foxworth Hall, is it?"

He paused as if he wasn't sure he should tell me and then nodded. "Sure is," he said.

Foxworth, I thought. I had seen the property only once, and not really close up, but all of us knew the legends that began with the first building, before the first fire. More important, my mother had been third cousin to Malcolm Foxworth, which made me a distant cousin of the children who supposedly had been locked in the attic of the mansion for years. So much of that story was changed and exaggerated over time that no one really knew the whole truth. At least, that was what my father told me.

The man who had inherited it, Bart Foxworth, was weird, and no one had much to do with him. If anything, the way he had lived in the restored mansion only reinforced all the strange stories about the Foxworth family. He had little to do with anyone in the community and always had someone between him and anyone he employed. They called him another

Phantom of the Opera. He had family living with him, but they had different names, and people believed they were cousins, too. One of them, who lived there only a few years before dying in a car accident, was a doctor who worked in a lab at the University of Charlottesville. Except for him, the feeling was that insanity ran in the family like tap water. At least, that was the way my father put it when he was pushed to say anything, which he hated to do.

"I'd like to come along," I said.

Three years before my mother had died, Foxworth Hall had burned down for a second time. I was just five years and five months old at the time of her death. I really didn't know very much about the place until I was twelve and one of my classmates, Kyra Skewer, discovered from gossip she had overheard when her mother was on the phone with friends that I was a distant cousin of the Foxworths. She began to tell others in my class, and before I knew it, they were looking at me a little oddly. Because everyone assumed the Foxworth family was crazy, many believed that their madness streamed through the blood of generations and possibly could have infected mine. The stories about the legendary Malcolm Foxworth and others in the family were the kind told around campfires at night when everyone was challenged to tell a scary tale. This one's parents or that one's uncle or someone's older brother swore they had seen ghosts and even unexplainable lantern lights in the night.

Few tales were scarier to me or my classmates than this one story about four children locked in an attic for more than three years. All of them got very sick, and one of them, the youngest boy, died. Some believed that their mother and their grandmother wouldn't take them to a doctor or a hospital. From that, others concluded that either both or just the grandmother maybe wanted them all dead. Part of the story was that the young boy might have been buried on the property. And on Halloween, there was always someone who proposed going to Foxworth, because the legend was that on that night, the little boy's spirit roamed the grounds looking and calling for his brother and two sisters, even after the second fire. Some of my friends actually went there, but I never did, nor did Lana or Suzette, my other close friend. The stories those who did go brought back only enhanced the legend and kept the mystery alive. Some swore they had heard a little boy moaning and crying for his brother and sisters, and others claimed that they definitely had seen a small ghost.

Whatever was the truth, the stories and distortions made the property quite undesirable ever since. Since Bart Foxworth had abandoned the property, it had been quite neglected and eventually fell into foreclosure. So it was curious that someone was considering buying it. Whoever it was obviously was not afraid of the legends and curses. Bart Foxworth, in fact, was said to have believed that his reconstruction of the original building still contained evil, and that was why he left it and didn't care to keep it up. It was said that he believed that God didn't want that house standing. It was as though a dark cloud never left the property.

People accepted the curse. Where else could you find a house with that kind of history that had burned to the ground twice? Who'd want to challenge the curse?

"Well if you want to come along, Kristin, get moving. Put on some boots and maybe a scarf. I have a lot to do there and want to get home for lunch and watch the basketball game this afternoon," Dad said, and he clapped his black-leather-gloved hands together. "Chop, chop," he added, which was his favorite expression to get someone moving.

My father had a construction company, simply called Masterwood, which was our last name. "With a name like mine," Dad would say, "what could I eventually do but get involved in construction?" Masterwood employed upward of ten men, depending on the number of jobs contracted. My mother used to keep the books, but now Dad had Mrs. Osterhouse, a widow five years younger than he was whose husband had been one of Dad's friends. I knew she wanted Dad to marry her, but I didn't think he would ever bring another woman into our home permanently. He rarely dated and generally avoided all the meetings with women that anyone tried to arrange. For the last five years, I did most of our housework, and even when my mother was alive, Dad often prepared our meals, especially on weekends.

Right after serving in the navy, where he got into cooking, he had been a short-order cook in a diner-type restaurant off I-95. He met my mother before he began taking on side work at construction companies. She was a bookkeeper at one of them. Two years later, they married and moved here to Charlottesville, Virginia, where they both put their life savings into my father's new company. They didn't deliberately come here because she'd once had family here. My mother had never been invited to the Foxworth mansion, and hadn't ever spoken to Malcolm or anyone else who had lived there. Dad said they not only moved in different circles from the Foxworth clan but also lived on different planets.

"Okay," I said. "Wait for me."

I ran upstairs to put on warmer clothing. I was actually very excited about going with him to Foxworth. I always thought Dad knew more than he ever had said about the original story, and maybe now, because we were going there, he would tell me more. Getting him to say anything new about it was like struggling to open one of those hard plastic packages that electronic things came wrapped in. When I came home from school armed with a new question about the family, usually because of something one of my classmates had said, he rarely gave any answers that were more than a grunt or monosyllable.

My cell phone buzzed just as I was turning to leave my room. It was Lana. In my excitement, I had forgotten about her.

"What time are you picking me up?" she asked. "We'll have lunch at the mall."

"Change of plan. I'm going with my father to Foxworth."

"Foxworth? Why?"

"He has to estimate a job, and I promised I would

help, take notes and stuff," I added, justifying my going there. "Someone wants to build on the property."

"Ugh. Who'd want to do that? It's cursed. There are probably bodies buried there."

"Someone who doesn't care about gossip and knows the value of the property," I said dryly. "It's what businessmen do, look for a bargain and build it into a big profit."

My father said I had inherited my condescending, often sarcastic sense of humor from my mother, who he claimed could cut up snobs in seconds and scatter their remains at her feet "like bird feed."

"Oh. Well, what about Kane and Stanley? We were supposed to hang out with them, me with Stanley and you with Kane. I know for a fact that he's expecting you."

"I never said for sure, and he was quite offhanded about it."

"Well, you never said no, and I know you liked him before when we were out. Emily Grace told me her brother told her Kane said he thinks you've grown into a pretty girl."

"I'm so grateful for his approval."

She laughed. "You like him, too. Don't play innocent."

"That's all right. You never want any boy to take you for granted," I said. "It's good to disappoint him now and then." She was right, though. I really wanted to be with Kane, but I wanted to go to Foxworth more. I couldn't explain why. It had just come over me, and when I had feelings this strong, I usually paid attention to them.

"What? Who told you that? Are you reading some advice to the lovelorn or something? You're not listening to Tina Kennedy, are you? She's just jealous, jealous of everyone."

"No. Of course not. I'd never listen to Tina Kennedy about anything. Gotta go," I said. "Dad's waiting for me. I'll call you later."

"Don't touch anything there," she warned. "You'll get infected with the madness."

"You forgot I had the shot."

"What shot?"

"The vaccine that prevents insanity. It's how I can hang out with you," I added, and hung up before she could say another word. Besides, I knew she wanted to be on the phone instantly to spread the news. I was returning to some ancient ancestral burial ground, and surely the experience would change me in some dramatic way. They all might even become a little more afraid of me, but probably not Kane. If anything, I was sure he would find it amusing. He could be a terrific tease, which was one of the reasons I was a little afraid of him.

Laughing, I bounced down the stairs. I had my blond hair tied in a ponytail, and because of the length of my hair, the ends bounced just above my wing bones. Both my mother and I had cerulean-blue eyes, and part of the legend of the attic children was that they all had the same blue eyes and blond hair. The fact that I supposedly looked like them only enhanced the theory that I could have inherited the family madness.

I had never seen a picture of them, and Dad told me that he and my mother hadn't, either. In fact, no one had seen any picture of them when they were shut up in the attic or even soon afterward. There were some drawings in newspaper stories, but their accuracy was always in question, as were the facts in the stories. Supposedly, the children who survived the ordeal never talked about what had happened, but that didn't stop the tales of horror. They were always reprinted around Halloween with grotesque drawings depicting children scratching on locked windows, their faces resembling Edvard Munch's famous painting *The Scream*, making it all look like someone's nightmare. In a few weeks, those stories and pictures would appear again.

Years later, three of the children, as the story goes, returned to Charlottesville just before the second fire. Dad said neither he nor my mother had ever met any of them. Some people believed that the older sister had begun an affair with her mother's attorney husband and that her mother was driven to madness and had actually been the one responsible for setting the first fire, which had killed Olivia Foxworth, Malcolm's wife, who was an invalid at the time. The details remained vague, and none of the facts had been substantiated, even after the mansion was rebuilt and another Foxworth moved in many years later, which only made it all more interesting.

I could never understand it. If the story about the

children locked in an attic was true, why would the children want to return to Charlottesville, let alone to Foxworth Hall? That would be like a prisoner wanting to return to his jail cell. Why revive such painful memories, unless those memories were really just the product of someone's wild imagination? And why would her mother's husband want to have an affair with a girl that young?

Maybe more important, why would she want to have an affair with him? No one knew where the older brother and sister were now. Some say they changed their names or left the country. The cousins who moved into the second mansion never told anyone anything, either, and even if Bart Foxworth had said something, it wouldn't have been believed. It was like that campfire game where you whisper a secret into someone's ear and they whisper it to the person next to them, who does the same, until the secret works its way back, and by then, the original secret is so distorted it barely resembles what the first person told.

It was like pulling teeth to get Dad to tell me anything. If I brought home another tidbit and persistently asked him about it, he would finally say, "I wouldn't swear to any of it being true. As your mother used to say, exaggerations grow faster than mold in a wet basement around here. I told you, Kristin, forget about all that. Just thinking about it could poison your mind."

Just thinking about it could poison my mind? No wonder the Foxworth property was an ideal Halloween hangout, populated with ghosts and moans and screams. But how could I help wanting to know more? I didn't tell Dad about it because I knew it would upset him, but on many occasions when new kids were introduced at school or at parties, someone would say something like, "You know, Kristin is related to the famous Foxworth children on her mother's side."

Inevitably, the new kid would ask, "Who are the famous Foxworth children? Why are they famous?"

Then someone would go into one of the versions of the story, with everyone looking to me to tell them more. They were very skeptical when I said, "I don't know any more than you do about it, and half of what you're saying is surely the product of distorted imaginations." I'd walk away before anything else could be said to me, not as if I wanted to hide anything but acting more like I was bored with the subject. Of course, I wasn't.

Why should I be? Everyone is interested in his or her family background. It's only natural. I'd been in many of my girlfriends' homes for dinner when their parents brought up memories of their grandfathers and their uncles and aunts and cousins. Pictures of relatives were hanging on walls. I couldn't imagine my mother ever putting up a picture of Malcolm Foxworth or Olivia Foxworth, not that she'd had any. She had some very old photographs of relatives, but to this day, I didn't know who was who, and if I asked Dad about any of them, he would claim he couldn't remember. Maybe he was telling the truth, or maybe he was just avoiding it.

Everyone's family had black sheep, but also relatives they were proud to mention. My family background on my mother's side had this big, gaping black hole full of terror and horror. Was it a good idea to try to fill it, or was it better just to cover it up and forget? Forgetting about it was just not very easy, at least not for me.

It was like everyone knew that your cousin many times removed was Jack the Ripper. Despite the distance in relationship, they were always looking for some sign, some indication that you carried the germ of evil. Instead of Typhoid Mary, I was Madness Kristin. Get too close to me, and you might become a blabbering idiot.

Dad was already outside checking something on his truck engine. The truck was practically a member of our family. I couldn't remember him not driving it. When I asked him why he didn't buy a new one instead of constantly tinkering with it, replacing parts, and filling in rust spots, he replied in one word, "Loyalty." When I looked confused, he continued, reciting one of his favorite lectures. "Problem with the world today is everything in people's lives is temporary. It spreads from their possessions to their relationships. They throw away their marriages as easily as they dump their appliances. This truck's never let me down. Yes, it's old, and it ain't pretty, but it's used to me, and I'm used to it."

Fortunately, once I got my driver's license, he had decided that I should have a modern car with all the safety bells and whistles. However, when he had to trade in my mother's car to get mine, he was almost as upset as he was the day she died. To this day, he refused to give away her clothes and shoes. They were all stored in our attic with some of her other things like hairbrushes, curlers, and perfume. It was almost as if he hoped she would turn up at the door, smile, and say, "My death was a terrible mistake. I wasn't supposed to be taken yet, so I'm back." That was why he loved watching the movie *Heaven Can Wait*.

More than once, I caught him staring at an empty doorway or listening keenly for the sound of her footsteps on the stairway.

People never really die until you forget them, I thought.

I couldn't ever blame him for believing she might return somehow. From what I remember and from what people tell me, no one expected my mother to die like that. She was a very healthy-looking thirty-four-year-old woman. They called it a cranial aneurysm. Something just exploded in her head, and she keeled over one day at work. She didn't die right away. Dad had a very difficult time talking about it for years, but when he did talk to me about it, I could see he was always amazed at how well she had looked in the hospital bed.

"It's why I couldn't believe the doctors," he told me. "I sat there thinking any moment she would wake up and bawl me out for putting her into the hospital to start with. That was your mother," he would add. He would add that to almost anything he told me about her, "That was your mother," signifying in his mind and mine that she was a very special person.

I had good memories of her, but a girl of almost five and a half certainly hadn't experienced her mother long enough to know her as well as she should. Without her now, I could hear nothing much about her side of the family. She was an only child. My maternal grandfather died very young from heart failure, and my maternal grandmother, who also had health problems, died when I was only seven, so I didn't get to know them that well, either.

The only uncle and aunt I had were on my father's side. My father's younger brother, my uncle Tommy, lived in California, where he worked as an agent in a talent agency. He never married or had children. Dad had a younger sister, Barbara, who was also unmarried and worked at a bank in New York. Dad's father had been killed in a car accident. He was only in his early fifties at the time. My paternal grandmother had lived with Dad's younger sister, Barbara. She eventually succumbed to emphysema and then pneumonia. She had been a heavy smoker, as was Dad's father. Dad wouldn't permit anyone who worked for him to smoke in his office or on any of his jobs. He actually made them sign an agreement and did fire a young man who smoked on a site.

I spoke to my aunt Barbara occasionally and visited with her in New York City last summer, which was one of my best trips without Dad. She was constantly inviting me to return so she could take me to shows and wonderful restaurants. Of course, she invited Dad, too, but he hated big cities.

"I'm just a small-town boy," he would say. "You

can take the boy out of the country, but you can't take the country out of the boy." I kidded him often about being stuck in his ways. He never denied it. "I am who I am," he would say. "One size Burt Masterwood fits all. Besides, you'll do all the traveling and discoveries in this family, Kristin. I did enough when I was in the navy."

Would I travel and make discoveries? I would go to college, but I still had no definite idea what I wanted to become. For a while, I thought about being a teacher. Lately, I considered going into medicine, maybe research. Perhaps it was because I had lost my mother when I was so young, or maybe it was because of the Foxworth legend that hovered over me, but sometimes I felt I was lost in a fog, the most difficult thing to know being my future. I dreamed of marrying someday and having my own children, but that also seemed more like a vague dream, something coming sometime, somehow, like a handsome prince riding in from some mysterious place.

"'Bout time," Dad said when I popped out of the house and closed the door. "Let's go."

He closed the truck hood with the same gentleness he employed whenever he did anything on his truck. He did treat it like some revered old friend, full of mechanical arthritis but still ambulatory. Sometimes I would catch him just looking at it and stroking it affectionately, lost in some memory or maybe just thinking about my mother sitting beside him.

"What's wrong with Black Beauty today?" I asked as I opened the door to get in. The black leather seats were creased and faded, but there wasn't a tear in either of them, and the carpeting on the floor was always kept up or replaced.

"Got to change her spark plugs. She reminds me every morning. Just like a woman, nag, nag, nag," he said, and started the engine. He listened to it and nodded. "Spark plugs," he repeated, and then backed out of our driveway.

We had a modest two-story Queen Anne–style home with recently renovated aluminum siding, black shutters, and panel windows in the bay Dad had built in the living room. All the bedrooms were upstairs, the wall paneling redone. Recently, Dad replaced the balustrade on the stairway with a rich dark mahogany, saying that it was something my mother would have liked. He was still doing things he knew would have pleased her. I was so used to him being able to fix and refurbish everything in our home that I grew up thinking every man could do that. I would smile incredulously when my girlfriends' fathers had to call a repairman to repair a window casing or a plumber to fix a toilet. Besides being a licensed general contractor, Dad was a licensed plumber and electrician.

"I'm a hands-on man," he would tell me proudly. "Your mother wasn't above bragging to her friends about me, making me out to be Mr. Fix-It. But that's how she was."

Our house was on a side road next to a working horse and cattle farm. We were nearly twelve miles outside the city of Charlottesville in the eastern foothills of the Blue Ridge Mountains. All of my friends were within what Dad called "striking distance," so I never felt any more isolated than anyone else, although I did especially enjoy spending time with Missy Meyer, whose father, Justin Anthony Meyer, was an important attorney and who lived in a classic 1900s brick Victorian home in the Belmont neighborhood of Charlottesville. It was only a block away from the Pedestrian Mall. Dad had done some renovation work for Mr. Meyer, laying down new pine floors and later redoing a bathroom.

"How many people died in the first Foxworth fire, Dad?" I asked once we were on our way, hoping to get him to start talking more about it.

"Far as I know, only two, the old lady and her son-in-law."

"That attorney who had an affair with one of the granddaughters?"

He looked at me. I could see he was making a decision. Until now, it was clear that he didn't want to contribute any more to the dark details that surrounded my mother's cousins and the events that had occurred in that grand old mansion. He had scared me when he'd said that just thinking about them could poison my mind, but now that I was older, maybe it wasn't as dangerous.

"That's what I was told," he said, "but I don't consider anyone I know to be anything of an authority on it. The Foxworths were very private people, and when people are that private, the only way you get to know anything about them is second- or thirdhand. Worthless."

"Did you really believe that the children's grandmother wanted her own grandchildren dead and was somehow responsible for the little boy dying?"

"No one as far as I know proved anything like that," he said. "It's a nasty story, Kristin. Why harp on it?"

"I know, but probably not much nastier than what they're showing at the movie theater."

He nodded. "I'll give you that."

"There are lots of stories like it on the news today also, Dad."

"Look, I'm like most people around here, Kristin. What I know about the Foxworth tragedies I know from little more than gossip, and gossip is just an empty head looking to exercise a fat tongue."

"Do you think the little boy's body is buried somewhere on the property? You must have some thought about that."

"Not going to venture a guess on that, and I'm not going to be one to spread that story, Kristin. You know how hard it is to sell a house in which someone died? People get spooked. Look how long it's taken to move this property, and there's no reason for that, even though the house on it burned down twice. It's prime land."

"How did it burn the second time? I heard an electric wire problem."

"That's it," he said. "It was abandoned, so no one noticed until it was too late."

"I also heard the man who lived in it burned it because he believed it had the devil inside it."

Dad smirked. "There was no proof of arson. All that just adds to the rumor mill."

"The same house burns down twice?" I said.

He looked at me and then looked ahead and said, "Lightning can strike twice in the same place. No big mystery."

He made a turn and started us on the now-infamous road to Foxworth, passing cow farms along the way. There had been a number of times when I was tempted to use my new driver's license and take myself and one or two of my friends out to Foxworth, but somehow the aura of dark terror hovered ahead of me when I considered it, even in broad daylight. And I didn't want any of my friends to know I had an interest in the Foxworth legends. That would only encourage their insinuations that I might have inherited madness.

"Did Mom ever talk about what happened, Dad?"

"You mean the first fire?"

"No, all of it, especially the children in the attic."

"Her girlfriends were always trying to bring it up, I know, but she would say something like, 'It's not right to talk about the dead,' as if it was some Grimms' fairy tale or something, and that would usually end it. But that didn't mean they didn't keep trying. A busy-body has got to keep busy."

"Did she talk about it with you?"

He gave me that look again, the expression that told me he was considering my age and what he should say. "I told you, Kristin, it's all hearsay, even what your mother knew and what we were told years later."

"I'm all ears," I replied.

He shook his head. "I'm going to regret this conversation."

"No, you won't, Dad. I won't be the one to tell stories out of school," I added, which was another one of his favorite expressions. I knew he loved that I used them, remembered them.

"Your uncle Tommy once claimed he had met someone who said he had known one of the servants in the original house at the time the children were supposedly locked in the attic. He went out to Hollywood to pitch the story for a movie, and Tommy heard it. He called us immediately afterward."

"What did he say?"

"He said the man claimed it was true that they were up there for more than three years, a girl who was about twelve when they were first locked up, a boy who was about fourteen, and the twin boy and girl about four. Their father was killed in a car accident and supposedly didn't leave them enough money to fix the heels on their shoes. Malcolm Foxworth was pretty sick by then, but he hung on for a few years more. The story was that he wouldn't put his daughter back in his will if she had children with her husband."

"Do you know why? Did he say?"

"He was vague about it. Tommy, who hears lots of stories, said he was sure the man was making most of it up as he went along just to season his story enough to sell it for a movie."

"Did it fit with anything you had heard or knew already?"

"I told you, I never really knew what was true and what wasn't. What I do know from what the old-timers tell me is that Malcolm Foxworth was a real Bible thumper, one of those who believed Satan was everywhere, and so he was very strict. Whatever his daughter did to anger him, forgiveness was a part of his Christianity that he neglected. That's what your mother would say. She didn't even like being known as a distant relative, and to tell you the truth, she would cringe whenever anyone brought that up. She'd be angry at me for telling you this much hearsay."

"So?" I asked, ignoring him. "At least tell me what else Uncle Tommy told you." Despite his reluctance, I thought I had him on a roll. He had already said ten times as much as he had ever said before about the Foxworth family story.

"According to the story the man pitched, the kids were hidden up there so Malcolm wouldn't know they existed."

"So that part is really true?"

"I told you. The guy was trying to sell a story for a movie."

"But even in his story, why did that matter, not knowing they existed?"

"I guess Malcolm thought they were the devil's children. Anyway, your uncle says that this servant who was the main source for the story swears the old man knew and enjoyed that they were suffering."

"Their own grandfather? Ugh," I said.

"Yeah, right, ugh. So let's not talk about it any-more. It's full of distortions, lies, and plenty of ugh."

I was quiet. How did the truth get so twisted? Why was no one sure about any of it? "What a mess," I finally muttered.

"Yeah, what a mess. So forget it." He smiled. "You're getting to look more like your mother every day, Kristin. You lucked out. I have a mug for a face."

"You do not, Dad. Besides, if you did, would Mom have married you?"

He smiled. "Someday I'll tell you how I got that woman to say 'I do.'"

"I already know. She married you because she knew you could fix a leaky faucet. And that's just the way she was."

He laughed. If he could, he would have leaned over and kissed me, but he didn't want to show me any poor driving habits, especially now that I was driving.

We rode on. It was right ahead of us now, and I could feel my breath quicken.

It was like opening a door locked for centuries.

Behind it lay the answers to all the secrets.

Or possibly . . . new curses.

Somehow I sensed that I was finally on the edge of finding out.

I was disappointed as we approached what was left of the second Foxworth Hall, which supposedly was a duplicate of the first. It looked more like a pile of rubble than the skeleton of a once proud and impressive mansion full of mystery and secrets. There were weeds growing in and around the charred boards and stones. Shards of broken glass polished by rain, snow, and wind glittered. Anything of any color was faded and dull. Rusted pipes hung precariously, and the remains of one large fireplace looked like they were crumbling constantly, even now right before our eyes.

Most of the grounds were unkempt and overrun, bushes growing wild, weeds sprouting through the crumbled driveway, and the fading grass long ready to cut as hay. Four large crows were perched on the stone walls, looking as if they had laid claim to the place. They burst into a flurry of wings and, looking and sounding angry, flew off as we drew closer. They, along with rodents and insects, surely had staked title to all of it years ago. Otherwise, it looked as quiet and frozen in time as any rarely visited graveyard.

Another truck was already parked near the wrecked mansion. I recognized Todd Winston, one of the men who had been with Dad for years. Todd had married his high school sweetheart, Lisa Carson, after she had gotten her teaching certificate and begun to teach fifth grade. Three years later, they had their first child, a girl named Brandy, and two years later, they had Josh. Dad was only about ten years older than Todd, but Todd treated him more like a father than an older brother. He was always looking for Dad's approval. He had a full strawberry-blond beard and a matching head of hair that looked like it was allergic to a brush most of the time.

"The property has a lake on it fed from underground mountain streams," Dad told me. "It's off to the left there, about a fifteen-, twenty-minute walk, if you want to see it," he said. "We're going to be here a good two hours or so. No complaints about it," he warned. "You wanted to come along."

"I won't complain. I've canceled all my important appointments for the day, including tea with the governor."

"Wise guy," Dad muttered, clenching his teeth but smiling.

"I've already seen two raccoon families who won't appreciate us bulldozing all this away, not to mention those crows," Todd said as soon as we got out of the truck. "Hi, Kristin. Your dad putting you to work in construction already?"

"No. I'm just along for the ride."

"The ride?"

I nodded at the wreckage. "I just want to see it all close up," I told him, and he nodded and looked back at what was left of the mansion.

"Hard to believe it was once the place people describe, with a ballroom and all, magnificent chandeliers, elaborate woodwork, and stained-glass windows. People who live in houses like this usually don't get burned out. The rich don't die in fires."

"Hogwash. Fire and water don't discriminate," Dad said. "Besides, that's how the world will end if we don't find a better way, and goodness knows, we're working on it."

"Thanks for the cheery news, Burt," Todd said. "Where do you want to start?"

"We'll begin on the east end here." He stared at it all a moment and then nodded. "They don't build foundations like this anymore. It's the original one. Who'd build one like it now? It's the instant gratification generation, including instant house slapped together with spit and polish."

"Amen to that," Todd said.

He'd say amen to anything Dad uttered, I thought. He didn't have much of a mentor in his own father, who Dad said was as useless as a screw without a head. He spent most of his time nursing like a baby on a bottle of beer and was one of the fixtures at Hymie's Bar and Grill just southeast of the city.

Dad looked at me with those expectant eyes. Now that I was here, he was anticipating my disappointment. There was nothing sensational to see, no clues to what had happened here either the first or the second time. There was no way to understand how elaborate the mansion had once been. I saw legs of tables and chairs and crumbled elaborate stonework, but remnants of beautiful pictures, statues, curtains, and chandeliers were burned up or so charred that they were unrecognizable. There was certainly not much for me to do.

"I'll be fine," I said. "I'll take that walk to the lake."

"You be careful," he said.

"Watch out for ghosts," Todd called.

"Mind yourself," Dad told him, and Todd laughed.

They started toward the foundation, and I walked around it all first. I kept looking up, trying to imagine the way the mansion stood, how high it really was, and where exactly the attic loft in which the children spent most of three years would be. Would they have had any view? Maybe they could have seen the lake. And if they had, would that have made things easier or harder, looking at places they couldn't go to and enjoy? The surrounding forest was thick, the trees so tall that from my position, I could barely make out some of the hills in the distance, and only the very tops of them at that. But it had been decades since they had been here. The trees weren't so high back then.

I saw Dad and Todd begin measuring parts of the remaining structure, moving charred wood, and inspecting the walls of the foundation carefully, as if they anticipated something grotesque jumping out at them. Right now, it was difficult to imagine anything frightening about Foxworth. It looked like one of the structures devastated in bombings during the Second World War that we saw in films in history class. However, I knew there were even adults who believed that if they stood inside the wreckage at night, they could hear screams and cries, even laughter and whispers.

Do all houses keep the sounds of those who have lived in them, absorb them into their walls like a sponge would absorb water, and then, in the quiet of the night after they are deserted or left waiting for the wrecking ball, free the memories to wander about the rooms, resurrecting happy times and sad ones?

I started to make my way to the forest and then walked slowly through the cool woods. Most of the leaves were gone because of the recent wind and rain, but some had clung determinedly to their branches and flooded the forest with their bright yellow, brown, and amber colors. Where there were thick pine trees, there were shadows. I saw rabbits and thought I saw a fox, but I wasn't sure, as it moved so quickly out of sight. About fifteen minutes later, I reached the edge of the lake my father had described. The ducks had already gone south. There were few birds, in fact, not even the crows I had seen. The lake was still, desolate, and silvery with clouds reflected in the surface and small circles here and there created by water flies.

Almost halfway around the lake, I saw what looked like a collapsed dock, most of it underwater. I drew closer, looking for signs of fish or turtles in the water as I walked, and then suddenly, I stopped and shuddered. The rocks and grass beneath the surface of the pond in one spot had somehow taken the shape of a small child. I knew it wasn't real, but it looked so much like a skull and skeleton that I gasped and backed away.

A dead little boy very well could be in the lake.

Why not?

A lake would be a perfect place to hide a dead child, weigh him down, and let him sink to the darkness below. When I closed my eyes, I imagined him staring up from the bottom with his glassy eyes. I was suddenly much colder than I had been. I thought I heard an owl, but that was unusual in the daytime. What was it? I hugged myself, turned, and started back, moving more quickly now, actually trotting and then slowing down.

When I stepped out of the forest, I could see that Dad and Todd had moved around three-quarters of the property, making their evaluation. Dad looked up, saw me, and beckoned.

"Did you find the lake?" he called as I approached.

"Yes, but it looks so cold and deserted with so much overgrown around it. I'm sure it was once very pretty." I didn't want to mention the strange sound I had heard. Todd might start teasing me again.

"Probably good duck hunting in the spring," Todd said. "But the land's been posted for years."

"We found something," Dad said when I reached them. "From the looks of it, we think it was part of the original house. When the second Foxworth Hall was built, they didn't do much about the original basement."

"No one can read what happened to a house like your father can," Todd said. "You know he's been called in to evaluate some properties that burned down where there might have been a murder or somethin'."

"All right. Enough of that," my father said.

I didn't know about those things, but right now, I wasn't as curious about other houses or stories as I was about this one. "What did you find?" Had they found the remains of the child? Probably not. He wouldn't sound so casual about that.

"Todd moved some boards that had to have been in the original basement and shifted a few things, and that appeared." Dad nodded at a dark brown metal box about seven or eight inches long and six inches wide. "It's locked," he continued. "Might mean something valuable is inside it."

I knelt beside it. There was a lot of rust.

"Look at what was scratched on the side," Todd said, and I turned it to look.

"It's a date: '11/60.' That's November 1960. More than fifty years ago," I said.

Todd nodded as if we had found something that belonged in a museum alongside Egyptian ruins. "Maybe there are millions of dollars in jewels inside it," he said. "Old jewels are worth more, aren't they?" he asked my father.

"Maybe a hundred-year-old cameo or something," my father offered.

I looked up at him. Was he serious? "Really?"

"Or thousands in cash. People used to keep money under the mattress, especially someone like old man Foxworth, who I heard was a real tightwad unless it was for the church," Todd said, wishing that we would find money.

Dad smiled at him. "Well, he's not wrong. People still hide money in their homes. They're afraid the banks will find a way to steal it. Anyway, Kristin, we waited for you to open it. Ready?"

"Sure."

He pulled a hammer out of his tool belt and knelt beside me. Then he put the back of the hammer under the latch and began to force it up. It gave way quickly because it was so rusted through. He handed the box to me. "Yours to open," he said.

Slowly, I lifted the top and gazed down into the box. There were no jewels, and there was no money. There was only what looked like a leather-bound diary. I plucked it out carefully and showed it to my father and Todd.

"Maybe it has a treasure map in it or something," Todd said, disappointed.

I opened the cover carefully, as the pages looked

yellowed and fragile. "No, it's actually someone's diary," I said.

"Unless it's Thomas Jefferson's, there's no money in it," Todd declared mournfully.

Dad smiled and shrugged. "He's probably right. We're about finished here. The foundation is in pretty good shape. Whoever the buyer is could build on it if he wants. I'll just make a few notes, and we'll head out."

I put the diary back into the box and went to our truck. After I got in, I put the box on the seat and then sat back and took out the diary again.

The very first page identified whose it was. It read: *Christopher's Diary.*

I thought for a moment. Christopher? Who was Christopher? Was he one of Malcolm Foxworth's servants or relatives?

I read the first page.

When I was twelve years old, I read "The Diary of Anne Frank." First, I was interested in it because it was written as a diary, and when someone writes a diary, he or she usually doesn't expect anyone else will read it. A diary is like a best friend, someone to whom you could confide your deepest, secret thoughts safely. I really didn't have a best friend. This would be it. I thought that whatever was in a diary had to be the most honest words anyone could write about himself or herself and about the people he or she loved and the people he or she met.

How do you lie in a diary?

I looked up when Dad opened his door to get in. He unwrapped his tool belt and put it behind the seat.

"So, whatcha got?" he asked as he got behind the wheel.

"A diary written by someone named Christopher."

"Really?" He started the engine.

"Do you know who it might be?"

He started to turn the truck to drive off. Todd beeped his horn and waved to us, and Dad waved back.

"Christopher, huh? Well, it could be one of those kids in the attic. I seem to remember now that the older boy *was* named Christopher." He glanced at me. "It might be nothing but someone's silly ramblings, Kristin. More garbage about the Foxworth family. I wouldn't waste my time reading it."

He looked at the diary. I put it away.

"What a place this was," he continued as we pulled away from the property. "Land with a lake on it like that. I'd buy it myself if I had the money. Too bad there wasn't any in that box, or at least valuable jewelry. We'd make an offer."

I looked down at the diary again. Maybe it was worth more than Dad thought. There was no way to know without reading it, but I didn't want to read it while we were driving. I never liked to read in a car or in the truck while it was moving. It made me dizzy. The writing was all in script, but it was a careful, neat script that, although it was slightly faded in places, was quite legible.

We had to stop at the quick market for some basic groceries on the way home, so for a while, I put the

diary out of my mind and concentrated on what we
needed. When we got home, I helped carry the bags
of groceries in first. After everything was put away, I
went back to the truck and got the metal box.

Dad was on the phone making a report to the pres-
ident of the bank about the property. I went past him
and up the stairs to my room. I took off my sweater
and got comfortable before I fixed my pillows and sat
on my bed with the box beside me. Then I opened it,
took out the diary, and again, very carefully, began to
turn the page after the line *How do you lie in a diary?*

Years later, I would remember "The Diary of
Anne Frank" for another reason, a more dramatic
reason. Just as Anne Frank was forced to hide in an
attic, my sister Cathy, our twin brother and sister,
Cory and Carrie, and I were forced to hide in our
grandparents' attic. We weren't hiding from Nazis,
of course, but the way our mother described her
father and the way our grandmother Olivia treated
us, we probably didn't feel much less afraid than
poor Anne Frank.

Anne Frank's father had her diary published.
He wanted the world to know her story, their
story. Everyone sees the same story in a different
way. My sister saw our story one way, and I saw
it another. When I began writing this, I didn't do
it because I thought it was so important to tell it
from my eyes and ears and memories. But now I
do. So I'll be more careful about what I continue
to write.

I paused to catch my breath. Is this what I thought it was? Dad's guess about who Christopher could be was right, but more important, this was not some silly rambling, as he had said. It was so well written. I was excited, and I wondered if I should call Lana or Suzette. All my friends would like to know about this. I reached for the phone and then stopped.

No. I thought there was something about a diary that demanded respect. Although Christopher wrote that he had come to the point where he wanted his view of everything to be known, I felt very special being the first one ever to read it. I should read it all first and not tell anyone about it until I was finished, I decided. It was almost a sacred trust. Maybe I was meant to be the one to discover it because I was a distant relative.

Others might not see it that way. They might just see it as something sensational and tell me to send it to a supermarket rag or something. I could just hear Missy Meyer saying, "You could get lots of money for it, maybe. I'll ask my father to look into it for you. The local newspaper might pay you and serialize it. You'll be famous and make a lot of money!"

No, thanks, I thought. This was too special. I returned to the diary, now determined to read as much as I could before I went to sleep.

There are times now when I think back to what our lives were like in the mid-'50s and remember it all the way you might remember a dream. Often, with dreams that are so vivid, you're not sure how much of it was fantasy and how much of it was real. There is so much of it that I want to be true, but I'm not the kind of person who is comfortable fooling himself.

I've always had a lot to think about, so it's not really so unusual for me to have decided to keep a diary. My thoughts are very important to me. This diary will be a way of keeping my history, our history, authentically. Nothing Momma has said, nothing Cathy has said, and nothing Daddy has said will be as easy to recall later on when I'm much older if I don't remember to write down what was important as soon as I can.

I didn't do this right away. I kept telling myself diaries were something girls kept, not boys. Then I read about some famous diaries in literature and, of course, ships' captains' logs, all written by men, and I thought, this is silly. There's nothing absolutely feminine about writing your thoughts down, about capturing your feelings. I just wouldn't do something silly like write "Dear Diary." I'd just write everything as it happened and be as accurate as I could.

I bought this diary myself with my allowance, but I never told anyone I had, not even my father, who was interested in everything I did and thought. It seemed to me that the whole point of keeping a diary was keeping that secret until it was time to let others read it, if that was your purpose.

And it would be no good if it was done cryptically
so that people had to figure out what I meant here
and what I meant there. That's why I have to be
as honest as I can about what I saw, what I heard,
and especially what I felt.

Like Otto Frank, I think it's important that
more people know what really happened to us
before and afterward. Cathy used to call us flowers
in the attic, withering away. It helped her to think
of us that way. But we weren't flowers. We were
young, beautiful children who trusted that those
who loved us would always protect us even better
than we could protect ourselves.

Besides, I can't ever think of us in any
symbolic way. We weren't the creations of
someone's imagination. We were real flesh-and-
blood children. We were locked away, not only
by selfish greed but by cruel hearts that used the
Bible like a club to pound out the love we carried
in our innocent hearts. How that happened and
what became of us is too important to just let it
disappear in the dying memories of those who
lived it.

"Hey, you," Dad said from my doorway. I was so involved in my reading I didn't hear him come upstairs.
He said he had been calling up to me.

"Oh, sorry, Dad. I didn't hear you."

"Aren't you having any lunch today?"

"Oh, is it lunchtime?"

"You have a nice watch, Kristin, and four clocks in this room."

"I don't have four. Just the teddy bear clock and the Beatles alarm clock you found in an old house."

"Okay. I'm going to make myself a ham and cheese sandwich. You want one?"

"Thanks, Dad."

"You didn't tell me if you wanted the chicken with pasta or the meat loaf tonight."

"I'm a fan of your meat loaf, Dad. You know that."

"Uh-huh. So what's got you so involved? What is that, anyway?"

"You were right. It is the diary of the older brother, just as you thought it might be. He's telling their story from his point of view."

"Really? The whole story?"

"I think so. I just got into it."

He stood there thinking. He narrowed his eyes and bit softly down on the left corner of his mouth as he always did when something troubled him. "I don't know if you should read that, Kristin."

"I won't be corrupted by it if I haven't already been corrupted by other things I've read."

"Hmm," he murmured. "There's always a first time."

"Oh, Dad. Besides, finally, I'll know what really happened. *We'll* know," I said.

"I wasn't dying to find out," he replied. "And that still might not be the truth. Lies can be written as well as spoken, you know." He started to turn away.

"I'll be down in a few minutes," I said.

"Does this mean you're not going to mall-rat it today?"

"Yes, Dad, that's what it means," I said, laughing.

He was smiling himself as he walked away.

I returned to the diary like someone starving for news from the outside world, just like someone locked in an attic for years might be.

First Days

Cathy likes to think of us as regular middle-class people living ordinary lives in the small city of Gladstone, Pennsylvania. She bases this on the fact that our house isn't any larger or much smaller than any other house on our street and that our father drives a modest Chevy. I don't know why it's so important for her to think of us as ordinary. I will never think of myself that way.

When I told her that today, she looked at me strangely. She even seemed a little angry about it. I think she believes being ordinary makes her safe or something. I know she thinks all the kids from wealthy families are snobs, especially Lucille Tompkins, whose father owns four jewelry stores. One of her girlfriends told her what the word "snob" means, and she is worried that someone might call her that. I have the feeling someone told her I was a snob and she didn't know what to say or how to defend me.

She remembers that we weren't the first to get a television and acts as if that's something to be proud of, but we did get one about the same time as our neighbors, the Milestones, got one, and Mr. Milestone was manager of the closest supermarket. Actually, Cathy's the one growing into a snob. She thinks we're better than rich people even though we don't have as much, because rich people don't love each other as much. I told her that was ridiculous, and she told me I was the ridiculous one. I don't know why I even bother explaining things to her now. Her brain isn't developed enough to comprehend serious or complicated thoughts. Actually, I can sympathize with why she's always so confused about us.

Momma doesn't have an expensive fur coat, but she has very nice, fashionable clothes, often saving whatever she can to buy herself something in style.

In fact, Cathy doesn't know this, but I have seen Momma search through Daddy's pants and jacket pockets looking for money he had forgotten was in there. I even know where she hides it in a shoe box at the bottom of her closet. If Daddy notices her thievery, he doesn't say anything as far as I know. Of course, I've wondered why she doesn't just ask him for the money. Maybe he would think the things she wanted to buy were silly. Or maybe she just feels guilty about spending money on anything other than necessities. She can rationalize it if she steals the money, because it was in his pocket and looks like small change. I wouldn't say this to her face, but Momma rationalizes often. When I learned what that meant, I nodded to myself. It's like saying white lies, making excuses, but doing it to tell yourself you're protecting someone else, keeping someone from being hurt, often mostly yourself. Daddy works so hard for what we have. She would feel bad if she believed she was taking advantage of his trust.

No one wants to look average, especially our mother. I would agree that she had a modest engagement and wedding ring, but over the years, Daddy did buy her some fairly expensive necklaces and earrings and bracelets, probably even when we couldn't afford it. Maybe he got good deals from Lucille Tompkins's father. The jewelry, however, was nothing that would make her look ostentatious. My father has a very good sense of taste.

He often told us that something didn't have to be big to be beautiful or outstanding. I remember him recently telling Cathy and me, "Subtlety is as effective in life as it is in advertising, children."

He should know, I thought. Daddy is in public relations for a computer manufacturer that needs a great deal of promotion.

Cathy's too young to understand what he meant by subtlety. Afterward, I tried to explain it to her, but she shook her head and told me

that I use too many big words and if I keep filling
my head with bigger and more words, it will
explode. I don't know where she gets these idiotic
ideas. She hates to read. I think she hates doing
anything alone, and that's why she doesn't read
much.

She's two years younger than I am, but I'm
confident I could have understood what I was
telling her when I was her age. I am and always
was an avid reader, and with the exception of
one B in fifth-grade history last quarter, unfairly
given to me by Mr. Firth, a stuffy man with
sagging cheeks and a belly that looked like he
had swallowed a whole watermelon, I have always
been an A-plus student. Mr. Firth has corn-yellow
teeth from smoking every chance he gets. I see
him rush into the faculty room between classes or
during lunch to light up. He always has redness
around his eyes that I recently diagnosed as
ocular rosacea, a chronic condition that has many
possible causes.

My father gave me a "Merck Manual" this year,
and I devoured it. He bought it for me because
even at a young age, I was asking questions about
diseases, illnesses, and surgeries neighbors had.

"We've got a potential doctor in our midst,
Corrine," he declared at dinner one night, and
then produced the manual. It looked used, but
that doesn't matter to me. Books can get wet and
crinkle, and old book pages can turn yellow, but
the words don't disappear for a very long time.

Daddy said, "A good book is like good wine. Its wisdom ages and becomes more valuable with time." He winked at me when he said it, because he knew I believed that, too. Momma just shook her head as if Daddy and I lived in our own world, and Cathy grimaced and said, "Ugh. Old books smell."

I know that other boys my age get ecstatic over new bikes, Erector Sets, electric trains, new sleds, and baseball gloves, but this manual is the most exciting gift Daddy has ever gotten me, and it is my most prized possession. He even wrote inside the cover: "To our future Dr. Dollanganger. Heal and protect those in pain. Love, Dad."

I read and reread that dedication almost every night. For me, it's sort of a prayer. Probably the man I respect the most next to my father is our family doctor, Dr. Bloom. He has an office in his home and lives with his mother. He's not an old man, but he's older than most men are when they get married. I don't think it's because he doesn't like girls or anything. I think it's because he's too devoted to his sacred work of healing. He just hasn't found the right woman yet, the woman who will tolerate his rushing out to make hospital calls at all times of the night and leaving parties to care for someone who's suddenly very ill.

Dr. Bloom looked at my hands once and said, "You've got a doctor's hands, Christopher, strong fingers. You could be a great surgeon someday."

I don't think anything anyone ever said to me made me feel any better about myself. I told Daddy and Momma at dinner that night, and Cathy gave us her usual "Ugh" when she understood that surgeons put their hands inside people's bodies.

"Get an appendix attack, and you'll be happy to have a doctor do it," I said.

Her eyes nearly popped. "Don't frighten her, Christopher," Momma said.

"People do get appendix attacks, Momma."

Cathy had tears of fear in her eyes.

"Now, now," Daddy told her, embracing her quickly. "You won't have an appendix attack." He gave me a look that said, Be careful, Christopher. She's just a little girl.

I nodded.

He was right. I had to control my tongue and think harder first before I spoke.

Doctors especially have to know how to do that. You have to learn to keep certain things secret for the patient's own benefit.

I heard my father call to me.

I put the diary aside and hurried down for the lunch he was preparing. All I could think of was to eat and get back up there to continue reading. My father had our sandwiches out and a jug of water and glasses.

"Thanks, Dad," I said, slipping into my chair. He

looked at me and sat. "What?" I asked before I took a bite. I could always tell when he had something on his mind.

"You didn't call any of your friends yet about that diary, did you?"

"No. I thought I'd read it first."

"Good. I don't want you to tell anyone about it for a while. Maybe never." He bit into his sandwich, and I bit into mine.

"Why not?" I couldn't imagine he had the same reason I did for keeping it to myself.

"For now, I don't want to broadcast that we found that. All I need is for this new prospective buyer to get second thoughts like so many others have over the years since the second fire. I don't want to perpetuate any of those Halloween stories. The bank wouldn't be happy with me. And the bank could confiscate that diary. Technically, they own everything on the property."

"Okay. It's our secret . . . and Todd's."

"Todd doesn't know what you found. He was too disappointed that it wasn't jewelry or money. I'm sure he's forgotten it was anything else by now."

"What if Christopher tells us in the diary where his little brother was buried or something?"

My father stopped eating. "What?"

"It could be in there is all I'm saying. I'm not saying I read it yet. He did write early in the pages that his little brother suffered a horrible death."

"How horrible? What does he say happened to him?"

"I don't know yet, Dad. Maybe he really was poisoned; maybe it was something worse."

He sat back. I could see I already had revealed too much, but as my mother often said, "Words are like toothpaste. Once they come out, you can't put them back in."

"I don't like this. Now you're scaring me. You gonna go and have nightmares after this?"

"I don't have nightmares. Stop being a worrywart," I said, which was another one of his own expressions. I asked my English teacher what it meant, and he told me with a shrug that it just meant someone who worried so much he caused others to do the same. "It's just . . . a diary."

"A diary written by a kid kept locked up in an attic of a nuthouse for more than three years," Dad said. "Madness is madness no matter how you cut it. Maybe he's making it all up, including the way his brother died."

"I'm not going to go crazy reading it, Dad. Will you stop?"

"You let me know when you're finished with it."

"Why? Will you burn it or something?"

"Just let me know, and don't ask so many questions, or I'll take away your what, who, where, why, and how."

We stared at each other a moment, and then we both smiled. The world I was about to enter through this diary was so unlike mine. I couldn't even begin to imagine how a grandmother would so harm her own grandchildren, but I was just beginning the diary. It wouldn't be long before I would find out the truth.

Maybe.

Maybe at the end, I would discover that Christopher never knew himself. The diary could simply be his attempt to get to know himself, and perhaps he was writing what he thought he should and not what he knew to be true. Reading it would be like taking a ride to see someone who wasn't there. Dad was always telling me to consider my time the most valuable asset I had. "Try to spend it wisely. A minute lost can't be made up like you can make up a dollar lost," he lectured. "I don't mean you shouldn't relax and have fun, but try to make it worth something."

I cleaned up the lunch dishes. Dad went into the living room to watch a basketball game. He called to me when he heard me starting for my room.

"Kristin?"

"Yes, Dad?"

"I'm serious. Don't you go blabbin' about that diary."

"I promise. I won't. Stop worrying about it."

"I don't like your reading it. I should have paid more attention when you told me what it was," he mumbled, but I didn't reply.

I didn't charge up the stairs, but I didn't walk up slowly, either.

Moments later, I was reading again, but now, after the concern Dad had exhibited at lunch, I couldn't help being nervous about it. I knew the power of the written word, how too often people were influenced by something they read and how it changed their behavior. As Mr. Feldman, one of my English teachers, would tell us, "If reading wasn't so important and influential, why would they ban books in dictatorships?"

Nevertheless, nothing would stop me from turning these pages, I thought, and began again.

Our lives are full of secrets. Cathy likes to think love is what floats about the most in our home. She thinks this way because she listens in on our parents talking to each other whenever she can. I see how she does it. She pretends to be busy with something and not be paying attention, but she's hanging on their every word, especially the way they express how much they love each other. I know when she comes running into my room to tell me about something they've said that she is probably exaggerating.

Cathy can be very dramatic. I think she believes we live in a movie or something and that our mother and father are famous stars because Daddy is so handsome and Momma is so beautiful.

She came running in this afternoon to tell me that Daddy practically "swooned" over Momma when he saw her. I had the feeling that she got the word "swooned" from our mother, who probably has told her that Daddy swooned over something she did with her hair or clothes. Cathy would never have come up with a word like that on her own.

Our mother had gone to the beauty salon

earlier today and had her nails done. Momma lets
Cathy go into her bathroom when she's taking a
bath in her perfumed bubble water sometimes.
They leave the door open so I can see them.
Momma isn't shy about being naked in front of
us. I know she is very proud of her figure, which
is a figure most women envy, but she also knows
I try to think of the human body the way a doctor
should. There have been times when she'll ask
me to wash her back for her. Cathy stands to the
side, watching enviously, so I have to let her do
it, too.

Cathy often sits on the edge of the tub and
listens to our mother go on and on about beauty
tips so that when she's old enough, she'll be
ready. On more than one occasion, I've seen
Cathy imitating her, luxuriating in her own bath
and pretending to put on makeup the way Momma
does. She comes into my room when she does her
hair and puts on a dress to ask me how she looks.
Twice this week, she asked me to wash her back
the way I would wash Momma's. Usually, I do it
too quickly, and she complains.

"Am I as beautiful as our mother?" she always
wants to know.

"No," I tell her. "Not yet. You're too young to
be beautiful like our mother."

She hates my answers. "You're so correct all
the time, Christopher. Ugh!" she cries, frustrated,
and charges out to complain about me.

I am correct. It's important to me to be correct, and I don't want to live in some fantasy, some movie. Facts are more important than dreams.

Cathy's a girl. She may never believe that facts are more important. I do know some women who do, especially some of my teachers, like Miss Rober, who teaches math and taps the blackboard so hard to make a decimal point that she often breaks the chalk. Miss Rober is fifty-something and has never been married. But that doesn't mean she doesn't wish she was.

Last week, I told Momma that, and she looked at me funny and asked, "How do you know she does? Some women don't, you know."

"She's not a nun, Momma. She wears her clothes to attract men, very tight sweaters and skirts. She likes to show cleavage."

"Christopher Dollanganger! I do believe you're getting too old for your age," she said, which at first I thought was just a funny misstatement but later understood.

Maybe she won't be asking me to wash her back as much or will close her door whenever she gets dressed. She won't come in on me when I bathe and will avoid looking at me when I get dressed.

There will be something between us that has never been: embarrassment.

I hope it doesn't come to that, but then again, I know it's as inevitable as facial hair and shaving.

I paused to take a breath. I couldn't remember when my father had looked uncomfortable looking at me when I was naked. Until she became ill, Mom would help me bathe. Once I was old enough to bathe or shower myself, even she stayed out of the bathroom. And of course, my father was embarrassed even to see me in my underwear now. In fact, it was Suzette's mother who took me for my first bra. When she volunteered for the job, Dad was visibly relieved. Mrs. Osterhouse was always offering to help me do things when it came to female necessities, but until now, I was pretty independent. Dad trusted me to do the right things anyway.

Still, I couldn't help but envision the Dollanganger household, especially a mother parading around naked in front of a son who was almost ten.

Was Christopher really so adult about this so early in his life? Was this the way young men and young women thought of family members naked when they were destined to become doctors?

I was torn between blushing at the thought of all this nudity and trying to think like they obviously did about one another, thinking that there was nothing about them that they should be ashamed to reveal. I wanted to admire them for that, but I couldn't help thinking about Suzette telling Lana and me about the time she saw her older brother, Jason, exploring himself and what happened as a result. I could never look at Jason afterward without thinking about it. How far would Christopher go when it came to all the sexual questions that were bound to come? Right now, he seemed so . . . indifferent. So like a scientist.

Was he capable of love? Did he ever have a girl-friend?

I returned to the pages, now feeling more like a voyeur, someone peeping in through a window and seeing the most intimate moments in the life of a family. There was a part of me that wanted to close the diary, that felt guilty about it and thought maybe my father was right, but a stronger part of me wanted to go on until I knew and understood what had really happened.

My father's job takes him away from home for as long as five days sometimes. Whenever this happens, Momma tells me I am the man of the family until my father comes home. She brushes my hair back, smiles, kisses my cheek, and tells me, "As long as I have you, Christopher, I'll always have a man around the house. Like I told you, some women don't need men, but I'm not one of them."

Out of the corner of my eye, I would see Cathy watching us. She wouldn't be smiling. She'd look almost angry about it. If I told her to do something afterward, she'd say, "You're not my father, Christopher." But in the end, she'd do it. That's Cathy.

She is always the first to greet Daddy when he comes home. She bursts ahead of me as soon as she hears him call out to us when he enters. I know that is important to her, so I always let her get to him first. He winks at me and lifts her and covers her face with kisses, describing how much he has missed her. She always glances back at me with that superior, self-satisfied look to show me Daddy loves her more.

How childish, I would think but never say. Daddy would hug me, too, but he always shakes my hand as well.

"Everything okay here, Christopher?" he would ask me with his slightly tilted head, his eyes a little narrow. Of course, Cathy was afraid I'd mention something bad she had done, some request of Momma's she didn't follow, but I never do. I don't have to. Daddy understands. We almost have telepathy. I once told that to Cathy, and she squinted and raised her nose at me as if she smelled something bad. If I tried to explain it, she'd wave me off and tell me she had something important to do, which she didn't. She's getting to be more and more like that, fleeing from anything she sees as complicated or in her eyes unpleasant.

While Daddy greets us and gives us whatever little gifts he has brought, Momma waits behind us. Sometimes she is smiling, basking in the love Daddy shows us, but lately I notice that she looks annoyed at how much time Daddy is spending on Cathy especially. I think Daddy knows or feels this, too. Yesterday, when he put Cathy down and went to embrace our mother, he held her like he had thought he might never have been able to do it again.

Momma always knows exactly when he will return, and she is always perfectly made up, even though he swears aloud that she doesn't need makeup or pretends to be surprised when he finds out she is wearing any. She's always wearing something special, like a dress he brought back from a previous trip or something he gave her on her last birthday. If she's wearing something new that she bought with money she secretly collected, Daddy never complains or asks her how or when she bought it. He simply compliments her.

I don't know if there is any wife anywhere who knows how to please her husband as well as Momma knows how to please Daddy. I guess I would want to have a wife like that, too. She wouldn't have to be as intelligent as I am. Momma isn't as smart as Daddy, but I know how much she pleases him, and I suppose a man needs that sort of comfort. It's a form of security to know who and what is waiting for you at home.

"You get more beautiful every day, Corrine," he told her today. "Seeing you makes me think I was in dark, cloudy weather the whole time I lived without you."

I could never think of things like that to tell a girl. I'm not romantic enough. I don't know if I will ever be. I guess I'm hoping that the girl I find to marry won't need me to be that romantic.

I don't know if there is such a girl.

When Daddy said she was more beautiful every day, Momma's face brightened, and the glow was so great it was like sunshine for us all.

Well, maybe not as much for Cathy. I've watched her carefully during Daddy's homecomings. I know all about Electra complexes and sibling rivalries. Whenever I read something new about child psychology or something medical, I watch for symptoms. It seems to me that the older Cathy gets, the more she seems jealous of our father's dedicated love for our mother. It's as if she wants to absorb all his love, capture all that he is capable of giving to anyone, even our mother.

And yet Cathy will always be the first one to tell me or anyone else how beautiful our mother is. If there is one thing she wants in her life, it is surely to be as beautiful as our mother. Whenever Momma does anything to enhance her looks, Cathy is there listening, watching, and learning.

"Beauty isn't something you can create with makeup, you know," I told her yesterday when she was pretending in front of her mirror. "You can improve it, maybe, but don't think it comes in some powder or lipstick."

"Yes, it does!" she fired back at me with her eyes. "Momma says a plain woman could look very attractive if someone showed her how to put on makeup and do her hair right." Then she quickly added, "But she said I'm not plain."

I smiled at her. "Beauty is a matter of opinion sometimes," I said.

She squinted and crinkled her nose. "It is not. You don't know anything about it. You're just too . . . smart," she said, and ran to Momma to complain about me.

Cathy can whine and cry better than anyone I know. When she returned to her room, I told her she would win the whining and crying Olympics.

Later, she brought Momma into the living room to tell me I was wrong, but I knew Momma was just trying to get her to stop complaining.

"The man of the house doesn't tease his women," she said. She tried to look angry at me, but she wasn't doing it too well.

Cathy stood there with her arms folded, nodding at me.

I knew Momma was really depending on me to be the man of the house and keep any childish behavior at a minimum. When she looked at me like that, even pretending, I did feel guilty.

"I'm sorry. I didn't mean to tease you, Cathy. Momma knows a lot more than I'll ever know when it comes to being beautiful."

"Or handsome," Momma said, smiling at me. "And I have the most beautiful children. How could I not, with a husband as handsome as your father?"

Cathy was beaming. Her mood quickly changed. She complains about me correcting her all the time and proving I'm right about things because she loves to be right even more than I do. I know winning is very important to her, and more often than not, when we play a game, I will let her win. I do it well. She really believes she has won. Whenever I do this, I glance at Momma, who is usually watching us, and I see that soft, angelic smile on her lips, and I know she loves me more than she could love anyone or anything.

I remember that when Daddy gave me the medical books, Momma said, "There's no doubt. We'll have a famous and wonderful doctor in our family. He'll take care of us when we're old and feeble, and he'll never let his sister get too sick, even when she's married and has a family of her own."

Cathy squinted and looked like she would regurgitate. She was still too young to think of herself as a married woman with children of her own, especially since I'd taken her aside and explained how children really come to be, not just children of animals but people, too.

"You're making it up, and you're as disgusting as poop," she said, and ran off.

Maybe I was wrong to explain it to her while she was still so young. I'm making that mistake often with her and with other kids my age. I just assume they are as ready as I am to learn what is real and what is fantasy. I can't help it, I guess. I feel I have an obligation to protect Cathy, and protecting her means teaching her important things. What is more important than knowing about sex?

Sometimes . . . sometimes I think Cathy
believes we'll never change; we'll never get
older; we'll never be anything more than the
Dollanganger children.

I would never tell anyone this, but writing it in
the diary right now is all right.

Sometimes I go to sleep fantasizing about
that, imagining us forever and ever, the perfect
little family who couldn't be changed by time, by
bad weather, by sickness, or by anything, for that
matter.

But almost as soon as I do this, I snap myself
back to reality and berate myself.

You can't be a child, Christopher, not now,
not ever.

Is that good or bad?

I'm still not sure.

I put the diary down to think about what he had written. After my mother died, my father would have
preferred the human species to be asexual. At least,
that was how I saw it now when I recalled the way he
would react to any questions I had when I was nine
and ten. It wasn't until I was eleven that he asked my
aunt Barbara to have a more intimate conversation
with me. I overheard him talking to her on the phone.

"I've seen some of the other girls in her class, Barbara. Maybe something's changed in the air or something, but some of these sixth-graders have the bodies
of older teenage girls. Kristin can't be far behind. I

think she and her girlfriends are already talking turkey, if you get my drift. I mean, I know they teach them stuff in school, but it can't be the same as what goes on outside the school, right? I'd just like it to be someone in the family."

My dad wasn't a prude, but he was quite shy when it came to what went on between men and women. There were so many times when I saw him redden after one of his workers or someone else made a remark he considered R-rated, especially if it happened in front of me. Usually, however, it was something that went over my head.

Anyway, he impressed Aunt Barbara enough with the need for my special talk even at my age that she made a quick trip to Charlottesville to see us, or *me*, I should say. She pretended she had come just to visit, but I knew and anticipated our tête-à-tête. It happened the second night she was there. After dinner, when I went up to my room to do my homework, she knocked on the door and came in.

Aunt Barbara was not an unattractive woman by any means. She had been engaged when she was in her mid-twenties, but her fiancé was in the army and was shipped to Afghanistan, where he was fatally wounded in a roadside bomb explosion. I know it took her years to get over that, and from the way my father talked about her, she had trouble with every date she had afterward. None of the men who asked her out wanted to be compared to her fiancé, and apparently, she let them believe they would be.

She did have another steady boyfriend for almost two years, but they broke up when he cheated on her. Most of her energy after that went into her work and taking care of my grandmother.

She sat on my bed and smiled at me. "You are growing up fast," she began. "Your father says you're thinking about boys already."

I shrugged.

"Do you have a boyfriend?"

"Not really," I said.

"But there's a boy you like?"

I nodded.

"I was a little older than you when my mother talked to me about all this. You know how she began?"

I shook my head.

"She said, 'I'm going to tell you about yourself and how you will be when you get close to a boy, and I'm going to warn you about things, but you know what, Barbara? You're going to do what you want anyway,'" she said. "Every girl does, and any mother who thinks differently is just fooling herself to make herself worry less. So let me tell you how it was for me the first time I did more than kiss a boy," she began.

I don't think I ever paid stricter attention to anything anyone had ever said. When I looked back on that evening and the way she followed up with me often, I thought that even though Cathy had a mother and a brilliant older brother, I was the luckier one for this part of life. At least, that was what I suspected, but I knew I had to keep reading to see if I was right, to see if Cathy ever paid any attention to her brother Christopher's information about men and women or if her mother gave her the education my mother couldn't.

Today, Cathy and I were both surprised but for different reasons. I should write that Cathy was more shocked.

We learned something I was beginning to suspect.

I noticed some physical changes in Momma and went to the "Merck Manual" to confirm my suspicions.

When we came home from school, I knew immediately that something was very different. Momma wasn't at the door or even moving about the house. She was sitting in her favorite chair by the fireplace and knitting what looked like a tiny sweater.

She put it aside to hug us both. Cathy's eyes never left the sweater. I knew she was thinking it was probably for one of her dolls.

"It's freezing out there today, Momma," I said, and moved to the fireplace.

Cathy never stopped staring at the knitting.

"I have news for you both," Momma began. "I was at Dr. Bloom's today."

"You're not sick," I said. If anything, she looked healthier. After reading what I had, I suspected what she was going to say.

"No. I'm pregnant, children. Here, Christopher," she said, and urged me to feel

her stomach. She watched me carefully. I think I
realized what she was waiting to hear me say.

"There's a lot of movement in your womb."

"What's a womb?" Cathy asked.

"A room for a fetus," I said, looking at
Momma.

She smiled. "Very good, Christopher. They
heard two heartbeats," she said.

"Twins?"

I looked at Cathy, who was acting very
strangely now. She began to back away as if
Momma might explode. She looked angry, too.

"Do you understand, Cathy? Momma is going
to have at least twins. I hope two boys," I said.
"Identical twins, and not simply fraternal."

"You'll be a wonderful older brother, no
matter what they are," Momma said, and looked at
Cathy. "And you'll be a wonderful older sister."

Cathy didn't say anything. She continued to
back away and to shake her head as if she was
looking at a ghost.

I rose. "What's wrong with you?" I asked her.

"I don't want twins!" she cried. "I don't care
about being a good older sister. I don't want any
more babies."

"Cathy?" Momma said as my sister turned
and ran out of the room and to her own. "What's
wrong with her?" she asked me.

"Sibling rivalry," I declared, and Momma
looked at me as if I was speaking Chinese.

Slowly, she rose. "This is ridiculous," she

muttered, and went off to Cathy's room to speak
to her.

I went to mine to start my homework.

Because of how I acted afterward, Cathy thought
I was as upset about Momma getting pregnant as
she was. I'll admit here that I wasn't overjoyed. I
would describe it more as being disappointed in
both our parents, especially Daddy.

I thought Daddy was a very smart man, even
though he wasn't what anyone might describe as
rich or the top man in his field at the moment.
Actually, I was under the impression that he was
getting ready to make some very brilliant move.
Whenever we were alone lately, maybe watching
the news, which usually bored both Momma and
Cathy, and there was a story about someone who
had done something very important or made a
lot of money, he would say things like, "That's
the way it will be for us someday, Christopher.
Someday we're going to live in a really nice
house, a big house, and your mother will have
all of the things she spends hours admiring
in magazines or reading about in one of her
romance novels.

"Cathy will train with the best to be a dancer,
and you're going to attend one of the better
medical schools. We won't have to worry about
the cost of anything. We're going to travel a lot,
too. I always wanted to do a lot of traveling.

"You get your curiosity about life from me,
you know, even though I was never interested in

medicine. Oh, I always respected doctors and still do, but I want to take us all on European trips and trips to Asia and safaris in Africa. The nicer ones, of course. Your mother won't stand for camping out in tents. Nothing like that. We'll always go first-class.

"We'll even go on the 'Queen Mary,'" he said.

Sometimes, when I sat with him and listened to him talk like this, it seemed to me he was just thinking out loud. He wasn't even looking at me. He was just going on and on about owning a boat or a very expensive automobile and a wardrobe of the finest custom-made clothes.

I would never think of him as a dreamer. I thought he was voicing real plans. Someday soon, he would come walking into the house and announce that we had it. He would either have a bigger, more important, very high-paying executive position or have made a wise investment, and we would be very rich.

Why wouldn't I think this about my father? Until now, he had never made a terribly foolish mistake. At least, as far as I knew.

So even though I had my suspicions, when Cathy and I came home from school today, the furthest thing from my mind was that Momma would tell us she was pregnant. Maybe I had snuffed out my suspicions because I didn't want to believe them.

See? No matter what Cathy says about me, I am not Mr. Perfect, and I will admit when I make a mistake. I don't need to go to a therapist to know why I snuffed out the truth that was as plain as day, and it's not because of sibling rivalry. I'm far above that.

First, I don't want to think my father is that careless, and second, I don't want to see my mother worn down by caring for babies.

Just think of it. I am nearly ten, and Cathy is nearly eight. That's a long time between children. Momma isn't used to being up all night and changing diapers and doing feedings, and with Daddy's travel schedule, he won't be that much of a help.

What I know in my heart is that if Momma starts looking dragged out and sees her beauty being sacrificed, she will be one very, very unhappy woman.

Daddy cherishes his private time, too. He loves going with his friends to play tennis when he's off or to play golf with his business associates. He doesn't have all that much time off. There have been many weekends when his travel has taken him into Sundays, too. It's not hard to imagine Momma telling him she is working seven days a week, so when he is free, he is going to have to lend more than just a helping hand now. He is going to have to give her free time to do her window-shopping or have lunch with her girlfriends, not to mention taking us shopping.

At this point in their lives, why did they decide to take on new children? I didn't think they would have sexual accidents. I thought Daddy would be

more careful, or if he wasn't, my mother would
certainly be. There is something going on here
that I don't know. Did Daddy promise our mother
something if she would agree to have more
children? Our lives are too cluttered with secrets,
and I don't like thinking that whatever they are,
they are deliberately being kept from me.

I'm going to stop writing in the diary for a
while. I'm afraid of the things I might write.

I think I might just be as upset and angry as
Cathy is, and I don't like it.

My cell phone rang. I hated the interruption, but I answered it because I knew she would keep calling.

"So?" Lana began. "How was your visit to the
house of horrors?"

Funny, I had read only a small portion of the diary,
but I was beginning to feel an attachment to Christopher and Cathy and to think of them as people I really
had known. It was as if the diary was making us closer
relatives. I suddenly didn't like the idea of anyone
thinking of them as sick, mad people doing horrid
things to each other.

"It was just a pile of rubble, nothing remotely
frightening about it. I think anyone who tells you they
heard screams or cries or saw ghosts is crazy himself."

"So it was a waste of time?"

"No. My father did what he had to do, and he's
helping to move the property off the bank rolls. He'll
get lots of work out of it."

"I don't mean your father. I mean you, dummy."

"I went for a nice walk and saw the lake. It will be a very pretty property again. It's actually very pretty now in a primitive, natural sort of way."

"Boring," she sang. "Kane was very disappointed, by the way. I told him I'd call you to see if you wanted to go to the movies. They'll meet us there."

"When?"

"Tonight, dummy. When else?"

"I can't tonight. And if you call me 'dummy' one more time, I'll tell everyone what you first thought a tampon was."

"All right, all right. I'm sorry. So why not go to the movies tonight?"

"I have to do something very important for . . ."

"For who?"

"My family," I said.

"What?"

"I'll call you tomorrow. Maybe we'll do something during the day."

"Are you serious? You're going to blow us all off?"

I looked at Christopher's diary. Was I really going to give up going out on a date because of this? Maybe I was a little crazy. "Never more serious. It's important." I said.

"Well, what is it? Maybe I can help."

"No," I said, suffocating a laugh. "But thanks for offering. I'll call you," I added, and hung up before she could say another word.

And then I turned the page.

"See what you can do about her," Momma told me after she and Daddy had spoken to Cathy, assuring her that neither would love her any less just because there would be new children in our family. "She can pout better than I can. She'll make pure mush out of the man she marries."

Of course, I was happy Momma came to me for help with Cathy, but I noticed something I hadn't noticed until now during the days that followed. Momma seemed to have less tolerance for Cathy. She was criticizing her more and more at the dinner table and afterward. Cathy's sulking over the twins that were coming was no longer cute or understandable.

"Your sister is just selfish," Momma muttered to me one day. "You should know that it's not easy for a woman when she's pregnant. Look at my figure. Look at how difficult it's getting for me to move around. I feel . . . like a truck. I don't know why I even bother with my makeup or my hair. Your father says I'm as beautiful as ever, but I know he's just trying to please me. You're the only one who knows the truth and is not afraid to say it, Christopher. You will be a wonderful doctor, because you will always say what's true and not what someone wants to hear. Go on. Tell me."

I shrugged. She was right. I didn't like telling lies or distorting facts. What was true was true, and pretending it wasn't wouldn't change it. People who lived like that were weak and foolish. Putting off reality just made it more difficult to face

it. I know this attitude doesn't go over well with
my classmates, but there's none whose opinion
really matters that much to me.

"You can't look the way you looked before
you were pregnant, Momma. Of course, you don't
have the same figure, but your complexion is rosy.
You look healthier than ever," I told her. "It's
characteristic of pregnant women who take care
of themselves, take their prenatal vitamins, and do
whatever their doctors tell them to do. Women
were made to be pregnant."

She looked at me and half-smiled. "I hope you
won't always couch your compliments in some
medical observation. Any girlfriend you have won't
think that's very romantic, Christopher, but thank
you anyway," she said. Then she thought about
it for a moment and shook her head. "I think I'd
rather hear your father tell me I'm no different.
Little lies are okay if they make you happier." She
walked away, smiling.

I went to see Cathy, who was pouting as usual.
She was being destructive, too. She had practically
torn apart one of the dolls Momma had bought
for her and ripped most of the clothing. The gifts
Daddy had been buying her to make her happy were
piled up in a corner as if they had been discarded.

I sat across from her and stared at her.

"What?" she asked. She could never stand my
staring at her with a sour expression on my face.

"You don't want anyone to treat you like a
baby, but you go and act like one."

"I don't care. Momma is mean to me, meaner than ever. Maybe those twins are making her meaner. I wish they'd fall out and go away."

"All right," I said, sighing and sitting on her bed. "Let me try to explain things. When a woman first gets pregnant, a married woman, she's usually very happy about it."

"So?"

"As time goes by and the baby grows and she gains weight, she gets depressed. You remember what that means."

"So?"

"She needs to be comforted and loved even more than before she became pregnant, Cathy. Someday you'll be in the same condition."

Her eyes widened. "I'm not going to get pregnant. I don't want to care for a real baby and change diapers full of poop and wipe drool."

I laughed. "Sure you will, but"—I narrowed my eyes—"if you really love Momma, you will stop making her feel even worse. You'll do more to help her. Daddy is upset with you, too," I added, because I knew that would have more effect.

"He is not."

"You know he tells me things he doesn't tell you."

She looked down. "Momma loves you more, and now, with new children, she'll love me even less," she said. "There won't be enough love to share, and I don't want to share."

"A parent doesn't love one of his or her
children more than the others."

She looked at me strangely. I must admit that
it was the first time she had ever looked at me like
this. It was disturbing, because it was the look of
someone who believed I was either lying to myself
or completely fooled. I didn't think she was
capable of seeing through my words. Of course,
our mother loved me better and always would.
She depended on me more. But I wasn't going
to admit that to Cathy. She would be even more
miserable and say hurtful things to our mother.

How intensely she could glare back at me,
though. No one else could make me look away.

"Just think about what I said and see if you can
be nicer," I told her, and left.

She was right to give me that look, of course.
Maybe Daddy loved her as much as or a little more
than he loved me, but he respected me more and
always would.

Knowing that and writing it will help me sleep
better tonight.

Christopher's words resurrected old memories. I had
often wondered why my parents didn't have another
child. I never asked my mother about it, but I did ask
my father once, and all he said was a cryptic "It wasn't
in the cards."

I imagined Christopher being here with me right
now and my turning to him to ask him to explain what
my father had meant.

He'd surely shrug as if there was no mystery, but I had heard my father say that when I was just ten. I wouldn't shrug. Maybe I was more like Cathy than like him.

"There must have been some physiological reason your mother didn't have another child," he would tell me. "Men and women usually don't feel comfortable talking about it, because one or the other was unable to make it work. Understand?"

Yes, I understood. I understood years later but never brought it up again for exactly the reason my imaginary Christopher was citing. If there was one thing I would never want to do, it was make my father feel uncomfortable about anything, least of all himself.

Still, after reading some of what went on between Christopher and Cathy and anticipating how their lives were about to change when the twins were born, I couldn't help wondering what my life would have been like if I had a younger sister or brother, or even an older sister or brother.

Cathy was obviously afraid that her parents wouldn't have enough love for that many children and that she would suffer the most. Reading between Christopher's comments, I realized she must have felt inferior even at that young age, inferior in the sense that she could see or feel that her mother loved her brother more and that her father held her brother in higher esteem. Both depended on him. She was still too young to be anything more than someone who needed care.

What is our capacity to love? I wondered. Does a

mother who has six or even ten children love each of them equally or as much as someone who had only one child? Was that even possible? Was Cathy really so wrong to be afraid and upset?

"Hello, up there!" I heard Dad shout. I looked at the clock and leaped out of bed. It was way past time for me to set the table. When I appeared at the top of the stairs, he looked up at me and just shook his head, walking off. I hurried down.

"Sorry," I called, and headed to the dining room to unfold the tablecloth.

"Don't you have any homework for Monday?" Dad asked when I came into the kitchen to get the dishes and silverware. "Something else to read or do?"

"I'll do it tomorrow," I said. "I don't have that much. I always stay a little ahead, Dad. You know that."

"Um," he said. He looked at me. "I want to remind you that what you're reading doesn't necessarily have to be the truth. Kids lie occasionally, or they exaggerate. Maybe he was too young to understand it all."

"I know that, Dad. Don't worry. I'm not gullible. The meat loaf smells good," I said, eager to change the subject.

He didn't say anything. I set the table and returned to the kitchen to prepare a small dinner salad.

"Seems I recall your mentioning seeing some boy," Dad practically mumbled.

"I've gone to a few things with Kane Hill. Nothing formal. Just met at the mall or at the movies."

"Still looking him over."

"Something like that," I said. "But it's not like buying a new pair of shoes," I added, and he laughed.

"I've done some work for Stan Hill. He has about ten car dealerships. Don't know much about the family. Is he a nice boy?"

"Yes."

"Well, it's Saturday night. Nothing for you to do socially? No parties, no meeting friends?"

"I wasn't in the mood," I offered.

He had his chin down and his eyes up when he looked at me. "Is this a female thing?"

I smiled. "Not exactly, but I don't know any boys who would use not being in the mood as an excuse, claiming it's a male thing, so maybe it is only a female thing."

He nodded. "What's a bigger mystery than a woman?" he asked.

"A man?"

"Please. We're so obvious it's pathetic," he told me, and continued to work on dinner.

When Dad worried about something, the wrinkles in his forehead would deepen. I knew it was a nervous habit, but his ears would quirk, too. In fact, he was one of the few people I knew who could actually move their ears at will.

"I have muscles everywhere," he would tell me.

I complimented him again on the meat loaf, and he went into one of his familiar stories about his days as a short-order cook, which usually led to a story about his time in the navy. Eventually, that would lead to him describing how Mom enjoyed his cooking on weekends so she could have time off.

"Nevertheless, she'd always find something to do for me and not herself," he said. "Selfishness just wasn't in her vocabulary. We used to argue about who loved who more. Finally, I told her I was bigger. There was more of me, so there was more love in me. She just shook her head, smiled, and walked off. That was how she was. I don't think I had one real argument with that woman. Why . . ." He stopped himself.

"What's the matter, Dad?" I asked.

"I gotta get to some paperwork on an estimate I promised someone tomorrow," he said. I knew he wasn't telling the truth. This happened often. He would realize how much he was talking about Mom and how that was only going to make him and me suffer the pain of our loss more. Neither of us ever said such a thing to the other, but it was out there, hovering between us like words caught in our throats.

I cleared the table and cleaned up the kitchen. When I looked for him, I saw him at his desk, just staring down at whatever paperwork he was making for himself. He wasn't reading it or writing anything. He was still lost in his memories. I didn't say anything. Quietly, I returned to my room and the diary, which to me had become a gold mine of memories. I hoped only that what I came up with at the end would help me in my own life.

I should have realized there was something going on when Daddy began staying home more and more to take care of Momma during the last weeks of her pregnancy. Why wasn't he needed more at work? Was he just drawing from his vacation time?

Momma was more irritable than ever, impatient, complaining that Dr. Bloom had her delivery date wrong. He wanted her to move around, but she resisted, some days lying in bed most of the day. I told her that wasn't good, that everything I had read about pregnancy indicated she should keep active.

She even snapped at me. "You're not carrying this weight, Christopher. Go find thirty pounds and tie it around your waist and then tell me how it feels and let me see how active you are," she said.

I agreed that she was too heavy, but every time I commented about the candy Daddy brought home for her or the bowls of ice cream she ate, she glared at me. Then she would just start crying.

"It will come off quickly," Daddy assured her. He looked at me to be sure I didn't contradict him.

Finally, one night just before dinner, our neighbor Bertha Simpson came over to prepare the meal for Cathy and me. I knew something was happening, but Momma and Daddy's bedroom door had been closed for hours. Suddenly, it opened, and he practically carried her out, warning us to be good.

"Her water broke?" I asked as they made it to the front door. He nodded, and they left.

"What water? How can water break? You can't break water," Cathy said. "That's stupid."

Mrs. Simpson looked as interested as Cathy when I explained what that meant. "I never saw a little boy as young as you know so much," she said. She shook her head as if that meant I was into witchcraft or something.

"Christopher is not a little boy. He's a genius," Cathy piped up. No matter how jealous she might be of me or how angry about something I had said or done, she never failed to defend me if anyone outside of our family dared criticize me or chastise me. I couldn't ask for a better watchdog or bodyguard.

I tried to keep Cathy occupied after dinner. Although serious complications with baby deliveries were not as common as they used to be, I couldn't help being a little worried as the hours went by. Maybe one or both of the twins had died. I didn't even want to think about Momma dying, and whenever Cathy asked me why it was taking so long to push two tiny babies into the world, I acted as if it was supposed to. I told her it takes double the time, which seemed to quiet her for a while. I kept her watching television until her eyes began to close and I knew she wouldn't fight going to bed. Mrs. Simpson wanted to help me get her to sleep, but I told her I didn't need her help. She looked at me oddly and followed me to Cathy's room.

"I don't think you should be doing that," she

said when I began to undress Cathy, who was almost comatose by now.

"I'm just getting her pajamas on her."

She stood back with her arms folded and didn't leave the room until Cathy was under the covers and asleep.

"I'll be going to bed myself," I said. "You don't have to stay, Mrs. Simpson."

"Of course I have to stay," she said. "Would I leave two young children alone at night?"

"There isn't anything you can do that I can't do for myself and Cathy," I told her, then shrugged and left her standing in the hallway.

I was up almost all night, waiting to hear Daddy come home or for the phone to ring, but he didn't, and it didn't. Finally, just before dawn, I fell asleep. I woke with surprise and washed my face before I hurried out. The house was so quiet. Cathy, grinding the sleep out of her eyes, ventured into the hallway. She was still in her pajamas.

"Did Momma bring the babies home?" she asked.

"She wouldn't bring them home so quickly," I said, but I was very concerned.

She followed me into the living room. I could hear Mrs. Simpson working in the kitchen. Cathy and I looked at each other, and then the front door opened and Daddy came in. He looked like he had slept in his clothes, but his face was beaming.

"Twins, all right," he announced.

Mrs. Simpson came to the living room.

"Boys or girls?" he asked us.

"Boys," I said.

"Yes," Cathy said. I knew she was hoping for that. She didn't want to compete with another daughter.

"Amazing," he told Mrs. Simpson, and then he looked at us and said, "We have one of each. And they're perfect, as perfect as you two. Let me get washed up and changed, and I'll take you to see your brother and sister."

Cathy smirked.

"Have you thought of names yet?" Mrs. Simpson asked him.

I perked up at that. Never had I heard them discuss names. I had all sorts of good ideas for names, but they had never asked me.

"Cory and Carrie," Daddy replied. "Everyone important to me has a name starting with C . . . Corrine, Cathy, Chris, and now Cory and Carrie."

"We'll all have the same initials," Cathy said, which surprised me. She had thought of that so quickly. "You can't give us anything with just our initials on it."

Daddy laughed. "Don't you worry about that. Your full name will be written on everything I give you." He picked her up, kissed her, and spun her around and then headed to his bedroom to get ready.

"You two should eat something and get dressed," Mrs. Simpson said.

"I don't want to go," Cathy said, pouting.

"Stop thinking about what you want, and start thinking about what's good for Momma," I told her. "Let's eat breakfast."

I seized her hand and pulled her into the kitchen, with her yelling that her arm was coming off.

Later, at the hospital, we saw our new brother and sister. I watched Cathy carefully. The resistance in her face melted away. Her eyes danced with delight. She glanced at me and then turned back to them. I was confident that her jealousy would wane and disappear.

I had come to a page with just a smudge on it. It looked like Christopher had started to write something and then stopped. Toward the bottom of the page was something that looked like a doodle. It had no shape or meaning that I could see. I turned it quickly, afraid that this was the end, that he had written no more.

When I saw the words, I breathed a sigh of relief. What a disappointment it would have been. For a moment, I was thinking that perhaps he stopped writing in the diary when they were brought to Foxworth. Nothing really would be learned, then. Of course, my father might be happy about that, but I'd be left wondering forever.

As if he knew I was reading it, he began by telling why there was this empty page.

I haven't written in my diary for some time now. To be honest, I thought I never would again. I spent many days and nights thinking about whether it had become silly, even stupid, to do it. I don't believe I'll ever give it to someone to read. I might change my mind. There might someday be someone I would trust enough to expose all my thoughts and feelings about myself and my family. Right now, I doubt it, but I have decided to continue and catch my diary up to where I am now and what has happened since I last sat down to write.

I have plenty of time to do it. I'm upstairs in an attic in a mansion, and the door is shut for all of us Dollanganger children. I write mostly at night when the twins and Cathy are asleep. Sometimes I don't put on any light but sit by the window and use the moonlight.

Actually, now I am very happy I started to do this. It helps me cope.

Nevertheless, it's very difficult for me to write about these early years, with the four of us needing more and more of not only love but the things growing children require.

As Cathy grew, she became more interested in herself. She was always crying for new clothes or new shoes, complaining whenever any of the girls in her class had something she didn't have.

I never came right out and said it, but it was Momma's fault. She had turned Cathy into this little replica of herself, spending hours and hours on beauty tips, fussing with hair, modeling new clothes, craving more jewelry. She let Cathy wear earrings when she was eleven, and although Momma didn't know it, Cathy and some of the other girls in her class were already into lipstick and sometimes toying with eye shadow and mascara. Of course, Daddy knew nothing of that, and even if Momma knew, I didn't think she would make as big a deal of it.

"Cathy's growing up too fast," I might tell her.

She would look at me askance. "My problem," she told me, "was I didn't grow up fast enough, Christopher. Innocence is not an advantage for a woman in this world."

I will have to admit that I didn't think all that much about it. I helped with whatever chores were necessary when it came to the twins, but Cathy had moved into that role smoothly as the years passed. By the time the twins were four, Cathy was as good at feeding them, bathing them, and putting them to sleep as Momma was. Cathy would be the one to read them bedtime stories and keep them occupied by playing games with them. In fact, I will admit here that Momma took advantage of Cathy, leaving her to do what she should have been doing just so she could go off with some of her girlfriends or shop. She told us she had to do that; she had to look more for bargains because Daddy was struggling to keep a home with four children.

And a wife who wasn't cutting back, I thought but again never said.

Still, despite the strain all this put on our

family, I wouldn't say we were unhappy. No matter how difficult things had become for him, Daddy never came home without a broad smile on his face, bathing himself in the laughter and kisses his children had for him. Momma was always ready to celebrate something, always eager to dress up and go somewhere.

Birthdays came and went for all of us, but one special birthday loomed in our near future, because it was Daddy's. We always liked to fuss over his birthday. He enjoyed it, pretending he was a little boy again, excited about presents and blowing out candles. This birthday was his thirty-sixth. Momma was determined to make it special by having a surprise party. The neighbors she invited were sworn to secrecy. All of us contributed to dressing up the house, hanging balloons and crepe paper. Cathy made a big "Happy Birthday, Daddy" sign and had the four of us write our names on it. Momma signed it, too, with "Forever your love, Corrine."

My fingers tremble as I write this. I always believed it was very important for me to have full control of my emotions. A doctor couldn't think about the patient he was treating too personally, or his feelings might cloud his judgment. I want this diary to be as close to the truth as possible, but it's not easy to put all your feelings off to one side and just write facts, especially when those facts are about your family.

Here are the facts, however. The police arrived close to seven p.m. They told Momma that Daddy had been in a very bad traffic accident, that it had been fatal. All of us refused to believe it until they brought in some of his possessions and his overnight suitcase.

It was as if a door had slammed on all our sunshine, now and forever. Cathy was the most emotional about it, even more than Momma. As with everything these days, I was asked to help with my brother and sisters, occupy their minds, and be the man of the house now that Daddy was gone. The only ones who saw me cry at all were Momma and occasionally Cathy. Ironically, Cathy criticized me for not crying or acting as devastated as she was. I overheard her tell Carrie and Cory that I went into a corner to cry and that she had seen me crying often.

What I did cry over was the realization that I was just getting to know my father the way I had always wanted to know him. He always thought of me as older than I was, but lately, I could feel him observing how much I actually did in the house, how much I did for Momma and my brother and sisters. I would never say he saw me as an equal, not yet, but he saw me as mature enough for him to be more revealing about himself and his own dreams, faults, and experiences.

Cathy never knew how much time Daddy and I spent alone together. He wanted to be sure to have that important father-son talk about sex and girls. I made it much easier for him, because I knew so much about the human body. It was

during one of our last talks that he told me he was
a little concerned about Cathy.

"She has a flair for independence," he said.
"That's a euphemism for defiance. You see how
difficult she can be sometimes when she's told to
do something. Lately, she's always asking why.
She's quickly passing the point where she will just
obey. I'm not saying I'm any sort of expert when it
comes to females, but I can tell you Cathy's going
to be a handful when she starts dating."

I agreed with him and promised I would
always look out for her. It was almost as if he
had a premonition about his own fateful birthday.
There was so much left for me to learn from him
and about him. There should be some natural
law preventing any child from losing either of his
parents until he has had enough time to really get
to know them both.

But enough of feeling sorry for myself. It was
pretty clear that our lives would never be the same,
all our lives.

I set the diary aside because my tears were making it
hard to see the words, and I didn't want to drip any on
the pages.

I was crying for the Dollanganger children and
Corrine, but I was really crying more for myself.
What Christopher was saying about losing his father
too soon was just as true for me; I had lost my mother
far too soon. How I wished I had had a brother or a
sister back then. For Christopher, siblings were a good

distraction, but there was something more important. He had a sister who was old enough to fully understand their grief. He could share his grief with her whenever he wanted, even though he was not one to show his emotions.

I shared the loss of my mother with my father, but his grief was different from mine. A man's love for his wife is different from a child's love for her mother. Yes, he was lost for a long while. I could remember him going from room to room as though there was no place he could go for any comfort because every place in our house had some reminder of Mom. A grown man needed a grown woman, especially the one with whom he had shared all his dreams and fears. A daughter would never, could never, be enough.

I knew that he went off to cry where I could not see him, just as Christopher wrote he had done as often as he could. And just like Christopher, I mourned all that I could have known about my mother and had lost the chance to discover. I wanted to talk to her when I was older and could understand more and, just like Christopher, be trusted with information reserved for more mature young people. I wanted to hear about her childhood fears and see if they were the same as mine. I wanted to have her guidance when it came to boys and sex and romance. All that had been taken away from me, and so my grief was different from my father's, just like Christopher's was different from his mother's.

I rose from my bed and went out into the hallway, standing by the top of the stairs for a few moments and listening. Daddy was watching television now. I suspected he might have fallen asleep watching it, which was something he did when he watched alone and even occasionally when I was watching something with him that really didn't amuse or entertain him. He'd watch it for me, but the day's work would catch up in his muscles and bones, and he'd drift off. Rarely did I wake him before it was time for me to go to sleep.

Christopher's brief factual description of his father's death had brought me back to the afternoon at the hospital when Dad came out of Mom's room before I could enter. I had been brought from kindergarten. I didn't realize it then, but later I understood that Dad had remained with Mom for hours after she had passed away. He had sat at her bedside, holding her hand. The nurses and the doctor urged him to leave, but he wouldn't listen, and no one bothered him. I think he wanted to be sure I had arrived first.

"Your mother has gone, Kristin," he said with a broken smile on his trembling lips.

"Gone?" In my childish imagination, I assumed he meant she had gotten up from the hospital bed and left. Maybe she was already home.

"She's gone to be with God," he continued. "When you look at her, you will see she is peaceful. She has no pain. I want you to go in and just look at her. She'll know you are there, okay?"

"Will she look at me, too?"

"Not the way you think. You'll understand someday. I promise," he said.

In his grief, my father looked strangely younger. They say people seem to age overnight with the death of a loved one, but he looked more like a little boy who wanted to believe in fantasies. That's how I remembered him at that moment.

I did what he asked. Mom did look peaceful, but there was something about her that told me she really was gone. I didn't cry loudly. I felt the tears streaming down my cheeks, but I barely made a sound. I thought if I did, I might somehow ruin her trip to see God or something. I was afraid to kiss her, and Dad didn't encourage it. I think he was afraid of what I would say after my lips felt her cold skin.

He took my hand again and led me out.

It had been a while since I had thought about all this. Christopher's diary seemed to have the power to open old wounds or revive closely held memories and secrets that lay dormant for both me and him. More important, I wanted them revived. I wanted to relive my childhood feelings and vividly recall some of my wonderful moments with my mother. It was like passing through a portal to go back in time, a fantasy I could make real. As quietly as I could, I went up the short stairway to our attic and opened the door. The light switch was on the right side.

Our attic was about the width of the whole house, with two panel windows that faced the front. The previous owners, who were the original owners, had left some old furniture up here. Dad called them pack rats and claimed there were many people like them, who couldn't get themselves to throw away or give away anything.

Some, he said, believed the possession would become valuable with age, and others clung to the idea that eventually, they would find some relative or close friend to give the item to, even though they rarely did. Because of the refurbishing and remodeling work he often did, Dad often came across what he called "prime examples of dying memories."

In our attic, the previous owners had left a hardwood wardrobe with a walnut veneer and embossed cherubs on the doors, another antique that now contained most of Mom's clothes; a cherry wood chest, which had many pairs of her shoes; a large dark maple full-length oval mirror; a dark brown leather settee with ugly thick armrests and legs; and some dark maple chairs from an old dining-room set. There was also a scattering of some of our own possessions in cartons lined up along the far right wall. Dad said the attic floor was well constructed, and except for one spot where there had been a leak many years ago, there was a decent-looking insulated ceiling. I suspected that he came up here from time to time to do just what I was about to do, open the wardrobe and look at Mom's clothes.

Most people give away the clothes that belonged to the ones they loved. I knew that my father had trouble doing that, and that even though he was probably past the reluctance, he would rather not think about it. He would rather feel that there was something more of my mother with us besides old photographs and videos, something she had touched and that had touched her. Too many years had gone by for the scent of her perfume to be on her clothes, I thought, but when I brought some of the dresses and blouses to my face, I was sure the scent had lingered. With it came flashes of her face, her smile, and the sound of her voice when she sang or read to me or just asked me to do something.

I was thankful that being in the presence of her clothes didn't make me cry. It brought me some comfort. I wondered if Christopher would talk about something similar later in his diary. Sharing the loss of a parent drew me closer to him. I sat on the old settee and looked at the opened wardrobe, imagining Christopher seated beside me, talking to me in a very adult manner, explaining everything about memories and sorrow and moving on with your life.

"Neither your mother nor my father would want their death to destroy us," he would surely say. "I had the feeling my father believed I would be all right no matter what, and I'm sure your mother had great faith in your father."

Yes, I thought. Yes.

I rose, closed the wardrobe, and shut off the attic light before I went downstairs to the living room, where I found my father asleep in his chair as I had expected. I turned off the television, and just like always, his eyes popped open.

"What?" he said.

"Time to wake up and go to sleep, Dad," I told him.

He rubbed his cheeks, glanced at his watch, and nodded. "Were you watching television with me?"

"No."

"Still reading that diary?"

"Yes."

"Don't tell me about it," he said, standing and holding his hand out like a traffic cop. "I, personally, want to get a good night's sleep."

"I thought you just did, watching television."

"Ha, ha." He turned to leave but paused. "Let's get the week's food shopping done tomorrow. I think I'm looking at a busy workweek."

"Okay. I'll make a list."

"Good. Good," he said, and lumbered up the stairway. He paused again and looked back at me. "Don't stay up too late. Give your eyes a rest."

"Will do," I said.

He muttered something to himself and continued up the stairs. I went to the kitchen and began to work on the list. I wouldn't read any more of the diary tonight, I thought. I'd take a long break.

If I could . . .

Settling into the Trap

❦

"Hey," Kane Hill said as soon as I picked up my phone. "What happened to you last night? Thought we had a date."

"I don't remember making it definite," I said. "I was just tired. I felt I might be coming down with something, so I decided to rest."

"Yeah, you came down with boredom. It's catching around here. How about hanging out today?"

"I have to go shopping with my father and get to my homework. I left it all for the last minute."

"You? You're the leading candidate for valedictorian, aren't you? You're in all the honors classes."

"Whatever. I'm not worrying about it, Kane."

He laughed. "Sure. Anyway, I'm having a house party Friday night to start the three-day weekend. My parents are going to Richmond."

We had Monday off because of teacher meetings. Most of our teachers, knowing we had an extra day off, usually piled on the homework to make up for it.

"Do your parents know about the party?"

"More or less," he said. "I wanted to be sure I got to you early enough to get it onto your busy calendar."

"I can just squeeze you in," I said, and he laughed again.

"Lana says you've been hanging around at Foxworth."

"Hardly hanging around. I went with my father when he went to do an evaluation for the bank."

"Well, how was it?"

"How was what?"

"Being there."

"I took a nice walk to the lake on the property and then just watched my father and Todd Winston go through their inspection of the foundation. It's the original one. Someone might buy the property and build on it again."

"My father's always toyed with that idea, but my mother gets the shakes just talking about it."

"There's nothing to get the shakes about. It's just an overgrown tract of land with rubble."

"Safe place for lovers to park at night, maybe, huh?" he asked. I was sure that his mind was full of imaginary scenarios.

"I gotta go, Kane. I'll write Friday in big block letters on my calendar."

"See you at school."

"Okay," I said, and hung up.

There was a lot about Kane that I liked. He was one of the better-looking boys in our school, but I think what I liked most about him was his casual, relaxed manner. I rarely saw him hyper or upset. He was famous for his James Dean shrug. About two years ago, there was a James Dean revival in one of the movie theaters, and many of the boys were trying to imitate him, but Kane really did have that offbeat smile and relaxed way about him. When he smiled at me now, especially since the last time we had spent time together at the mall and he took me home, it was as if he and I were sharing some big secret. I knew most of my girlfriends, especially Lana and Suzette, were more than a little jealous and were dying to know what had happened between us. I didn't say anything, because I knew they would be disappointed. Not enough had happened to please them.

It wouldn't be hard to break new sexual ground with Kane. He kept his light brown hair midway between the top and the base of his neck. Strands were always falling over his forehead, threatening to block the vision of his soft hazel eyes. Sometimes I thought his self-confidence had just a little more arrogance than I appreciated, but part of that was also just what everyone assumed the son of one of the wealthiest men in Charlottesville would possess, although his older sister, Darlena, was not stuck-up by any means. Kane was an above-average student, athletic, and, as Lana would mutter sometimes, "drop-dead gorgeous." She said it was her mother's favorite expression for every stud she saw in real life and on television.

No matter what, though, I didn't want to be taken for granted by any boy. Actually, I thought that what attracted Kane to me most was my fairly obvious indifference. It challenged him to work harder at winning me over, and for now, that was the most interesting thing about our new relationship.

I did everything I told Kane I was going to do. Dad and I went shopping at the supermarket. Every time we did, he never failed to tell me how much he had depended on my mother to do the week's grocery shopping.

"You know, I can do it all by myself now, Dad," I told him. "I drive."

"That's all right. I don't have that much opportunity to spend time with you, Kristin."

"This isn't spending time with me, Dad. It's spending time with chopped meat and potatoes," I told him, and he laughed.

I think he wanted to shop with me because it kept my mother's memory vivid for him. More and more these days, he was telling me how much I resembled her. He said that any father wants his daughter to look more like her mother than like him. "After all, she's the one he fell in love with, right?"

Thinking about this reminded me about Christopher's sister Cathy, who he said wanted more than anything to look like her mother. It was clear from what I had read so far that his mother really must have been very beautiful and also very aware of that. From the way he was describing her, she was obsessed with it. The implication was that she spent too much time on her makeup and hair and clothes, pushing her responsibilities onto both him and Cathy. Maybe Cathy loved her father more, but I sensed that she loved the idea of becoming as beautiful as her mother most. I wasn't sure yet how Christopher felt about that. Did he want her to be as beautiful as their mother? Did he think she really could be?

I noticed that whenever any of my friends complimented another on how handsome or beautiful their older brothers or sisters were, they seemed surprised. Was there something about being a brother or sister that made you feel weird or guilty if you were a girl and thought your older brother was handsome or if you were a boy and thought your older sister was beautiful? No one would deny that his or her mother was pretty.

My mother was very attractive but in a more natural sort of way. We had the same hair and eyes, but I thought she had fuller lips and higher cheekbones whenever I compared myself to her now. I would hold her picture up beside me and look at myself in the mirror. Was that something Cathy Dollanganger would do? My mother didn't use very much makeup, as I recall. According to Dad, she didn't go to the beauty salon as often as most of her friends.

"But she could gussy up," he told me, "whenever we had a fancy affair to attend." He said that expression was something he had picked up from his grandmother, "gussy up."

"All I have to do is use that once, and I'll be marked for life in my school," I told him.

"It says a lot more than cool, girl," he replied, and we both laughed.

More than once, I'd wished I had been born in an earlier time. Maybe Dad was exaggerating or saw things as having been better when he was younger because he wanted to think of them that way. One of my English teachers, Mr. Stiegman, once told us that nostalgia was nothing more than dissatisfaction with the present. Anything looked better than now, even harder times. It was a fantasy that people accept. Not according to my father, however. Besides harping on loyalty and complaining that youth was wasted on the young, he seemed genuinely happy with the twists and turns he had made in his life.

It took a few hours to shop and then get everything put away. While Dad planned our dinner and then watched a basketball game, I went up to my room to do my homework. No matter what I was working on, my eyes would drift toward Christopher's diary. It felt as if it was really calling to me: *Read me. I need you to read me.*

But I resisted. I needed to concentrate on my work. Kane was right. I was neck-and-neck with another student in our class to be valedictorian, and I so wanted that to please my father and in my heart to please my mother, too. Ironically, that thought gave me pause again and drew me to look at the diary.

I had felt Christopher's pride in his accomplishments and how they pleased his parents. He wanted to be a doctor almost more for their sake than his own, but Cathy struck me as being far more self-centered. Was that because she was so young? On the other hand, young children are always looking for their parents' approval. That was why she was so afraid when the twins were announced. She thought she might lose that approval or have it diluted. After the twins were born, she was, according to Christopher, becoming more and more of a help to her mother and to her father before his death. Maybe she wanted the twins to love her more than they loved their mother. Maybe that was her sweet revenge.

What a complicated family they had been, or were all families really just as complicated? Dad and I basically only had each other. We were a simple family now. After reading only part of Christopher's diary, I made a mental note to pay more attention to my friends and their relationships with their parents and siblings to see if there were any sorts of resemblances to the Dollangangers.

In an eerie sort of way, Christopher's diary was gradually taking over my everyday thoughts. Was there something magical about this book, something supernatural just like Foxworth itself in people's eyes? For a long moment, I wondered if it would actually change me in some dramatic way. I had the strong impression that my father suspected that or feared it. Maybe, just maybe, he already knew what I was about to discover when I continued reading the diary, and that was why he didn't want me to do it.

If my mother were alive, would she let me read it? One thing my father could have said that might have stopped me would be "Your mother wouldn't want you to read that," but he didn't say it. He would never use my mother or the memory of her to get me to do something.

It took all my self-control to finish my schoolwork and go to sleep without turning another page of Christopher's diary, but it was the first thing on my mind in the morning, and I knew that when I arrived at school, I was behaving differently from the get-go. First, I didn't want to have any homework to do after school, so instead of wasting my time in study hall, at lunch, and between periods, I attacked every assignment and ignored my friends, who were full of gossip from the weekend. Second, I wanted the school day to end as quickly as possible, and when Kane or Lana or any of the girls invited me to do something after school, I turned them all down, claiming I had some important household chores. Most shrugged, some smirked, but only Kane gave me a knowing look and a small smile.

"I hope there's not another man involved," he whispered after the last class of the day ended and we all started out of the room.

I just smiled back at him. You see, there really was another man with whom I was involved—Christopher Dollanganger—but I wasn't about to mention it or even hint at it. I just couldn't outright deny Kane's half-facetious accusation, and because of that, his curiosity brightened. I even thought he might follow me home to be sure that was where I was going. I wondered how he would react if he knew the truth, relieved that it was only someone in a diary or spooked that I would be so drawn to it?

I couldn't blame him for either reaction.

I could tell that my father had been home, which was unusual on a workday. My first thought was that he might have decided to get the diary away from me. He might have been thinking about it all day. Panicked, I hurried up to my room. It was there where I had left it, but it looked like it had been picked up and placed differently. Had he thought of doing that but changed his mind out of fear of how I would react? Of course, there were parents who forbade their children to read something or view something. They believed that they were doing it to protect their children, but it had been some time now since my father had treated me like a young, impressionable girl.

Oh, he issued standard warnings about driving carefully, not staying out too late, avoiding bad influences, but he did it almost mechanically, as if it was something he had to do but didn't believe was as necessary with me as it would be for other girls my age. He had confidence in me that came from our mutual pain, the loss of my mother. We trusted each other in ways I could see my friends' parents didn't trust them. Because of how his father's death had only sped up his already quickened maturity, it occurred to me that Christopher's mother might have had the same sort of attitude toward him that my father had toward me.

Was I deliberately looking for these resemblances between us, or were they simply there and too obvious to deny?

I held the diary reverently in my hands. It was as if it could give me psychic powers. Now I felt sure of what had occurred. Sometime today, at some moment, maybe because of something someone said or something Dad remembered, he had come home to dispose of this book. When it came to doing it, he retreated, but that didn't mean he wouldn't come for it again. I made up my mind to hide it well from now on. I didn't like keeping secrets from my father, not now, not ever, but this had become too important to me. I would see it through to the end. It was a promise I had made to Christopher and a promise I would keep.

I sat on my bed and opened the diary.

What happened to us next, I knew was coming. Oh, it was obvious that Cathy would go into a deep depression. She didn't care about anything, not her schoolwork, how she dressed and looked, or even how the twins were getting along. Whenever she was home, she was in a sulk, sleeping more than ever, and practically bursting out in hysterical tears every time Daddy's name was brought up or she saw something of his.

Momma depended mostly on me to get her to snap out of it. She tried to comfort her occasionally, telling her the expected things like we should be grateful for the years we had Daddy. Nothing comforted Cathy. I wasn't all that much help, either. I was hurting just as deeply as she was, and I was full of the same rage that this had happened. In all my dreams, my father was out there in the audience looking up proudly while I

accepted my diplomas from high school and from
college. Now those dreams had evaporated or
burst like bubbles.

But something else was going on, something
I anticipated simply by looking at the growing pile
of bills on Momma's desk. She had no job. Our
neighbors had been helping, bringing us food from
time to time, but something deeper and darker
was surrounding our devastated family. I was afraid
even to dream of college and medical school.
The twins were crying and complaining more, and
Cathy's rage against the injustice of our father's
unexpected death and the God who had taken
him from us boiled over nightly. Momma looked
like she was sinking in the quicksand of one tragic
thing after another.

In the beginning, whenever I tried to have
a serious conversation about our situation, she
would start to tear up and wave me off. I felt like
I was making everything more painful by asking
realistic questions. There was nothing to do but
wait until she was ready.

The time came when she finally was.

One night, while the twins were occupied with
themselves, she pulled Cathy and me aside and
told us how dire things were.

Incredibly, Daddy had not kept up a life
insurance policy. There would be no money
coming from that sort of thing. All of the
possessions we had that were bought on time

would be reclaimed. We couldn't keep up the
payments. With every sentence she uttered, it
felt as if the roof was falling lower and lower and
would soon bury us.

I wondered why she was so busy every night
writing letters. Surely, she was asking someone in
the family somewhere for help, or maybe she was
applying for a job. Even I was shocked by her next
revelation.

"I have been writing to my mother," she said,
"asking her to help us."

Neither Cathy nor I could speak for a
moment. All my life, I had wondered about our
grandparents, our family. Neither Daddy nor
Momma wanted to talk about them. They never
mentioned them and always avoided answering
questions, so I stopped asking.

"She has agreed to our living in their house in
Charlottesville, Virginia," Momma said. Her face
was suddenly bright with the happiness and hope
we hadn't seen since Daddy's death. "We're not
just going to live with two elderly people who need
us to care for them or anything. My parents are
rich, very rich, as rich as some kings and queens."

She went on to describe the house, and then
she almost casually dropped the news that froze
me in my shoes, news that Cathy couldn't quite
comprehend.

We were going to leave that night on a train.
The reality of what she was saying took hold

as she continued to describe how she had grown
up in a big house with servants and how our lives
would be wonderful again. Now Cathy began to cry
and complain about leaving her friends.

"What friends? You've been ignoring them for
weeks anyway," I told her. She looked at me as if I
was betraying her for not complaining about this as
hard as she was, but the cold truth was staring us
in the face. We had no income; we were in debt.
We could even be evicted!

Cathy grew coldly quiet again, until Momma
described how little we could take with us. She
wanted us to take no more than two suitcases
for all four of us. Cathy began to wail about all
the toys and dolls she would be leaving behind.
Momma promised she would have far more when
we were living with her parents.

But we hadn't reached the worst fact of all
yet. I could see it in Momma's face. She had
one more thing to tell us. She tried to make it
seem less frightening and astounding than it was
by beginning with "There is, however, one small
thing."

Small thing? It was like telling passengers on
the Titanic that there were no more life jackets.

Momma had been written out of her father's
will. The reality was that whether we were here or
there, we were just as poor.

"Did Daddy know this, Momma?" I asked
her. I was thinking about all the times he had sat

with me and described the great things we were
going to do and have, the trips, the expensive
clothes, the college educations, all of it. Was he
anticipating inheritance?

"Yes," she said. "He knew I was disinherited,
but he kidded me about it and said I had 'fallen
from grace.' How foolish I was. I laughed, too,
back then. I never dreamed we'd be . . . in this
situation."

How foolish <u>she</u> was? What about Daddy?
What were all those plans? Just the ramblings
of a dreamer? While he was dreaming, our bills
were accumulating. Why didn't he think about
all possibilities, the most obvious being that
something could happen to him and we would be
in desperate trouble?

It was as if my rose-colored glasses were being
shattered. Did both my parents live in fantasies?
Daddy had permitted Momma to buy all these
things. Even if they were on payment plans, they
still had to be paid for, and there was all that
accumulating interest. Where was the father I had
seen, the one who was moving up the ladder and
would be a highly paid executive? And now this,
trapped into going to live with grandparents who
didn't care enough about their own daughter to
keep up with what was happening in her life. They
never called, they never wrote, and they certainly
had never visited us or invited us to visit them in
all these years. She wasn't just disinherited; she
was disowned. She no longer existed in their eyes.

I didn't know why. At the moment, that didn't matter. We were leaving, and we would have to live with them.

"So why are we going there, Momma?" I asked. "They don't sound like they really want us, especially if your own father cut you out of his will."

"I am confident," she said, pulling her shoulders up with pride, "that I can win back his love and have him put me back in his will. I once told you, I think, that I lost my two brothers, who died in accidents, so I'm the only one left. He's too proud to let his money not follow his blood. You'll see. We'll be fine. We'll be more than fine. We'll be very rich, too, someday soon. He's not a well man. He's been in and out of hospitals and now has a full-time nurse."

"So that's why we're leaving so quickly, tonight," I said. "You're afraid he'll die before . . ."

"Before I win back his love? Yes, Christopher. You're so bright. You understand. Thank goodness I have you," she said, and kissed me on the forehead.

I looked at Cathy. She seemed even angrier now. I knew it was because I was understanding and seeing things from Momma's point of view and not hers. I knew that in her mind, it was some sort of betrayal.

"There is one final little detail," Momma continued. "Your real name is Foxworth, not Dollanganger. Dollanganger was a name your father chose for us. It comes from some ancestor."

"What?" Cathy practically pounced. "Why would he want to change an easy-to-spell name?"

"It's all very complicated," she said, falling back into her chair. "I haven't time to explain every little detail. We have so much to do quickly. Let's just get on with it. We can think about other things later."

"You've gone over everything carefully, right, Momma? We have no choice anymore, correct?" I asked. "You've spoken to Daddy's attorney?"

I looked at Cathy when I asked the questions so she would listen carefully and see why I was willing to go along with what our mother wanted.

"Everything, Christopher, twice and again just in case. Trying to find another way has nearly exhausted me. Trust me," she said. She started to cry, telling us how she had tried to think of every possible solution, how disgusted she was with herself for not being able to simply take up the reins and take care of us herself. Through her tears, she again described how much we could have if she succeeded in getting back into her father's good graces.

"My mother assures me he will probably only last a few more months," she said, to drive home how important it was for us to get started immediately. Cathy began to complain again about all she was leaving behind.

I seized her hand. "Enough!" I said. "Let's get to packing."

I looked at Momma. She was smiling at me through her tears. I was truly her little man. I was no

longer just a son and a brother. I was the father we
had lost.

I set the diary down for a moment.

Their real name was Foxworth, and Dollanganger
was an assumed name? This would explain some of
the confusion with the way the stories about them
were told over the years. But how could Corrine be
Malcolm and Olivia's daughter and her husband be a
Foxworth, too? How closely were they related? The
point was, they were related. That part of the rumor
was accurate, then.

Were they close enough to be considered incestu-
ous? Was that why my father said Malcolm Foxworth
was unforgiving? Vicious and hateful? It certainly
might explain why Corrine was written out of her father's will and disowned by both her parents.

These poor children, I thought. They were caught
in the middle of it all, and so was this new widow with
no means of supporting them. What else could she do
but throw herself on the mercy of her parents? How
did people who had the most reason to love each other
grow to despise each other so much? Surely, Malcolm
Foxworth and Olivia Foxworth weren't that cruel.
Surely, once they saw their grandchildren, they would
soften. Uncle Tommy's source of information had to
be wrong. How could their grandfather enjoy them
suffering so much, locked up in an attic?

I heard Dad come home and instantly, almost
instinctively, slipped the diary under my pillow. He
was moving through the house. Once again, I had lost

track of time and not done anything to prepare for our dinner. I hurried out of the room, but he was standing at the base of the stairway looking up.

"Working on your homework?" he asked.

I think I'd rather have a tooth pulled than lie to my father. I saw the concern in his face and told myself that if I didn't lie, he would be more upset. "Yes. Sorry. Intense math. Pasta night, right?" I started down the stairs. I tried to avoid his eyes, which I knew was a mistake.

He didn't say anything, but he was hurt. "How was school today?" he asked instead. He always made some reference to it, but lately, he was too occupied with so many other things to ask standard questions.

"Great. Oh. I have a party Friday night. Kane's house."

"Okay," he said. "We might have some celebrating to do this week, too."

"What?"

"The live one is now a real one, and yours truly will probably get the cleanup contract to start."

"Foxworth is sold?"

"Looks that way," he said. "I hope the first thing the new owner does is name it something else and then build something so beautiful no one ever thinks of those horrid stories anymore," he added pointedly.

I nodded and went into the kitchen to make a salad and get the table set. Dad went upstairs to shower and change. As I worked, I felt a trembling inside me.

There was no question in my mind now that the diary wasn't simply the ramblings of some disturbed child. Christopher Dollanganger or Foxworth was a very bright young boy who was more than simply what my friends might call book smart. From what he was writing, I thought he was much more. I could tell that he was good at reading both people and books. Furthermore, he was not blinded by his love of his mother and his father to the extent that he refused to acknowledge and write about their weaknesses.

Was it cold for a child to look so clearly and closely at his own parents? He obviously had loved his father very much, but he was not hesitant to criticize him for having more children while he was struggling to provide for the two he had. More important, he now realized his father was more of a dreamer than an achiever. Anyone else would have been so shocked and disturbed that he couldn't go on. Whom could he believe in? Maybe only himself. Maybe that was enough for him, but it certainly wouldn't be for me, I thought.

In fact, I was so deep in thought about it all that I didn't realize Dad was standing in the kitchen doorway watching me.

"How many times are you going to cut the same carrot?" he asked.

"Oh."

"What's got you so deep in thought, Kristin? I hope it's not something you read in that diary."

"No, no, I'm okay, Dad. Don't you know that

teenage girls have a lot on their minds?" I offered. It was unfair, I knew. I used that whenever I wanted to sidestep something or take advantage. I knew my father regretted that there wasn't another female in the house to offer me advice, so it was an easy way out for me, but I never used it without feeling guilty.

"Boy troubles?"

"I'm trying to avoid that," I said. I paused and looked at him. "You know, you never told me if you had a serious girlfriend before you met Mom. Did you?"

"Oh, boy," he said. "I asked for it."

"Well, it's not fair. You can ask me about my relationships, but I can never know about yours."

"Let me put it to you this way, Kristin. When I met your mother, every woman I had met before slipped out of my memory like melting icicles. There was no longer any room for any of them in my thoughts."

I waved my knife at him. "You're very good, Dad. I'd put you up against any CIA interrogator."

He finally laughed. "Look who's talking, Miss Sidestep," he replied, and went into the kitchen to start his pasta dish.

He did talk about his early dates with my mother and how afraid he was of doing or saying something that would turn her off. When he talked like this, he looked so much younger to me. It was as if by resurrecting his good memories, he could actually go back in time, have a boyish smile on his face, and have dazzling eyes.

"So you believe in love at first sight?" I asked.

He paused and thought a moment. "Not for every-body," he said. "Only the lucky."

"What about the rest?" I followed.

"A shot in the dark at best," he said.

Now he was the one falling into deep thought. I watched him work. He was preparing spaghetti carbonara, working as carefully as a surgeon on his sauce, not out of necessity but out of love for what he could do. He always said, "When you prepare a meal for someone you love, you love the meal."

I went to set the table. Usually, when we had pasta lately, he would open a bottle of wine and let me have some. He said he was happy I was old enough now to partake with him, because there was nothing lonelier than drinking good wine alone.

What he had told me about him and my mother got me thinking about Christopher's parents, Corrine and Christopher Sr. Surely, they had to have fallen in love at first sight and so strongly and completely that they would defy whatever rules or morality stood in their way, not to mention her parents. It had to have been so strong a love for Corrine, in fact, that she would give up great wealth. At one point in her life, then, she wasn't obsessed with expensive jewelry and clothes and other luxuries, or perhaps she had so much faith in Christopher Sr. that she wasn't afraid to risk it.

Yet from what I had read so far, even though she must have known they were struggling financially, she didn't appear to have any regrets. She was even willing to have more children. Had she changed, or was Christopher Sr. so good at filling her with hope and deceiving her about what they had and would have soon that she would put aside her own demands? Christopher hadn't come right out and said it yet in his diary, but maybe his mother was very gullible and far more naive than she acted.

Without my even reading another word, it was clear that something changed in her, because she was willing to hide her children in a small bedroom and an attic while she worked on winning back her father's love. Was she fooling herself again, justifying that by believing she could soon give them far more? How did it all turn so ugly? Why?

All my friends seemed to live in fairly uncomplicated families compared with the Dollangangers. Certainly, I did.

Then again . . . maybe they didn't. Maybe everyone had deep secrets that appeared as soon as they closed their doors. Maybe they spent most of the time pretending those secrets and troubles didn't exist.

At dinner, I got Dad to talk more about his work, what he believed could be built on the Foxworth property this time, and some of his company's other jobs. I could tell that he knew I was doing everything I could to keep him from asking me any more about the diary. I could see it in his eyes and his soft smile, but for now, at least, he stepped back.

I would wonder later if I wished he hadn't.

After dinner, I watched a little television with him and then went upstairs to do some other reading in my history text. I still liked being ahead of the class. He looked in on me and saw that was what I was doing and then said good night.

I thought I would go to sleep myself, but then I remembered I had put the diary under my pillow. I took it out slowly, glanced at the clock, and told myself I'd read maybe a little more, just until I got tired.

Boy, was that a mistake.

The train ride was bizarre. We got off in the middle of the night in seemingly nowhere. There wasn't a house in sight, and I had overheard the conductor say we were a good hour's ride from Charlottesville. We certainly couldn't walk there. The twins were exhausted as it was. I should have realized that there was something very strange going on when the conductor called my mother "Mrs. Patterson," but after we disembarked, there was another big clue. Momma had left her luggage on the train, claiming the conductor was going to put it in a locker for her to get later. When I asked her about that, she said she wanted to be able to greet her father in the morning first, without us. She said she had it all worked out with her mother.

"Tonight you'll all be in a bedroom, and then we'll see," she said.

We walked on, finally seeing some houses and then the dark, enormous mansion silhouetted against the purplish mountains and sky. Momma said that when we saw it in the daytime, we would realize what a grand palace it truly was. As strange as it all seemed, that filled me with some hope. I saw how frightened and disgusted Cathy was, so I kept talking, asking Momma about fun things we could do here like ice skating. She told us about a lake not far away from the house, actually on her parents' property. In the summer months, we could swim in it. I flashed a smile at Cathy and she seemed to calm down some, now just as interested as I was in what was in the house and what our grandparents were like.

When we approached a rear entrance, a tall elderly lady opened the door as if she had been standing there waiting for us all night. She wasn't wearing anything expensive. I thought we were being greeted by one of the servants. Without speaking, she ushered us into the house and up a steep staircase. We had no time to look at anything. We were hurried down a long hallway, past many rooms, until she finally thrust open a door to a large bedroom with heavy drapes shut tight on the windows.

"Quickly," she ordered when we hesitated. "Get them ready for bed. And do everything quietly."

Momma nodded and began to undress Carrie. Cathy helped with Cory. Both twins were so tired and dazed they barely made a sound. I put one of our suitcases on the bed and started to open it to get out their pajamas.

"Not on the bed, you fool," the old lady said. "On the floor."

I put the suitcase on the floor and looked at Momma in disbelief. She was trying to smile, but her lips looked frozen tight.

"Well, you were right about your children being beautiful, but are they intelligent, or were they born stupid and ill?"

"They're perfect, Mother."

Cathy looked at me with probably the same expression of shock that was on my face. This ugly, grotesque, awkward, and stern-looking woman was our grandmother? Momma set Carrie on one bed, and Cathy placed Cory beside her. Then we turned and looked at our grandmother and our mother. I had trouble seeing any resemblance and hoped that she was indeed not really a blood relative; maybe she was a stepmother.

"You can't have boys and girls sleeping together," our grandmother said.

"They're only innocent children. Why do you think such evil thoughts, Mother?"

The old lady's cold smile put a chill down my spine and definitely froze Cathy.

"Why do I think evil thoughts? Innocent children? That's what your father and I used to think about you and your half-uncle. Surely, they've inherited that impurity."

Momma suggested that she give us separate bedrooms, and that was when things became even more puzzling. The old lady went on and on about how important it was that no one, not even the

servants, knew we were here. I kept looking at
Momma for some more explanation, but whatever
defiance and spirit she had had when we first
arrived seemed to have evaporated. I thought I
might protest, but before I could open my mouth,
our grandmother stepped toward Cathy and me,
towering above us.

"You're older. You'll keep the other two quiet,
or else," she said. "When your mother and I leave,
I'm locking the door."

"Locking the door?" I asked.

Her eyes widened with fury at my merely
questioning something she had said. "You must
not move around this house. You will stay here
until your grandfather dies. Until then, you don't
exist."

"Don't exist?"

"Stop repeating everything I say like some
idiot!" She looked like she wanted to slap me.

Momma shook her head at me, so I bit down
on my lower lip. The old lady went on and on
about why we had to be kept locked up in the
north wing but said that on the last Friday of the
month, we were to go up another stairway and
hide in the attic. She made it sound like nothing,
but Cathy looked at me and mouthed, "The
last Friday of the month?" I knew why she was
shocked. That was weeks away.

Our grandmother explained that she would be
the one to bring us food. Finally, Momma started
to get us into bed, whispering constantly, her eyes

teary, that this was only temporary, a few days, maybe a week, but we had to be obedient and not get our grandmother upset.

"It's our only hope, Christopher," she whispered in my ear.

I nodded. "Don't worry, Momma," I said, which brought her first real smile. She kissed my cheek and rose. I could see how reluctant she was to leave us. "We'll keep the twins entertained and quiet."

She looked at her mother, who only scowled back.

"I'll be back in the morning," our grandmother said. She practically pushed Momma out the door. We heard the lock snap shut.

"What was that?" Cathy asked. "Godzilla's mother? She was huge and awful. How can she be our real grandmother?"

"Cool it," I told her. "Don't say those stupid things in front of the twins, or we'll have a helluva time keeping them quiet. It will be hard enough as it is."

"What did the old lady mean when she said 'you and your half-uncle'? Who was Momma's half-uncle?"

"Let's not think about anything," I said. "Let's just get some sleep. It's not that bad in here. Besides, what's one or two nights?"

She looked hard at me, searching to see if I was just placating her or really believed what I had said. It was getting harder and harder for me to fool her. She shook her head, said her prayers, and curled up beside Carrie.

I lay on my back and looked up at the ceiling. The house was not completely quiet. We couldn't hear anyone talking or moving about, but I could hear creaks and groans as if the mansion was trying to warn us: Get out. Get out while you still can.

As if I had made the train journey and the walk in the night with them, I felt my eyelids slowly closing. I put the diary under my pillow and turned off the side table lamp. Almost immediately, I saw Olivia Foxworth in my mind, towering above the twins, Cathy, and Christopher. How could a grandmother be so hard and mean to young children who were obviously exhausted and frightened, especially her own grandchildren? I tried to push her out of my mind, and when I finally did fall asleep, I woke once in the middle of the night, imagining her standing beside my bed, looking down at me, and saying, "Don't you dare read another page!"

It took a while to fall asleep again, and then I did something I hadn't done since I was a little girl. I overslept. Dad was knocking on my door and poked his head in.

"Kristin, are you sick?"

"What?" I sat up quickly and looked at the clock. "Oh."

"You should have set your alarm," he said.

"I haven't done that for so long."

"Um. Maybe you're going to have to start again. I

saw your light was on late," he said, shaking his head. Then he backed out and closed the door.

I hopped out of bed. No matter what, even if I skipped breakfast, I was going to be late for school for the first time. Dad was waiting for me when I came down the stairway.

"I don't want you driving fast, now, Kristin. You're going to be late. I'll write some excuse for you, say we had a problem at the house or something."

"No need to lie, Dad. It's my first time. I'll get a warning, but I shouldn't get any punishment. I'll just tell the truth. I overslept."

"Why did you stay up so late?" he asked. "I thought I saw your light on. It was that diary, right?"

"Yes," I confessed.

He shook his head. "I'd like you to give it back to me, Kristin. I'll keep it somewhere safe and return it to you later."

"Why?"

"Look at what it's doing to you now."

"It's not doing anything to me. I lost track of time. That's all, Dad. It's not a big deal. I'll be more careful. Promise. I won't be late again, ever."

"I have to go to work," he said. "Think about it. And remember, no fast driving. You get a ticket, you go to court here first, and the judge is merciless. You'll lose your license in a heartbeat and have to go to months of traffic school."

I watched him leave and then went to drink some orange juice and have a piece of toast. Right now, I had little appetite. As I ate my toast, I looked up and thought about the diary. I didn't want even to consider it, but once again, I did. It was hard to believe that my father would go into my room and take it away from me, but it occurred to me after seeing his reaction this morning that he just might.

He had seen me intent when reading novels or even textbooks, so it wasn't just that. There was something more here. I felt certain now. My father knew something that he had never told me, and seeing me reading the diary so intently resurrected that memory. He was surely afraid I would read about it. Perhaps he had made some sort of promise to my mother. Whatever, I thought he never believed I would find a way to discover what he knew. I was confident that this was what was bothering him now, and it wasn't simply my oversleeping.

Rather than driving me away from the diary, it only stirred my curiosity about what I would read and learn. As far as I could remember, our family, even before my mother died, did not hoard secrets. Everything about my grandparents, uncle, and aunt was openly discussed. My parents were people who never hid anything from each other and, I thought, surely not from me.

Corrine and Christopher Sr. had a deep and serious secret to hide not only from their own children but from everyone who knew them. That was why Christopher Sr. had created their new surname, Dollanganger. A family born out of a lie couldn't end up well. Of course, it was understandable that neither would tell Christopher Jr. the truth and certainly not

Cathy, not while they were still so young, and maybe they had thought they never would have to tell them the truth. Christopher Sr.'s fatal accident made it almost impossible to keep the big secret. Up to where I left off, I had the impression that Christopher was hoping his mother would come up with some other explanation. Maybe their parents weren't related by blood or something.

I should have been more concerned about being late for school and my first class of the day, English with Mr. Stiegman, but my mind was totally absorbed by what I had read in the diary. I was almost surprised to find myself pulling into the student parking lot. I would have to go directly to the principal's office and get a pass to enter school and my class.

Our principal, Mr. Market, was a very easygoing forty-five-year-old man. He had been principal of our school for nearly eight years now and was very well liked because he was always fair. I sensed that he was fond of me and impressed by my grade point average. I didn't like to believe that I was treated with any more favor because I had lost my mother at an early age, but sometimes I felt it. There were many other students who lived with one parent, but that was because of divorce. Many of them had behavioral problems, and few were doing anywhere nearly as well with their grades as I was.

My father was never really on my back when it came to schoolwork. He was very proud of my achievements, but he never pressured me the way some parents pressured their children. I think what made me work so hard was my fear of disappointing him, even though he always made it seem like he would love me no matter what. Maybe that was why I worked so hard. He cared so much about me.

Did Corrine care as much for her children? She should have thought ahead and prepared for disasters. That was what adults did.

Mrs. Grant looked up from her desk with surprise when I entered the office. She was Mr. Market's secretary, and, like him, she took personal interest in many of the students.

"I'm late," I announced.

She stared at me a moment as if to confirm that I had said it and that I was really standing there. "What happened?" she asked, her face folding and crinkling as if it was composed of aluminum foil.

"I overslept. My father thought I was sick or something, but I forgot to set my alarm. I haven't done that for a long time, and I overslept."

She nodded and buzzed Mr. Market.

"Late arrival," she said. "Kristin Masterwood. No, no written excuse. She says she overslept."

She listened and then hung up the receiver.

"I have to give you a demerit and a pink warning slip," she said, as if she was having a toothache. "Next time, it's a week's detention."

"I know. There won't be a next time."

She smiled and gave me the slip, and I went to my first class. Everything stopped when I entered and handed Mr. Stiegman my slip. He shook his head, looking glum, and I took my seat. I didn't look at anyone, even though I knew all eyes were on me. I realized quickly where we were in the reading of *Macbeth* and turned to the page in my textbook. When the bell rang less than fifteen minutes later, I was barely out of my seat before Lana and Suzette pounced. Right behind them was Theresa Flowman, gloating. She was my competition for class valedictorian. If we were neck-and-neck after this semester, behavior would play a role in the faculty's choice.

"What happened to you? Why did you get a pink slip?" Lana asked quickly. I knew she was wondering why I hadn't come up with an excuse for lateness that would have avoided a pink slip. Everyone else managed to get their parents to concoct something. No one seemed to believe what my father believed, that little lies were like plaque in your arteries, building up until you had a ruined reputation that would destroy you. In his business, where trust was essential, that was, he said, equivalent to a heart attack.

"Overslept," I said as casually as I could.

"Maybe you're trying too hard to be valedictorian," Theresa said, intending her words to be little pins aimed at my self-respect.

"Theresa, you've got to stop thinking everyone is like you," I replied.

Lana and Suzette laughed, and Theresa sped off.

"That girl is so horny I wouldn't lend her a pencil," Lana said.

"Stop," I ordered, even though I couldn't help smiling under my disapproval.

"Speaking of which, Kane was looking for you in

homeroom," Suzette said. "Each time he appeared, he looked at your empty desk as if he had lost his best friend or something. Actually, I never saw him like that. He looked like a lost puppy. You know about his party, of course?"

"Yes."

When we started down the hallway to our next class, Kane suddenly appeared right behind me.

"Where have you been, stranger?" he whispered. "Foxworth?"

"What?" I said, stopping and spinning on him. It was frightening for a moment, as if he had somehow found out about the diary.

"Just kidding. I saw you were missing in home-room."

"I overslept. It looks like major news around here."

"Shows you how boring it is otherwise," he replied, and shrugged. He walked along with me. "My dad told us that Foxworth is being sold."

"How did he know so fast?"

"He's on the bank board, one of the directors. Your dad's going to do a lot of work there."

"He told me."

We paused outside my next class. My girlfriends were watching us and giggling.

"You know, I've never really been out there in the daytime," Kane said. "Maybe you can give me a tour this week after school, before it disappears."

"It wouldn't be much of a tour," I said.

"Any excuse to be with you works for me," he replied, giving me one of his dazzling smiles, and he went on to his own class.

I watched him walk away and thought about how I would feel returning to Foxworth now that I was getting so deeply into the diary. If anything, it made the property seem more forbidden. While I had read how Corrine brought her children through the darkness from the railroad stop, I was envisioning the path they took that brought them to the rear of the mansion. Now that it had been abandoned, that route was very overgrown, but I was already toying with the idea of walking it, bringing that whole scene to life for me.

Could I do that?

I hurried into the classroom. All I needed to do now was be late for my next class. That would really get me into hot water.

Before the day ended, Kane again suggested we go to Foxworth, maybe to watch some of the removal of debris.

"I'm sure your dad will think it's nice that you're interested in his work."

"Why is this suddenly so important to you?"

"I'm just interested in what you're interested in," he said.

"How do you know I'm interested in that?"

"I could tell. How about tomorrow? I'll pick you up for school so you don't have to worry about your car after."

"I'll let you know later," I said.

"Complicated?"

"I'll let you know," I repeated with more firmness. He gave me that famous shrug again and walked off. How could I explain why I had any hesitation? It wasn't only because I was reading the diary. I was afraid that my father would think I was so obsessed with it that I had talked Kane into going to Foxworth to watch the work. He might also believe I had disobeyed him and told Kane about the diary. I had to work that out without making Kane suspicious, too.

I had made up my mind before I left school for home that I was not going to touch the diary until much later, if at all today. I thought I should do that to ease my father's concerns. Besides, I had a lot to do at the house, and I did have more homework than usual.

When Dad came home, he found me vacuuming the living room.

"What happened at school?" was his first question.

"Pink slip warning. I'll set the alarm. Don't worry."

"Got a lot of homework?"

"Yes, why?"

"Herm Cromwell wants to take us to dinner."

"He wants to take *you*, Dad, not us. Don't worry about it. I'll make a turkey burger and sweet potato fries. I've watched you do it enough times."

He nodded.

"Oh, Kane Hill knows about the sale of Foxworth. His father . . ."

"Is on the bank's board. Figures."

"He wants to look at the property when you start

working on removal," I said. "I didn't say yes or no. I didn't mention anything else," I added quickly. "He's never been there in the daytime, and he has this nutty idea that some famous local site is about to disappear."

"What do you mean, in the daytime?"

"He probably made some visits on Halloween."

Dad nodded. "He can come whenever he wants."

"Tomorrow?"

"We're starting tomorrow, yes."

"He's picking me up for school. We'll show up after school."

Dad stared at me a moment. "A famous thing might be removed? I don't consider it a historical site," he said between his clenched teeth. "Best thing that was ever done for this community is getting rid of that wreckage and selling the property," he added, with such firmness and anger that I held my breath. "Let's get it out of our lives once and for all," he said, and went upstairs to shower and change for dinner.

I watched him go up and then finished vacuuming and started to prepare my dinner. Rarely did I see Dad that red with anger. Sometimes he'd bring home some frustration because of work, but he usually dropped it quickly when he saw me or, more likely, thought about my mother.

"Your dinner smells good," he said from the doorway when he had changed and come down. His tone was calmer.

"You'll have a good dinner, Dad, I'm sure."

"Yeah. Sorry I exploded out there over this Foxworth thing. I'm just tired of hearing about it. I get an earful at Charley's Diner from whoever hears about the job. They start talking about the nut who rebuilt it and all that. Makes me almost wish I didn't take the job. I'll be home early," he said, and kissed me before he left.

After I ate, I sat there for a while thinking about the last few pages I had read in the diary. This was a mystery wrapped in a mystery, I thought. They were only children. Why was it so important to my father to get them gone and forgotten?

I changed my mind. Maybe I would rush my homework, but I would be back in the diary tonight.

An hour and a half later, after making certain to set my alarm, I settled back against my pillow and opened the diary to where I had left off. I felt like Alice falling into a dark Wonderland.

From the moment they woke up, the twins complained. Cathy was just as vocal, which wasn't helping matters. While I went to the bathroom and washed myself, the grandmother from hell came in with our tray of food, along with a specific list of rules we were to obey. She ordered me to read them aloud to my brother and sisters, and before she left, she told us to beware, that God saw all and would see the evil and sin we were prone to commit. The only positive thing she told us was that we could go up to the attic, where we would have more room, but only after ten a.m.

I took one look at Cathy's face and saw that she was going to do or say something to show her defiance, maybe by pounding on the door. She

surprised me with her suggestion, a fantasy that
would take more root in reality as time went by.

"Okay," she said. "Since we're being deserted
by what family we have, we'll form our own.
Christopher, you're now the father. I'm the
mother."

I looked at Cory and Carrie and saw how the
idea gave them some relief. There was a chance
to have fun after all and get their minds off this
dreadful situation. Our grandmother had typed
out a list of rules for us to follow, and it was pretty
clear from them that she was either a nutcase
or simply sexually repressed. I found them so
ridiculous that I read them aloud, imitating her
voice and growly face.

"No being undressed in front of each other."

"Boys and girls cannot use the bathroom
together."

The one that got me most was "No handling or
playing with private parts."

The most ridiculous one was "Do not look at
the opposite sex unless absolutely necessary."

I could see I was going to have a time of it
explaining to Cory and Carrie what private parts
were. Cathy had that self-satisfied grin on her
face, enjoying my efforts to make it sound more
scientific than sexual.

There were actually twenty-two rules, mostly to
do with cleanliness and obedience. She threatened
to add more as time went by. Despite my satire
and my imitation, Cathy stopped smiling. She

looked around and then burst out with all her
pent-up frustration, bemoaning how much we
were hated for something we didn't do, whatever
it was, and declaring that this was all going to be
a disaster. I remained calm and assured her that
our mother would look after us and our demented
grandmother would settle down.

She calmed. "You're right," she said. "Momma
won't let this go on much longer."

I breathed a sigh of relief, but something inside
me warned that this was only the first of many crises
to come.

I set the diary aside for a moment and thought about
their grandmother's rules. Christopher had suspected
early on that his grandmother was sexually repressed.
I knew what a sexually repressed person was, but I
doubted, even from the little I had read so far, that
Cathy would have known at her age. Their grandmother would probably cut herself off completely
from the outside world if she were still alive today
and saw how we all dressed, what we read, what we
watched on television, and how many of us were
sexually active, not only before we had graduated high
school but also in middle school. For sure, there were
still people like her, who thought a liberated woman
was simply promiscuous.

How did Christopher's mother grow up in such a
household? Was she permitted to go on dates at least
by my age? What kind of clothes did they force her

to wear? What books and magazines were forbidden, and what about movies and television? Was makeup forbidden? Was she permitted to go to parties? Who wouldn't understand why she had an affair and ran from the world she was in? I was sure she felt more like a trapped animal.

Despite my aunt Barbara's willingness to teach me the facts of life when I was younger and her occasional phone calls, without a mother or an older sister, I had to fend for myself when it came to what I would call street sophistication. Aunt Barbara wasn't around every day or even every month, and I felt funny as time passed and I got older calling her for advice or intimate talk. I think she knew that, too, and during one of our last talks, she said, "You're pretty sophisticated for your age now, Kristin. I have faith in you always doing the right thing."

Maybe she did, but I wasn't convinced.

At nearly seventeen, I was still far from the most experienced and worldly girl in my class, especially when it came to relationships. Some of the girls had been going out with older boys since they were fourteen, and as we all knew, those boys weren't going to be satisfied holding hands and just kissing in the backseats of cars when they could really *be alone*. Some of them were from broken homes, but even those who weren't seemed to be on a long leash, staying out later than the rest of us. I imagined that their mothers, like Cathy's mother, were more absorbed with themselves.

Like any other girl, I guess, I wanted to see how

many bells would ring and how much control I would still have when those famous female hormones began calling. Both Lana and Suzette were still virgins. We talked about it almost every time the three of us were together at one of our houses. Even though they had mothers to advise them all the time, I suspected they didn't know much more about their own impulses and desires than I did. They thought that just because I was the best student in the class, maybe even in the whole school, I would know more than their mothers.

I smiled to myself recalling how I answered some of their questions, because I thought I sounded or replied the way Christopher would. I was almost as scientific. I also got the feeling that if I told them how little sexually I had done with Kane or how far I might go, they would find it a justification for doing the same. I didn't want to take responsibility for their actions, but they would surely come back at me with "Well, you did it."

Responsibility, I thought to myself—look at how it was thrust onto Christopher. Maybe it was just a game at first for him to play daddy, but it wasn't difficult to see how he would really have to be like a daddy. I knew that kids our age who lived in war-torn countries or in poverty had to grow up so quickly that childhood was a fantasy. But for a boy who came from a middle-class family, who once had all the advantages, to be dropped into this situation had to be mind-shattering. I knew how difficult it had been for me to lose my mother, but the way this was turning out, he and his brother and sisters were more like instant orphans.

I picked up the diary reluctantly this time. It was making me angry and depressed. I was developing a love/hate relationship with it. It was intriguing, yes, but also enraging. Dad might be right, I thought. It could make me bitter and cynical. Right now, it made my stomach churn the way it did just before I had to do something unpleasant, like go to the dentist, but I turned the page anyway, feeling that it was almost as necessary as having my teeth checked.

Our first foray up to the attic was like exploring another country. It was vast, probably the entire length of the mansion, and filled with endless antiques, leather-bound trunks with travel labels, giant armoires containing both Union and Confederate uniforms, and rows and rows of men's old fashions, women's clothing, dress forms, not to mention dozens of birdcages, rakes and shovels, and piles of framed photographs.

"These might be our relatives," I said. "Ancestors."

Cathy grimaced until she saw a pretty girl who was maybe eighteen. It was hard to tell. Both women and men in the nineteenth century looked older at our ages. I thought she was quite sexy, with her bosom rising out of a ruffled bodice. I saw how fascinated Cathy was with her.

"I'm sure you'll have a figure like that."

"How can you be so sure?"

"From the way you're developing already," I said, and she looked at me so strangely. "It's all right for me to notice, you know, despite what our monster grandmother says."

Cory and Carrie started to complain about the heat and stuffiness. I managed to open a window, and then I made a new discovery, a room that was half decent, with school desks. Cory found a rocking horse, and Cathy put Carrie on it, too. For the time being, we had plenty to occupy ourselves. Cathy and I gazed out the window at the view.

"It's like looking at a television with the picture stuck on something beautiful. You can't get tired of something beautiful," I told her.

She shook her head. "You're impossible, Christopher. You see something good in everything, even this. Why does our grandmother look at us and see nothing but sin? What have we done? We're just kids."

"I don't know how she's thinking yet," I told her. "Don't worry about it, anyway. We won't be here that long."

Carrie and Cory began to complain again, demanding that we take them outside.

"Now what, oh great optimist?" Cathy asked, and I quickly came up with some new games to play.

"We'll turn the attic into our own garden with a swing!" I declared, and spent hours building one for them. It kept them occupied for only a little while before they were screaming to go out again.

This wasn't going to work, I thought. We couldn't keep them locked up as long as Momma envisioned. Cathy looked at me and saw the

momentary weakness and doubt in my eyes, but I
quickly recuperated, chastised them like a father
should for whining and screaming so much, and
then gratefully accepted Cathy's declaration that it
was lunchtime.

These were early days, I told myself. Surely, it
would be worth it. This was a mansion, and they
were obviously very rich people to own so much
land. If we were able to share just a small part
of it, we'd be well-off, too, and coming from the
disaster we were in, this had to be a great idea, an
opportunity.

I could hear my father say, "Chin up, chest out,
shoulders back. You're in the Dollanganger army,
boy."

When I heard my father coming up the stairs, I shoved
the diary under my pillow and grabbed my history
text. The moment after I made the change, I felt terrible guilt. My father had such trust in me. Deceiving
him again, even with something most people would
call very minor, gave me a sick feeling.

How did people deceive the people they love or
are supposed to love? I wondered. From what I had
read so far and from what was common knowledge, I
knew that Corrine Foxworth would keep her children
locked in the attic for years, yet according to Christopher, she had told them they would be there a few
days, maybe a week, all the while knowing it would
have to be much longer. All parents tell their children
little white lies to keep the peace or keep them from

being afraid or impatient, but this was different. This was cold, hard deception. In a real sense, she was betraying them, betraying those she should have loved the most.

I already had a bad feeling about Corrine willingly shutting up her children in rooms far away from the servants and the grandfather. I didn't like the fact that the door was actually locked. What if there was a fire or something else terrible happened, like an appendix attack or an injury? How long would it take to get them help and assistance? How could a mother go to sleep at night knowing this?

I tried to think like Christopher and understand that Corrine was in a desperate place, practically penniless with four children, and in her way of thinking, this was a small enough sacrifice to make in order to gain the security and future for her children and herself that she envisioned. I told myself that I had to remember she had once enjoyed this opulent lifestyle, living in this large mansion with its beautiful grounds and the lake. Who could blame her for dreaming of being rescued?

It caused me to wonder about what sacrifices my father had made in his life after my mother's death, sacrifices he made for my benefit. I was sure that many evenings, he lay awake in his and my mother's bedroom, alone, looking into the darkness, unable to sleep, and probably dreaming of getting away from it all, fleeing the crisp memory of her movements beside him, her laughter resonating in the halls and rooms, the scent of her perfume still lingering around her vanity table and in her closet, perhaps the discovery of a strand of her hair. After her passing, every reminder was like a scratch on a scab, a wound. How much easier it would be to move to another city, into another house, and make new friends, friends in whose faces he wouldn't see the sorrow and the pity or the reflection of my mother in their eyes and hear the fragility of their words. Everyone was always afraid he or she might say something painful and vividly resurrect my mother's dying breath. I knew. I saw the fear in his face and felt it in my own heart.

Despite what he would tell me about being tied to the house and his work, about being comfortable where he was, and about being too old to start anew, I was well aware that he was holding on to it all for me. He didn't want my life disrupted. He didn't want me to have to find new friends and get used to new teachers and new surroundings. "People my age and younger are moved about this country like checkers on a board," he would say.

Being young is supposed to mean you're strong enough to be shaken up, even periodically, yet students like that don't do as well, and yes, they probably have many emotional and psychological issues, but they live. I would have lived through it, too.

And what about another woman, another wife?

Was it really impossible for him to take on another companion, or was he avoiding it just to please me? Yes, I hated the thought of another woman looking into my mother's mirror, working in her kitchen, putting her clothes in my mother's closet, and greeting my father with a kiss at the end of his workday. It was like losing my mother all over again, and yes, that was painful even to consider, but it was also selfish of me not to want it to happen.

My father, like any other man, had needs. I couldn't share everything with him. How many times had he turned down an invitation because he didn't think I would be comfortable accompanying him? How many times had he looked at another married couple laughing, holding hands, having dinner in a restaurant, or simply talking softly somewhere and felt the great emptiness and pain in his heart? Maybe he would never love anyone as much as he had loved my mother, but he would have someone on his arm, someone else to come home to. He was still a young man. It had to be difficult having no one to embrace in bed, no shoulder to kiss, no warmth to soothe him when he felt terribly alone. There was a wide hole in his heart, in his life, and I couldn't fill it completely. We were still a family, yes, but he was a man alone at times and places when he shouldn't be.

Who was making the sacrifices here?

Not me.

And certainly not Corrine Foxworth!

He knocked on my door.

"Come in, Dad."

"Just want to give you a heads-up on something," he began. "Herm Cromwell just told me that the *Charlottesville Catch-all*, that weekly paper, is doing a lead article on the Foxworth story because of the real estate sale. They're going to rake up the legendary horror for sure. Herm knows the editor, and there's going to be a mention of the fact that we're, through your mother, the only living Charlottesville relatives of the Foxworths now. You're not to talk to anyone from that newspaper about it," he added, as sternly as he ever said anything to me.

"I don't know very much about it, anyway."

He stared at me in that way he could with those brown eyes turning almost a dark orange when he focused them so intensely. "You're reading that diary," he said.

"What diary?" I smiled, and he nodded.

"Better keep it that way, Kristin. I know how descendants of people who committed horrendous acts are stained with bad blood no matter what they do or who they become. It's like walking about with ghosts clinging to your shoulders, understand?"

What he said made me cringe. Sometimes I did feel like I was carrying ghosts.

"I've already tasted that stale bread, Dad," I said. It was one of his expressions.

He nodded. I could see just the suggestion of tears in his eyes. He understood. "Okay. I'm going to demolish that place the way your mother scrubbed the kitchen floor," he vowed, and left, closing the door softly.

I put the history book down and thought. Maybe he was right. Maybe I should toss the diary into the garbage and forget Foxworth and the poor

Dollanganger children. What good would come of my reading it, anyway? I couldn't save them from whatever fate they had. It was too late. Dad wasn't wrong about not wanting to seek out any more horror than we get daily on the news. Why go looking for it?

I turned off my light and curled up against my pillow. Of course, it was only my imagination, but I had forgotten that I had put the diary under my pillow, and it was like I could hear Christopher calling to me, begging me to read on. Someone had to listen. Someone had to know the truth. Otherwise, they would suffer in the darkness. I was the only hope to bring in the light.

In the morning, I realized just how determined my father was to get this job done, and as quickly as he could. He was up and dressed a good half hour before I rose and came down to have breakfast. I saw he was about to leave me a note and get started. It was barely light outside. He was in his jacket and hat.

"Talk about the crack of dawn," I said.

"Oh. I got a new crew coming on this morning, backhoes and plows. They want some of the grounds cleared along with the rubble. The new owner's already talking about a pool and a pool house, fixing up tennis courts."

"Do you know who it is?"

"Nope. Never asked. Whoever it is, good luck to him," he said. "I put out your favorite cereal and have the bread ready to be toasted. So you're really coming over after school?"

"That's the plan."

"Okay. We'll talk about dinner then. This looks like a Charley's Diner night for us."

"Okay, Dad."

"Be careful," he warned. He never said good-bye. It was always "Be careful."

A quick kiss on his cheek sent him on his way. From the way his shoulders were hoisted and his arms were flexed, he looked like he was off to do battle. Maybe in his mind he was. I ate my breakfast and then went up to make my bed, taking the diary out from under my pillow. I glanced at the clock. I was a little ahead of schedule.

"Don't do it," I told myself aloud. "Don't you dare."

But I didn't listen. I opened to where I had left off. Just a page or two, I thought, and I'd be off.

I was thinking more like an addict than a sensible young girl.

Until now, and mainly because of our grandmother's warnings and her dark view of us, neither Cathy nor I thought anything about the other being present when either of us bathed. Neither our mother nor our father had ever forbidden it, and if they didn't see anything wrong about it, we certainly didn't.

Cathy thought we had to clean up before eating our lunch. We had gone through so much of the dusty attic, practically swimming through layers of old air, skimming through the history of the family, stirring up bookworms and moths, and sweeping away gobs of spiderwebs.

"I feel putrid," she declared. "We're all too dirty to put our hands on food." She immediately directed me to help bathe Carrie and Cory. As soon as they were done and she had dressed them, she stripped and got into the tub.

Suddenly, as if just realizing where we were and what we were doing, she stopped washing her face, turned to me, and asked what would happen if the grandmother (she avoided saying "our grandmother," as if calling her "the grandmother" made her sound more like the creature she thought she was) caught us like this.

I moved to the tub and embraced her. She put her head on my shoulder and choked back a sob.

How quickly it had all changed, I thought. I would do my best to hide it from her and the twins, but this did feel like being in a dungeon, no matter how lightly I treated it, and Grandmother Foxworth couldn't resemble a sadistic and cruel prison matron more.

"Forget about what she says," I told Cathy. "We're going to be rich. Think about that, about all the things we'll have and be able to do."

I knew she dreamed of being a famous ballerina. I had checked on the best schools for dance when Momma and Daddy mentioned such a possibility for her, and although they were expensive, I described them again. As I ranted on and on about the things we'd all have, I began to wash her back the way I often did, the way I washed Momma's back occasionally. If she could walk in our mother's shoes, she would.

Despite how insignificant I made our grandmother's warnings and innuendos sound, I couldn't deny that she had put new thoughts in my male mind. I had looked at Cathy's naked body so often while we were growing up, but I always thought of it the way a student of human anatomy might. She was my own private female specimen, maturing right under my eyes and confirming all that I had read and studied about the birth of sex. Her breasts were already little buds crowned with slightly orange nipples, and the beginnings of her pubic hair told me she was marching to the drumbeat of her stirring hormones.

The second I felt a stirring in myself, I dropped the washcloth and backed away from the tub. What shocked me was the power and speed with which my own sexual awareness sprang out of the dark pocket in which it normally slept. I restrained it but never treated it as I would an unwelcomed guest when girls I knew flirted with me or showed a little too much of their bodies, maybe deliberately brushing themselves against me to seize my attention, something Mindy Thompson used to do whenever we were in lunch line or leaving a classroom. This was different. This was my sister Cathy. Maybe, I thought, our grandmother was right.

Cathy glanced back at me, surprised.

"They're getting restless again. I'd better move things along, distract them," I told her, when I really meant distract myself.

She nodded and rose out of the tub. I thought she'd call for me to wipe her back, but she didn't, and I put all my attention on the twins.

We had our lunch, but almost as soon as it ended, they were complaining again. I rushed back up to the attic and found books to read to them. We broke out a checkers set for Cathy and myself. We stuffed every minute, every second, with something to keep them from crying and whining about being shut up in this house. They finally fell asleep and had their afternoon naps. Cathy and I fell asleep ourselves. The day waned, and before we knew it, we were all at dinner. The twins grew exhausted from their own endless complaining. It was going to be easy to get them to bed. It was now Cathy who looked like she would get hysterical any moment. She kept looking at the locked door and the windows and me.

"What?"

"How could she want to leave us like this? What if there's a fire? We'd have to tie sheets together and form a fire escape or something."

"Brilliant," I told her, and she brightened. "It's good that you think ahead. Most girls your age don't have any foresight."

She beamed.

"If we both think of sensible things like that, we'll get through it, Cathy Doll."

The dread left her face.

Years ago, our father's best friend, Jim Johnston, called us the "Dresden dolls," because we were all flaxen-haired with fair complexions. We looked more like fancy porcelain people. The name stuck, and even neighbors began to refer to us as the Dresden dolls. I knew Cathy liked it, liked to be thought of as someone special, even though I wasn't crazy about being called any kind of doll.

She nodded, hopeful again. "Okay, how about checkers?" she said. "I'm determined to beat you."

For a few minutes, at least, it was as if we were back at home. Cathy and I were playing checkers. The twins were comfortably asleep. All was quiet and well with the world. Maybe we could get through this, I thought. No, not maybe; we would get through this. Momma knew what she was doing, I decided. I felt cheerful again, buoyed up.

And then the door was thrown open, and she came into the room.

And it was like in one moment faster than a blink, all the air was sucked out of it.

I could hear the now-frantic sound of the buzzer. Kane had his finger on it and wasn't taking it off, so it kept ding-donging. At the same time, my phone began to ring.

"Oh, no!" I cried.

I had lost track of time. I could easily be late for school again!

"Where are you? I've been honking and pushing

your doorbell. I even called your cell, but it went right to your voice mail. I wasn't sure if you had forgotten and either gone with your father or driven yourself. What's going on?"

"I'll be right there!" I cried.

How could I be so absorbed that I wouldn't hear all that noise?

I shoved the diary under my pillow, grabbed my books, and practically leaped over the bed to get out the door. I flew down the stairs, nearly twisting my ankle at the bottom, and came close to ripping the door off its hinges to get out.

Kane wore a smile of incredulity. "What's happening?"

"Let's just go," I said, rushing past him. I turned because he was still standing there. "Hurry!"

I got into his car, and he moved quickly now to get in and start the engine.

"Sorry," I said.

"Don't tell me you overslept again."

I didn't answer. He looked at me and backed out.

I was grateful now that we lived on a practically dead street, because neither he nor I looked both ways. We just shot out onto the street, and he spun the tires. If my father had been home and seen this, I'd be as dead as one of his doornails.

"It's going to be close," Kane said. "Personally, I don't care. It'll be my first warning slip, but you . . ."

"Just don't get a speeding ticket, and don't go through any red lights," I ordered.

If we got into an accident or Kane got a speeding

ticket, I'd feel worse than Cathy in the attic. I'd probably be just as sick to my stomach when the principal
informed my father about my second lateness in a row.
I pushed the vision of my father's face of disappointment out of my mind.

"So? What's going on? Are you sick or something?
What happened?"

"Something," I said.

He looked at me and raised his eyebrows. "What?"

"Oh, no," I said. We were making good time, but
now my heart sank. There was one of those fender-
bender accidents just at the road where we had to turn
off to get to the school. Traffic was backed up. I knew
there was a way around, but it would add a good five
minutes and only that if we were lucky. Other people
were probably doing the same thing by now. I started
to tell him where to turn.

"I know, I know. Relax," he said. "We're not going
to be the only ones going to school who were caught
in this mess. It's actually a bit of good luck. Mr. Market will have to take that into consideration."

A little less than five minutes later, we turned into
the school parking lot. I could hear the bell ringing.

"We're late for homeroom."

"Stop worrying. I'll explain."

"I don't need anyone to explain for me," I replied,
a little too harshly, but I couldn't help it. I was enraged
at myself for putting myself in this position.

When we reached the front entrance, I looked back
and felt some relief. Four more cars were pulling into
the parking lot, with two more waiting to make the

turn. Kane was right. There would be enough of us in the same situation.

In fact, at the principal's office, there were three others ahead of us, all seniors. Mrs. Grant was writing out green slips, which indicated acceptable excuses. So the situation had already been explained and confirmed. Nevertheless, when it was my turn, she looked up at me with some disappointment in her face.

"I would have thought you would have left yourself lots of time, Kristin. You have to anticipate problems if you want to get ahead in life."

"Yes, ma'am," I said.

She shook her head but wrote out the slip.

"Who's she trying to be? Your second mother?" Kane asked after he got his green slip, too.

"I guess I need at least one," I said, and he immediately looked sorry he had spoken.

I made it just as the bell to end homeroom was ringing, so at least I wouldn't be late for my first class. Nevertheless, all my girlfriends, who didn't know about the traffic jam, were surprised and curious. Lana had caught sight of Kane and me entering the school together.

"Kane picked you up for school?" she asked. "It's out of his way."

"Yes, and yes," I said.

"And you were both late," Suzette said. All the girls smiled. I knew they were thinking Kane and I had been dilly-dallying and that was why we were late.

"It wasn't our fault," I said, even though I knew that it easily could have been mine. I rattled off a description of the car accident before anyone could ask anything else. Actually, I thought, it wasn't my fault. It was Christopher Dollanganger's.

I laughed to myself envisioning my meeting him someday and telling him.

I was sure he would say, "How I wish that was all I suffered in my teenage years, a late demerit in school."

My girlfriends looked at me as we walked, all whispering.

"She's just in love," Suzette declared loudly enough for me to hear, and they all nodded.

I wished it was as simple as that. I was in quite a daze all morning. Besides feeling like I had run the four-minute mile, I was reeling with images and thoughts that Christopher had described in his diary. In two different morning classes, I was caught looking like I was daydreaming and not paying attention. I missed a question or something my teachers had said. I couldn't help it. It was as if I was carrying Christopher along with me now wherever I went. Whatever I saw happening, whatever I heard said, I automatically wondered what Christopher would think of it.

"There's something different about you," Kane told me when we walked together to a table in the cafeteria at lunchtime. "I don't only mean your almost being late twice in a row, although for you, that's close to a capital crime and probably had you in a state of terror."

"It is not," I said, and tried to look sullen about his remark. He just smiled and slid in beside me.

"Okay. It's not a capital crime. So what's the worst

thing you've ever done?" he asked as he started on his sandwich.

"I'm not going to tell you something that personal," I replied, and he laughed.

"Sure. I bet it was something horrific, like drinking a beer at a girlfriend's house when you were twelve."

I punched him a little more than just playfully in the shoulder.

"Hey."

"Don't make me out to be some Sandra Dee."

"Who?"

"Didn't you ever see *Grease*?"

He thought a moment and then smiled. "Oh, yeah, I remember. 'Look at me, I'm Sandra Dee, lousy with virginity.' Right?"

I gave him a good smirk, and he smiled.

"So what exactly does that mean?" he asked. "Lousy with virginity? Are you or aren't you?"

"None of your business," I said.

"Methinks the lady doth protest too much," he kidded.

I turned away and thought about myself for a moment. Was I as virginal as Christopher and Cathy were? Did I reek of teen virtue because I was so devoted to my father and such a responsible and good student? Was I as responsible as Christopher had to be, both of us thrust into becoming older almost overnight?

I gazed around the cafeteria and wondered how my classmates really saw me. From what I had read so far, Christopher didn't appear to have had many school friends. He mentioned no one in the early part of the diary, during the time before they were going to Foxworth to live. He certainly couldn't have made new friends while he was there. I had friends. I wasn't really like him, and for some reason, even though I was fascinated with him, that gave me relief.

Strangely, though, that relief made me feel guilty. I didn't want to see him as in any way strange. The feelings and revelations about himself that I had read surely were normal. One day, he realized that his sister was becoming a woman. Unfortunately, it was happening under weird circumstances, but I imagined any boy would have had similar reactions when he found himself in the same sort of situation, seeing his younger sister's body developing.

I glanced at Kane. He had an older sister who was in college. If anything, the roles might have been reversed. I certainly wasn't about to ask him when his sister first realized he was a man. When did he realize it? I wondered. Do boys react to that differently? Maybe I was too cloistered, too naive and oblivious to things, looks, feelings I should know meant more than I thought. The diary, I thought, Christopher's diary, might be more of an education about myself than anything else.

The rest of the day went smoothly. I forced myself to be more alert and pushed everything else out of my mind. I aced a math quiz, and I knew from her reaction to her grade that Theresa Flowman had not done that well. I participated in some idle chatter with my girlfriends. I was surprised that Kane hadn't told anyone about us going to Foxworth after school. I was anticipating Lana or Suzette asking me about it. They knew I was leaving with him since he had brought me, but they both apparently assumed I was either taking him to my house or going to his. We had planned it all. I got the usual silly warnings, like "Don't do anything I wouldn't do, which means you can do it all."

For more than one reason, I was happy to be spending more time alone with Kane. We had known each other for years, but it wasn't until this year that he looked at me and showed some romantic interest. Once again, I thought about Christopher's suddenly looking at Cathy and seeing more than simply a young girl. It made me wonder about myself. Could it be that I had blossomed in so subtle a way that I didn't even realize it myself? My father treated me, and always would, as his little girl, despite the new responsibilities I fulfilled and my being old enough to drive and go on dates. Perhaps a father, or even a mother, for that matter, resisted accepting that a daughter was no longer a child. In a mother's case, that umbilical cord was thinning out, and in the father's case, there was the realization that soon his little girl would be looking to another man to love and protect her.

"So you're really into this valedictorian thing?" Kane asked after we drove away from the school.

"I don't live for it, no, but it won't hurt."

"You'll have to make a speech at graduation."

"My father says I do that daily."

He tossed his head to the side the way he usually did when something pleased him, along with that small, soft smile that could burrow its way into the hardest of hearts. Even though I believed he knew what a charmer he was, I didn't sense him conniving to use those dazzling eyes and nearly perfect facial features to work his way in with any girl or get some favor from a teacher. His popularity came so easily that he didn't obsess about it.

"So tell me," he said as we turned toward Foxworth, "what do you really know about this place and what happened there originally? Your mother was related. You should know as much as, if not more than, anyone else about the history."

"She never talked about them, with me at least, and my father hates talking about them. He's not just clearing land and getting it all ready for rebuilding. He's attacking it as if he was General George Patton going after Hitler."

Kane laughed aloud. "That's what my father said your father would do. I guess he's made his feelings about it pretty clear to anyone who gets him talking about it."

"My father isn't afraid of expressing his opinion about anything," I told him. "Not just Foxworth."

"So I should watch myself around him," he countered. "Right?"

"Well, I'm not afraid of expressing my opinion, either."

He shook his head. "Where have you been all my life, Kristin Masterwood?"

"Either in the room across the hall, the room behind, or the room ahead."

We drove on. His smile was becoming deeper, his

eyes drinking me in like some bon vivant tasting cherished wine.

I felt myself blush.

Where would this journey take me?

Maybe I should be keeping my own diary, I thought, and then I felt my body grow tense, much tenser than before when my father and I had approached the ruins of Foxworth Hall. Christopher's diary had put me inside it in a way I never imagined. For a few moments, as we drew closer, I didn't see the ruins of a great fire. I saw the mansion standing high, the windows dimly lit, and high above, two little children, Carrie and Cory, being held up by their brother and sister to look out at a world that had suddenly become forbidden to them. It was like going to the site of a massacre or a prison and still being able to hear the cries and screams.

During all the time they had been kept here, had anyone driven up and caught sight of them in a window? If they had, did they keep it to themselves? From what everyone had known of the Foxworths, they didn't just invite anyone to their mansion, and they certainly didn't spend time in the city talking with people unless it was strictly business. I doubted Olivia Foxworth had any friends her own age by the time the children were locked up in the small bedroom and attic.

We pulled up next to my father's truck and got out. He had all the machinery going full steam. The area around the rubble had been cleared, and a good portion of the charred boards, pipes, shattered fixtures, and other contents were piled into three large trucks to be hauled away. Two large brush cutters were clearing the property to the south, and two men were surveying the property on the east end.

"I'll say your father is out to get this done fast," Kane commented. "He's wiping out all traces of the whole clan."

Dad paused and looked up from a clipboard when Todd Winston nodded in our direction. I waved, and he indicated how we should approach safely.

"Hello, Mr. Masterwood," Kane said quickly. "This is some job."

"A lot to do. It was a big place, and there was a great deal of destruction," my father said. He looked at me as if he wanted to study my reaction to it all, waiting for my comment.

"I thought I'd show Kane the lake," I said, ignoring everything else.

"Good. You two watch yourselves. There are boards with nails sticking out all over the place."

"Looks like it was more like an explosion than another fire," Kane said.

"A fire *is* an explosion," Todd told him. Kane gave him his usual shrug. "We haven't found anything else of any value, Kristin," Todd told me.

My father spun on him, and he looked away quickly.

"See you in a little while," I said, and started away.

Kane followed but looked back at my father and Todd. "What was that about? What did they find that was worth anything?"

"Nothing, really," I said. "Todd is hoping to find buried treasure."

Kane nodded, but his eyes were full of new curiosity. I wondered why my father hadn't told Todd not to mention the metal box. Now I had to lie my way around it, and I could see that Kane had already figured out how to tell when I was avoiding telling him something. I had one of those faces that would make a detective's job a piece of cake.

I walked faster.

"This place must have been something," Kane said, catching up. "So much property and a lake. They were very rich people."

"Supposedly."

"You'd think they'd have had happy lives."

I paused and turned to him. I knew, just like everyone else, that Kane's family was one of the wealthiest in Charlottesville. "Is that what makes your family happy, money?"

He laughed. "Not according to my father. He keeps telling us he's not made of money, but we love him anyway."

"Obviously, these people were miserable here," I said, and continued to walk.

"Then why did that woman bring her children here and keep them in a small bedroom and an attic for years?"

"She was bankrupt. Her husband was killed, and he didn't have life insurance, and they were in debt when he was alive."

"So you *do* know more about all this than you're admitting." He pounced.

"That's all I know," I said. "Most everyone knows that much," I added, and pounded ahead, my arms folded across my breasts.

When we reached the lake, I stopped, and he came up beside me. "You look annoyed. Maybe coming here wasn't such a good idea. The place is cursed."

"Maybe it is," I said, and sat on a big rock to look out over the water.

He went down to it and dipped his hand in. "Freezing," he said. "And I was going to suggest we go skinny-dipping."

I didn't respond. He looked out at the water and turned back to me.

"It must have been quite beautiful here once, when that dock was good and the borders weren't so overgrown. It has a natural spring feeding it. I bet it was even good to drink. It's kind of serene, even now with all this overgrowth around it. I actually like it. It's more like undisturbed nature, don't you think?"

As if it had heard Kane's remark, a crow seemed to come out of nowhere and perched on a dead branch floating on the water. It seemed to be staring at us as if it was wondering why we had come.

"Hey, crow!" Kane called to it, breaking the tension.

The bird lifted its wings as if to reply. We both laughed. And then it flew off into the woods.

"Be nice to go rowing on this lake," he said. "Even now."

"Maybe the new owner will clean it up and make it attractive again."

He walked back and sat next to me. "I've been here before," he revealed in the tone of a confession. "But I never thought of it this way."

"When were you here?"

"I came up here a few times with the guys on Halloween."

"I thought so when you said you had never been to Foxworth in the daytime."

"It was stupid. There really wasn't anything scary about the place. If anything, it looked pathetic to me, a shell of something. Everyone tried to scare everyone else, jumping out of shadows and moaning."

"So why did you want to come here today?"

"Oh, I didn't in particular. I just wanted an excuse to be with you."

"You could have just come out and said it. We could have gone somewhere else."

"It's really not that bad." He leaned toward me and looked at me closely.

"What?"

"Your eyes are the color of the sky today. It's like you're one with the world, at least here."

"Am I?" I looked at the water. Did I have a special connection with Foxworth now? Would it burrow deep into my heart and be forever a part of me?

"You're a very pretty girl, Kristin. You don't notice me watching you most of the day, I'm sure, but sometimes I catch you looking almost . . ."

"Almost what?"

"Angelic. Like you're somewhere else, somewhere beautiful and alone, someone really undiscovered as if you were lost in time . . . like this lake."

"I don't feel particularly angelic, but I'll admit there are many times when I feel lost in time."

He smiled, and then he kissed me, softly, keeping his lips against mine just a little longer, like someone sipping the last drops of honey. When we parted, he kept his face close, his eyes locked on mine. "I'm smart enough to know you're special, Kristin," he said, and then he kissed me again.

This time, I really kissed him back, as if there would be a magic carpet taking us away from all that was sad and dark in this world, taking us someplace warm and comfortable, a place where we could breathe happiness and never know sorrow, a place I was sure Christopher Dollanganger and his sister Cathy had hungered to be in.

"Now I'm sorry I'm having a party Friday. Who needs anyone else there?"

"I don't know if my father would let me go to your house knowing your parents weren't home."

"So we wouldn't tell."

"You wouldn't tell!" My eyes widened, even flamed. "I have a special relationship with my father. It's based on honesty."

"Ouch," he said, holding up his hands. "Maybe you *are* Sandra Dee."

I punched him again, and he exaggerated the blow and fell off the boulder.

"Killed at Foxworth!" he cried. "And by a distant cousin. How appropriate. Oh, woe is me."

"Get up, you idiot."

I stood up, and he scurried to his feet. "Your wish is my command," he said. He leaned in to kiss me again. Then he took my hand. "You know why I really like you, Kristin?"

"You want me to help you with math," I said, and he laughed.

"Man, you are easy to fall in love with."

I stopped and looked at him. Was that true? And if it was, why? What made someone easy to love? What made it so easy for Corrine to fall in love with her half-uncle? What made it so easy for my father to fall head over heels in love with my mother? Was there something magical that happened? Was that happening to me, too? "Why?" I asked him.

I thought he would make a joke, but he looked very serious. I could see he was thinking carefully. "There are other pretty girls in school. I've gone out with one or two, but even though none of them is prettier than you, that's not the only reason. You're . . . naked," he said.

"Excuse me?"

"I don't mean without clothes. I mean there's nothing false and deceptive about you. Like your father, I guess, you say what you mean, and I bet the only time you hold back or fudge it a little is when it might hurt someone who can't defend him- or herself."

"Thanks, I think."

"But even that isn't all of it."

"So what else is there?"

"There's a mystery in you. I feel there's more to you than anyone knows, maybe even your own father. I don't know if I'll ever know it, but I'm intrigued. Most of all, you make me feel comfortable with myself. I think I could tell you anything," he added. "I once read that true love means no secrets, because the people in love are unafraid of each other."

I squinted suspiciously. "Since when have you become so poetic, Kane Hill?"

"Since I realized how much I like you," he replied, and then he shrugged.

I didn't say anything. He reached for my hand, and we walked back in silence, soaking in the delicious special moments we had created for ourselves, both afraid that any words spoken would shatter them and bring us back to reality. Was it because we were here? Because we went to this lake? I wondered if the Dollanganger children had ever once looked upon this place and seen it as something magical. I would know, I thought. Christopher would surely reveal it.

My father watched us approach and stepped away from the work to greet us. "So?"

"It must have been very beautiful here once, Mr. Masterwood."

"Probably," Dad said reluctantly. "Someone will make it beautiful again once the corpse is gone. I'll be done here in about an hour, Kristin. We're still going to Charley's Diner?" he asked, looking at Kane and perhaps thinking we had made other plans.

"Yes, Dad."

"Okay. Be careful, now," he warned Kane. "You've got precious cargo aboard."

"You don't have to tell me that, sir."

"I do have to tell you," Dad said. "You'll realize it when you're a father."

Kane gave him his famous shrug and a smile. Dad nodded at me and returned to his work.

"I like your father," Kane said as we walked to his car. He looked back at him. "You can just feel he suffers no fools."

I looked at Kane, surprised at the quote he used. "'Suffers no fools'?"

"Actually, it's my father who says that all the time. Occasionally, I listen to him when he tells me stuff," he added, and gave me that smile that made me want to kiss him again.

And again.

Which we did when he dropped me off at my house.

"I really enjoyed spending time with you at Fox Hell," he said.

"You think places get stained forever by the events that happen there?" I asked.

He grimaced like I was getting too heavy about it. But then he shrugged. "You mean like the Dallas Book Depository because of the Kennedy assassination? Sure. I don't know how well Ford's Theatre did after Lincoln was shot there, but I don't imagine it was a selling point."

"Seems wrong to punish nature for what happened at Foxworth. It's beautiful if you don't know what happened there."

"You sound like you'd like to be the one building a new house."

"Just curious," I said.

"Get curious about *me*. I'd like the attention," he said.

"Like you lack any," I replied, and got out of the car.

He watched me walk to the house, that teasing grin on his face. "None of it mattered before," he shouted after me.

I smiled at him and watched him back out, much more carefully this time. He waved, and I waved back, and then when he was gone, I went into my house and up to my bedroom.

I knew my father wouldn't be home as quickly as he had indicted. He would stop working, but he'd have a lot to do with locking down the machinery for the night. Knowing I was going out for dinner, I should have turned myself directly to my home-work, but just having been on the Foxworth grounds caused me to want to be back into Christopher's diary and his thoughts. It was as if I was touching him, all of them, more now. I even imagined what they all sounded like.

The door opened and my mother walked in looking like she had doubled her thirty-three years in a day. My heart sank. Something terrible had happened or would be happening, I thought. I wanted to hold the twins back, but they exploded with shouts and whines, complaining about being kept locked up, blaming us for being mean to them. Looking like it pained her to do so, Momma put both of them on her lap and almost in a whisper asked them to calm down. She forced a smile and asked how it really had been. The twins were relentless, especially Carrie, who only became more demanding and shrill, slapping at Momma and then leaping off her lap to slap at me for keeping them locked up so long. I would never say they weren't spoiled, but I couldn't blame her or Cory for being so upset. They felt betrayed.

Suddenly, our grandmother appeared, looking taller, larger, and meaner than she had, demanding that Momma shut up the twins. "Discipline them now!" she cried.

To both Cathy's and my surprise, the twins turned on her without fear. Carrie was even louder, and Cory was backing up her every syllable with loud syllables of his own.

I never expected what our grandmother did next. She seized Carrie's hair and literally lifted her off her feet. My sister howled in pain, and when Grandmother Olivia dropped her, Cory kicked her and attempted to punch her. Unlike anything I had ever imagined an adult doing when confronting a child this small, our grandmother swung at him and slapped him so hard he fell on his side and then, probably still stinging with pain, crawled beside his wailing twin, both now hugging each other. I looked at Momma to see what she would do. She just looked down, appearing even more defeated.

I'll never forget the way Cathy looked at me then. She was like someone who had just realized that the last bit of hope for saving herself, for saving us, had passed, and we were about to descend into a pit of hell darker than we could ever begin to imagine. We both turned to Momma, hoping she would end this. However, when she threatened to take us out of the house, our grandmother just smiled and dared her to do it. Momma seemed to crumble. I wanted to go to her and tell her to do it, but I held back, not wanting to burden her any further. Little did I know what would happen next.

Grandmother Olivia ordered our mother to take off her blouse. Momma pleaded, begged not to have to do it, but our grandmother was unmerciful and relentless. Slowly, Momma stood up and unbuttoned her blouse. She wasn't wearing her bra or slip, and at first, I thought that was what our grandmother wanted to demonstrate, but I felt my heart stop and start. Momma's back from the neck down was crisscrossed with welts, some having bled into crusty red. I looked at Cathy and the twins. They were literally holding their breath at the sight. I saw tears in all their eyes. My whole body stiffened. I clenched my fists. Why did they do this to her? This kind of punishment was medieval.

My grandmother, looking more superior than ever, told us the welts went down to our mother's feet. She sounded proud of it. There were thirty-three lashes representing her age and fifteen extra to represent the years she had lived with our father in sin. Our grandfather had ordered our grandmother to do it, and Momma had submitted to the punishment. Still gloating, our grandmother told us that we would be punished if we didn't follow her rules. She shoved the door key into Momma's hands and walked out, her shoulders hoisted, making her look like a giant hawk.

What kind of a creature was she? She not only had punished her daughter viciously but was eager to show it as if it was an accomplishment.

There couldn't be any of her genetics in me, or any of my grandfather's, I thought. I detested every cell in her miserable body and hoped my grandfather was suffering in pain somewhere downstairs in his own private hell.

I felt my throat close so tightly that I panicked when I tried to swallow and couldn't. Throwing down the diary, I rose and quickly went into my bathroom to drink some water from the faucet. My heart was thumping. A real whipping? Welts crusted with blood? To see your mother so tortured by her own mother and father had to be earth-shattering for those kids, especially the little ones. Did my mother know what kind of monsters the Foxworths were? Had she heard about this? Did my father know? How much worse was this going to get for those children if they would do such a thing to their own daughter?

A part of me wanted to throw the diary into our fireplace, but a greater part of me wanted to know more. It was as if I wanted to make myself angry and sick over it. I looked in the mirror and then splashed cold water on my face, because I looked like I had a fever, and I certainly didn't want my father seeing me like this. He'd rip that diary out of my hands and tear it to pieces right in front of me.

I returned to my bedroom, approaching my bed slowly, as if I believed the diary lying on my blanket could leap up and bite me or something. I paced about, glancing at it every few seconds. It was going to disturb me, I thought. I wanted to continue, I then thought, immediately. I needed to continue, but maybe I should ration my reading. I knew I would have trouble sleeping tonight as it was.

For now, the easiest escape was my homework. When my father arrived and came up to see me, he found me at my desk, finishing up my math.

"Hey," he said. "If you have a lot of work, I can whip up something fast instead of going to the diner."

"No, I have it under control. You need to relax."

He smiled. "And you know this how?"

"I saw how intensely you were working today. You can't do it all in one day and get it behind you, Dad."

"Yes, boss. I'll grab a quick shower." He started to turn and then stopped. "Oh."

"What?"

"I won't be getting away so fast, anyway. Herm brought the new property owner up to see me. Man by the name of Arthur Johnson. Only about forty but quite wealthy. He runs a hedge fund. He wants to make me his general contractor on his rebuilding. Seems he's already had an architect working. The new structure won't be as tall as Foxworth was, but it'll be just as wide and deep. Something like a Greek revival. Nice man. No dickering on price, either. It will set me and Todd up for quite a while." He paused, his eyes narrowing with suspicion. "What's wrong? You don't seem happy about this."

"I thought you didn't like being there."

"Not enough to turn down this kind of money. Besides, when I'm finished, there won't be the slightest resemblance to what was there. Johnson is of the same mind. Has all sorts of ideas for the landscaping. It will look more plush than it ever looked. No restraint when it comes to flowers and bushes, the way it was most recently. There'll be no resemblance to a monastery and no question that whoever lives there actually enjoys his wealth. With all the new business it might bring, I might have to put you to work this summer," he added, half-joking.

I glanced toward my bed. The diary was back under my pillow, but it was as if I thought Christopher could hear my father speaking. Maybe my father was right. In a relatively short time, Christopher and his brother and sisters' story, along with the story of the most recent inhabitant, would be buried and forgotten. The new building would be all that a new generation would see and know. Only the diary could keep the story of the Dollanganger children alive.

"We'll head out in twenty," my father said, and left.

I gazed at my homework. How could I concentrate now? My heart was thumping. I couldn't help it. In the back of my mind, a frightening thought was blossoming like a dark flower.

It was as if the Foxworths could feel themselves disappearing. Once the building was gone and there was a new owner changing it all, they would fade away. They were desperate. They wouldn't let go of us now.

Maybe not for a long time.

Maybe never.

I put it out of my mind and concentrated on what I would wear to dinner, even if it was only Charley's Diner. I was still going with my father, and I wanted him to be proud of me, proud of how I dressed, how I looked. He wouldn't harp on it; he wouldn't even mention it, because he assumed I would dress properly. I knew how he shook his head and muttered to himself when he saw the way some of my friends and classmates looked when they went out with their parents, even to fancy restaurants.

My father and I didn't go out to eat all that much, but I knew that whenever we did, especially when we went to Charley's, he enjoyed it, not so much because he and I didn't have to be in the kitchen as because it was his chance to meet some of his old friends and toss around stories and their form of gossip. Charley's Diner was just that sort of hangout for many other men who were involved with the construction industry. I saw all the pickup trucks and construction vehicles in the parking lot when we arrived.

One part of Charley's was like an old '50s diner with its faux-leather red booths with pleated white centers and chrome edges and tables. There was a long counter with swivel stools and lots of Formica and chrome, but there were also a good dozen or so retro dinette sets, again with lots of chrome and Formica. The floor was a black and white checker, and although some of them didn't work, there were miniature juke-boxes at the booths and on the counter. Consequently, there was always music but nothing anyone my age would appreciate.

Charley Martin was the original owner. He was well into his seventies, although he looked ten years younger, with his full head of salt-and-pepper hair swept back and to the sides as if he had just run a wet washcloth over it, maybe with a little styling lotion. He was stout, with the forearms of a carpenter, both arms stained with tattoos he had gotten in the Philippines when he was in the navy. Dad called him "Popeye." He pretended to be annoyed, but I could see he liked it. They loved exchanging navy stories.

By now, my father's tight community of construction workers, electrical and plumbing employees, and people who worked in Deutch's lumberyard, the one Dad favored, all knew about "The Foxworth Funeral Project," as it rapidly had been labeled. When I thought about it, I realized, what else could it be called?

It was inevitable, I guess, that new work on the property would revive the legends and stir up the stories, some quite exaggerated over the years since it had burned down a second time. Some spoke about old man Foxworth constructing a private church in the mansion that rivaled the church his evangelist ancestor had built to house his own form of preaching the gospel. Ray Pantel, whose family-run company did a great deal of the electrical work and repairs in the first mansion, said his father had told him Olivia Foxworth had skirts put on the piano legs because she believed naked piano legs were too suggestive. That set them all trying to outdo one another with stories describing the Foxworths' fanatical Bible thumping, which somehow always returned to Olivia and Malcolm's sexual repression.

"I heard they only made love enough times to have their children, and always in the dark at that," Jimmy Stark, a retired plumber, said. Everyone laughed.

"No wonder their daughter ran off," Billy Kelly, the manager of Deutch's lumberyard, declared. "From what I was told, she was practically forbidden to look at any boy, much less go out on dates. She might even have been forced to wear a chastity belt."

"She ran off with a good-looking young man," Jimmy said. He was at least fifteen years older than my father but had the genes of an immortal, as my father would say. He looked younger than men twenty years younger than he was. "My father saw a picture of him once. He had to go down into the basement to work on a water heater when Malcolm was still alive and saw this damp, rotten carton with some photos in it. The old lady found out he saw the pictures and threw the whole damn carton full into the furnace. That was the last time they called him to do any work for them."

Everyone mumbled and complained about how the most recent inhabitant had gone outside of the Charlottesville community for all his labor when he rebuilt the mansion. Ray said his father had told him that the nutcase had located the original plans and tracked down the builder's company outside of Richmond.

"Probably didn't want any local people snooping around. Who knows, maybe they found that little boy's body but were all sworn to secrecy."

I could see my father was starting to get annoyed with the discussion. At any moment, someone was going to ask him, as so many had, if my mother had mentioned any of this, and he might just explode. He glanced at me.

"Let's change the subject," he said, nodding in my direction. "Not everyone here has ears full of grime and grit and doesn't mind rusty garbage flowing into their head."

That worked, and they were back to talking about the hopeful surge in new housing, the economy, and politics. Gradually, they all peeled off to go their separate ways while Dad and I had our slices of Charley's famous apple pie.

"They can be a bunch of old women sometimes," Dad muttered, sipping his coffee and looking in the direction his friends had taken. Jimmy was still at the counter having his coffee.

"I resemble that remark," I said, imitating him

whenever I said something with which he might disagree. "Why not call them a bunch of old men?"

He nodded. "You're right. Chauvinistic. Anyway, that's why your mother hated gossip. Something begins with a nibble of the truth, and by the time it gets to where it's getting, it's as far from the truth as could be. Let's hope once I level what I have to and rebuild what Arthur Johnson wants, what I've always hoped happens."

"Which is?"

"That Foxworth dies a long-needed death."

I nodded, but I wasn't ready to go to that funeral, and he knew it. His eyes got smaller as he squinted and leaned in toward me. *Here it comes*, I thought.

"I won't stop you from reading that diary, Kristin, but I will be very unhappy if you talk about it, especially with other kids at school who might get their families talking about it all again and bring attention back to us, just when I don't want that. Understood?"

"Another warning? You couldn't have made it clearer if you wanted to," I said with a half smile.

He smiled, too. "I promise. I won't talk about it anymore," he added, raising his right hand.

I knew I should have been happy about that, but there was something about being alone with that diary and the story that made me tremble when I least expected it.

When we got home, I returned to my homework. I had the feeling I was rushing through it to give myself time to get back to Christopher, especially after hearing all those stories and rumors at Charley's. I tried

to resist, telling myself I needed a good night's sleep.
I set my alarm and got into bed, but moments later,
as if Christopher was calling me through the pillow, I
turned over, pulled out the diary, and turned the page.
How could I not? They were all in such pain.

It wasn't until Momma got herself together and,
all stunned, we were calm enough to listen to her
that Cathy and I fully understood who we were. I
hesitate to write "what we were," for everything I
knew and understood about good and evil in this
world kept me from accepting that we were as our
grandmother saw us, spawn of the devil, creatures
inclined to be sinners.

Slowly, as if the words were coming up from
her gut, regurgitated like sour milk, Momma began
to tell her story. She spoke in almost a whisper,
first describing how horrid her youth was, not only
for her but also for her brothers who had died.
Her parents wouldn't permit her and her brothers
to be normal people. They couldn't go swimming
because they would show too much of their
bodies. They couldn't go to dances because they'd
be too close to the opposite sex.

Cathy's eyes widened with every illustration
Momma drew up.

"You and your brothers were like prisoners,"
I said, not ignoring the irony that prisoners were
what we were right now.

"Worse. Prisoners could have their thoughts.
My parents would look at me and tell me I was

having sinful, dirty thoughts. She would listen in on my phone calls, read notes I wrote in my notebooks for school, read any card or letter addressed to me that came to the house first, and if she didn't like a word or something, she would burn it before I saw it. I would find out later that someone had sent me a birthday or holiday card. You can be sure if any boys did, I never saw them. I was never permitted to have a girlfriend in my room alone with me, and if any boy dared come to our house, he and I had to sit in the entryway. I couldn't even bring him into the living room."

"And your father put up with all this?" I asked.

"My father?" She laughed. "First, he would never challenge anything my mother said to us or did to us, and second, my father was cruel even to his own, seizing control of his father's estate when he died and cutting his father's second wife and son out of their inheritance. When she died years later, her son was brought to live with us, Garland Christopher Foxworth IV, but my parents wouldn't permit him to be called anything but Christopher or Chris," she said, and put her arm around me. She smiled. "Do you know who I mean?"

My mind was spinning. It was finally being brought home to us with details. Of course, Garland Christopher was my mother's half-uncle. They would still be considered close blood relatives. The word screamed and echoed in my mind: incest. We were the children of incest! It was true. All the innuendos and sly comments

made sense now. This was the horrible sin
my grandparents saw our mother and father
committing. I looked at Cathy. She was not
grasping it as quickly as I was, or else she didn't
want to grasp it.

Momma continued, describing our father's
arrival at Foxworth Hall, telling us they fell in
love at first sight. Both of them knew it. Her face
brightened when she described that feeling.

"Goodness knows, we needed love in
our house. I needed to feel some love, some
happiness. My brothers were already dead from
accidents. Neither of my parents smiled or laughed
much at all. For a while, that changed when your
father came to live with us."

She told us that her parents treated our father
like a son because of the sons they had lost. That,
I realized, must have only cemented and intensified
their fury over the romance she would have with
my father. To my grandparents, he wasn't only her
half-uncle; he had become a son, in their minds, a
brother to her.

"Didn't you realize they would be upset,
Momma?" I asked her.

"Of course. We both did, but someday you'll
see and understand how real love can blind you to
anything else but the one you love. Nothing else
matters but your and his or her happiness. Please
try to understand, even though I know you're
both too young to realize the power of romantic

love. Please don't think of us as anything but two lovesick young people. Not only didn't we think of the sin my parents accused us of committing, but neither of us would ever say that word. We never believed anything bad could come of a love so strong and pure."

I could see from the way she was looking at me that she was worried that I, especially, would condemn her, not from a biblical point of view but from a scientific one. From what I had read, children of incest could suffer genetic side effects. Perhaps there were things that would happen to us as we grew older, but right now, none of us looked less than perfect. With Momma at such a low point, I couldn't even let myself think of any of that. But I knew that I would, if not right away, then later when I had more time to consider it all.

Again, I glanced at Cathy. She looked like she was hearing a Romeo and Juliet story now. The pain, the suffering, and even the immorality of what our parents did were romanticized. I saw that dreamy, far-off look of fantasy in her face. Was it just a girl's characteristic? Momma didn't really pay attention to the stories Cathy brought home from school, but I knew she was already talking about boyfriends.

Maybe Momma's story was more of a Cinderella story than Romeo and Juliet. Our father was like a prince when he arrived and considering

the way her parents were treating him. Their
love was that magic carriage that would turn into
a pumpkin if they let it happen. I suppose our
mother saw romance and marriage to our father
as an escape from a horrid life. Never would she
permit herself to imagine that she would have to
return to it and bring us along. She was fitted with
a pair of rose-colored glasses early in her life, and
now I could see that she never took them off.

Once disaster struck, she went on about her
plan to get her father to forgive her and reverse
her disinheritance. She vowed to do anything he
wanted to get herself back into his good graces. I
wanted to believe it was not for herself as much as
for us. Then she looked at me again, suspicious of
my "thinking eyes," as she sometimes called them.
She insisted that there was nothing wrong with her
marriage to our father, and despite all her father's
predictions, we turned out to be so beautiful and
perfect. Yes, I thought, we were the Dresden dolls.
Both our parents always believed that.

I assured her that I had no contrary thoughts
and that if God had condemned her and our
father, we wouldn't be as healthy as we were.

"Maybe your mother is angry that we're not
deformed and ugly," I said.

She smiled. "Yes, she is having trouble
accepting that the four of you are the result of our
love. She mumbles that the devil always makes evil
look attractive, but I can see that she is having
trouble believing herself."

"And we won't do anything to make it easy for her to," I said. "I can promise you that."

How she beamed. She embraced and kissed me, thanking me for being so understanding and giving her the strength to do what she had to do for us all. My words seemed to energize her. It was as if she no longer felt any pain from that whipping. Even the twins seemed impressed with how quickly she had recuperated.

She made us join hands and promise never to think of ourselves as ugly or evil, but I wondered why she had brought us to such a terrible place with such a horrible woman to rule over us. We might have been better off living in semipoverty. She knew what her parents were like, how rigid and cruel they could be.

"Didn't you anticipate all this?" I couldn't help but ask.

She smiled. "You sound so much like your father sometimes, Christopher. Of course, I knew how cruel they could be, but I thought that after all these years, being alone, having no family, they would realize what they had lost and they would have changed." She went on to explain how her mother's letter had filled her with optimism, but, she said, smiling at me, "I know what's really eating away at her."

"What?" Cathy demanded. Maybe she hoped something was literally eating away at her and she would disappear completely.

Momma held her smile on me like a spotlight.

"Once she looked at Christopher, she saw his handsome father, and once she looked at you, Cathy, she saw me, and her rage came rolling back like thunder over the hills."

"Then she'll always hate us," Cathy said, throwing up her hands. "Why bother? Let's go."

Momma nodded reluctantly. For a moment, I thought she was going to pack us up and take us out of this hellhole. I could see Cathy thought the same and looked excited, hopeful, but instead, Momma came up with her plan.

She decided she would go to secretarial school and learn all the skills she needed to get a decent job and find us a big enough apartment. Then we could move out and not want for the basic things, at least. In the meantime, she wanted us to amuse ourselves, care for the twins, and put up with her mother's insane rules. Like the dreamer she could be when our father was alive, she drifted into her visions of the future, a future in which we would all realize our dreams. Of course, I knew that even if she did get a good job and a decent place for us to live, what we wanted to do for ourselves would take a great deal of money.

Nevertheless, I was happy, of course, to hear that she wanted to take us out of here. For a while, I feared that she didn't see how difficult all this was for us or that she was ignoring and pretending. I couldn't help it. I wanted to dream along with her, but Cathy was suddenly the more realistic one, asking her how long it would take.

"It won't take me that long. Maybe a month."

I looked at Cathy quickly. A month? Stuck here? I gave her my best "keep it to yourself" look, and she didn't start to rant and rave. Momma promised that in the meantime, she would have enough money to buy us things and bring them to us. Just before she left, she told us she was just as much a prisoner as we were, even worse, because she was under her father and mother's close scrutiny.

"If I just breathe wrong, they'll pounce."

I knew her technique so well. She hoped that if we felt sorry for her, we wouldn't feel as sorry for ourselves. I didn't say anything. Momma was who she was, I thought. I loved her more than any child could love his mother, but I wasn't blind to her weaknesses. I had to tolerate them. She needed me to be strong for her and for us all, now more than ever.

When we went to sleep that night, I persuaded Cathy to think only good thoughts. I teased her the way I used to and promised her that she would be the dancer she dreamed of being. I called her "Cathy Doll," which was the stage name she hoped to have. It worked. Yes, I was like Momma. I knew how to get my sister to cooperate, and together, I thought we could handle the twins. I'd start by teaching them things they should be learning in school. We'd make it through this, I told myself. We'd give Momma the time she needed.

I thought they had all fallen asleep finally, but

when I looked at Cathy, I saw her eyes were still wide open. She was thinking too hard.

"What?" I asked her. "What are you thinking so hard about?"

"We could have been born with horns and tails."

"No, that's ridiculous."

She sat up and looked at me. "But this is why we all have blue eyes and golden hair."

"There are scientific reasons for hair and eye color based on genetics, what you inherited. The scientific information isn't perfect yet." I said. I was tired now myself, very tired. Thinking can exhaust you, too.

"Still," Cathy said, pushing hope into herself. "If we follow her rules and she thinks we're good, she'll treat us like she should treat her grandchildren."

"Sure," I said.

She lay down again. "It will be all right," she whispered, more to herself than to me.

I looked at the locked door and then at my little brother and sister curled in fetal positions, dreaming good dreams the way children their age should.

I wanted to whisper, "It will be all right," to myself, too.

But my lips wouldn't let me.

Nor would my heart.

What a mistake reading Christopher's diary before I went to sleep was becoming. I spent a night tossing and turning, picturing the four of them shut up in that mansion and believing that their mother would find a way to rescue them. Normally, Christopher was too smart to buy into his mother's fantasies, but this time, lying right beside his intelligence was his hope. It was weaker, thinner, but he clung to it. What choice did he have? They were too young and needy to be able to do anything more for themselves. How would even three of them survive all this?

The more I thought about them, the more questions I had, and those questions were like tiny balls of hail pounding at my brain, making sleep almost impossible. I finally did fall asleep, but only a couple of hours before I had to get up, and thank goodness, this time, I had remembered to set my alarm.

I leaped out of my bed and nearly drowned myself in the shower to wake up. Usually, I gave myself plenty of time to dress, do my hair, and put on a little lipstick before I made an appearance. I was mumbling annoyance at myself all the way down the stairs.

"Heard your alarm go off," my father said as soon as I set foot in the kitchen. He turned to give me a scornful look. "How late did you stay up?"

"Not that late," I said, and dropped like a sack of potatoes into my chair.

He pulled the corners of his mouth in tightly and gave me his best look of disappointment. He had squeezed fresh oranges for my juice and was at the stove preparing French toast for both of us. The aroma helped me become more alert.

I stretched, drank my juice, and smiled. "You usually wait until the weekend to make that."

"Had a craving and thought you might, too."

"Maybe you should return to being a short-order cook, Dad. You're so good at it."

"Thank you, but no thank you. This Masterwood is not going to work for anyone else."

"Open your own diner. I'll be hostess, waitress. We'll call it Burt's Eats or something."

"How I wish I was young enough to have fantasies again," he said. "I wish I was eighteen again." He brought me a plate of French toast. He put the maple syrup next to it and the jar of Mrs. Wheeler's homemade jam. Mrs. Wheeler was a widow who lived five miles or so down the road and made jams, sour pickles and sour tomatoes, pies, and birthday cakes to supplement her income. My father was always drumming up more business for her. He said she reminded him of his mother, "who treated her kitchen the way most people treat a church."

He wished he was young enough to have fantasies? I thought. Corrine Dollanganger, a married women with four children, clung to them, and Christopher instinctively knew that without them, he and his brother and sisters wouldn't survive. Maybe fantasies were as important to our lives as bread. I wondered now about my own.

Since reading the last page I had read in the diary, all my dreams rang with more hope than reality to me. Just recently, I had been imagining myself becoming a super doctor who not only treated patients but on the side performed miraculous research and found cures for cancer and other serious illnesses. Had I let everyone fill me with so much hot air about myself and my brilliance that I would explode with the shock of reality someday, maybe sooner than I thought?

"What made you want to get into construction? And don't tell me your name again," I said, taking my first bites of the French toast. As usual, it was better than any we had out at any restaurant, including Charley's Diner. He had some secret in making it that he wouldn't even tell me.

He stood there looking down at me. "You're asking many more questions these days."

"Maybe I need more answers as I get older, even though parents supposedly say their young children never stop asking questions."

"That was you. You were born with question marks in your eyes."

"I'm regressing," I said, smiling. "This is so good, Dad."

"I'm glad," he said, and went to serve himself. "She makes really good jam," he told me as he smeared some of it on his toast. "Everyone has some talent hidden in themselves. It just takes the right combination of events to bring it out, I guess."

"You're giving me an answer?"

He ate and looked past me for a few moments. Then he nodded. "The moment I met your mother, I became more ambitious. When you care a great deal about someone else besides yourself, you want to do more. Short-order cooking for a living was okay when

I had no one but myself. I even put up with the dumb things my boss would do that made my work harder, but once I was with your mother, the world began to change, open up. She inspired me." He paused and waved his right forefinger at me. "You wait until you find the right person to inspire you, Kristin. It makes all the difference when you have someone besides yourself to be responsible for, someone you love and who loves you."

I nodded, but I wasn't thinking about myself. I was thinking about Christopher and how all that was happening was forcing him to be more mature. He didn't appear to me to be someone who ever pumped up balloons of false hope. He was simply too realistic about everything, even when he was much younger, but I had the sense that he knew the chances of him enjoying his youth were slipping away.

Was I really enjoying my youth? How much had my mother's death taken from me? After my mother died, all I wanted to do was escape from sadness, and the quickest way to do it seemed to be just get older, almost overnight. All teenagers wanted to rush their lives along, wanted to be on their own faster. It drove us to resist rules, take chances, and lie to ourselves. How many times, in how many different ways, did my friends tell their parents, "You're treating me like a child"? I never had to. My father sensed I was unfortunately taking on a seriousness born out of my mother's unexpected passing. She had slipped away like a shadow helpless against the morning sun.

"What do you have on for today?" Dad asked.

"Nothing special. I'm going to Kane's party tonight. You remember?"

"Driving yourself, or what?"

"Kane's picking me up."

He nodded. He looked thoughtful. I imagined he was thinking about me growing up so fast, but he surprised me. That wasn't in his thoughts right now. "I didn't want to mention this," he said after he sipped his coffee. "Don't want to encourage any thinking about it, but I know you'd want to know."

"What?"

"When we were going through a shed to retrieve anything worth saving before we knocked it down, we found a child's rocking horse. I'm guessing that it survived the first fire. Probably the way it fell under some metal, whatever."

"Really. Where is it?"

"Todd took it to refurbish it. He thinks it might sell as an antique. Was it mentioned in the diary?"

For a moment, I couldn't answer. Was he interested, or was he just testing to see what was in the diary? "Yes," I said. "The first day after they had been brought there."

He thought and nodded.

"Those children were told they had nothing after their father's death, right? And that was why she brought them to Foxworth? Is that what he wrote in his diary?"

"Yes. Corrine threw herself on the mercy of her parents. She sounds to me like someone very helpless. She was babied and spoiled, even though her parents were supposedly very cruel. I know now that her husband spoiled her."

He smirked and shook his head.

"What?"

"I don't know what's true or not true. We—your mother, I should say—understood differently."

"Meaning what?"

"She wasn't that desperate. She could have survived without her parents. But as I've been saying, who knows what really happened?" he added and rose.

"What do you mean? There was a life insurance policy? She had some money?"

"Like I said, who knows what was and wasn't true? It was too long ago, and the people who knew her well enough are either dead or gone."

"Didn't this Bart Foxworth who rebuilt the house ever talk to anyone about it?"

"Talk about it? He chased people off that property at gunpoint if they came around with that intention. You heard them talking at Charley's. He didn't have much to do with local people. There was something about them that brought out the hermit in him. Maybe they were termites in a previous life. No, he and his cousins or whoever they were only fanned the wild stories with their weird ways. First, he rebuilt the place and left it standing for years and years without anyone living in it, and then he abandoned it like a rat fleeing a sinking ship."

"I don't understand the second fire, then. No one was living there?"

"Hobos discovered it or . . ."

"Ghosts?" I said with a slight smile.

He shook his head and then pointed his right fore-finger at me like a pistol. "I don't want to hear you say something like that outside of this house."

"Don't worry. I won't. I'll get the dishes, Dad. I've got time this morning."

"Thanks to your alarm clock," he said. He looked at me and added, "Be careful."

"You, too," I shot back, and he finally smiled.

"Oh," he said turning back. "I nearly forgot. Your uncle Tommy is going to spend a day and a night with us next week. He's stopping by after some business meeting. Worked it into his schedule. Seems he wants to see how much you've grown or something."

"That's great!"

"Thought you'd be happy about it. Okay. If I'm not back before you leave, have a good time," he said.

Dad knew how much I liked Uncle Tommy. He had remained a bachelor, but he was not unattractive, and he did have a couple of very serious romantic relationships as far as I could remember. Dad claimed that was because he was in the mad Hollywood world. One of his relationships lasted about five years, and then his girlfriend broke off with him, probably frustrated with his lack of interest in a permanent relationship. Dad told me he once told him that he was afraid of commitment because he was afraid of being a disappointment. When I asked him what that meant exactly, Dad hesitated and then said, "He doesn't sing that song."

"What song?"

" 'I Only Have Eyes for You,' " Dad replied. "He's certainly not the first who couldn't be faithful to one woman, but he's rare because he admits it. Maybe he just likes emotional good-byes."

I didn't want to think of Uncle Tommy as weak or selfish. I certainly didn't like thinking he was deceitful, but I couldn't help comparing him with my father. There wasn't all that much age difference. Uncle Tommy was three years younger, but he always seemed much younger to me. It went back to Dad's point about wanting to be responsible for someone other than yourself, I thought. Uncle Tommy just wasn't cut out to be that way. Oh, he took care of my grandmother, but taking care of your mother was not the same thing. That, whether you liked it or not, was built into your DNA. At least, that was what I thought.

Was I cut out to be responsible for someone else? Many women were the primary wage earners in families these days. Or at least, they were on practically an equal basis. Did I want to have children sooner or later in my life? It was still harder for women to decide, even women who could afford nannies from day one. I didn't see myself as a mother who would gladly relegate her motherhood role to an employee.

It made me wonder again why Corrine wanted to have so many children. Was it more her husband's desire? Did she go along expecting something more for herself? Maybe she had made a deal first: she'd have the children, but he had to get her help and not stop buying her things. Then he died, and she was left with empty promises. Just from the little I had read about her, I could see she would regret having had four children, especially when it came to looking for a new husband. The man would have to be committed not only to her but to four children who weren't his own. She was smart enough to know that wouldn't be an easy task. On the other hand, if she inherited great wealth, none of it would matter. Was that always one of her goals? Had she discussed it with Christopher Sr.?

Could that rumor Daddy mentioned be true, that she did have some money, enough to take care of the family until she found employment? How conniving and dishonest was Corrine Foxworth? I wondered. With Christopher Jr. so observant and intelligent, she would have had to put on quite a show of desperation. There was no question that he believed her, believed it was happening to them. Did he want to believe her? Although he said he knew his mother had weaknesses, did he deliberately avoid seeing them?

Perhaps Dad was right. Perhaps she could have managed and not submitted to her parents' insanity and punished her children so, but not only their futures were at stake. Hers was, too, and she was a woman who liked to be pampered. Only lots of money would make her happy.

There were so many questions to answer. Could Christopher Jr. do that in his diary, or would he avoid not only the answers but the questions themselves? He said he was writing facts, but even he would admit that the facts were seen through his eyes and those eyes had their own prejudices and feelings. He could do nothing about it, no matter how hard he tried. I'd have to get better at reading between the lines, I thought.

And what was up with my father, suddenly telling me something about the Foxworths *willingly*? Was he subtly trying to warn me that what I read in the diary might not be the truth? Did he want to prepare me for something more terrible and fill me with skepticism before I had read it? I was back to the question that haunted me. How much had he and my mother really known?

I finished cleaning up our breakfast dishes and the frying pan he'd used and then headed upstairs to get my things and go. Because of his military experience, my father always made his bed before he left for work. When I was only five, I studied how carefully he did it and tried to do it for my own bed. Eventually, I became as good at it as he was. Keeping things clean and organized was also important to my mother. Dad was meticulous when it came to his tools at home. Anyone who saw our garage always commented on how neat it was. My father believed that how you treated your possessions said a great deal about how you treated yourself and others.

When I made my bed, I tucked the diary in under the pillow as I had been doing, and I thought about the messy world in which Corrine had permitted her children to be placed. Rats and mice, insects and dust, stale air and poor ventilation were not ideal, especially for the twins. Most mothers would be very concerned about their children's health, but from the way Christopher described her acceptance of it, she didn't seem to worry the way a normal, caring mother should. Was this the first clue concerning what eventually happened?

I was eating and sleeping this diary, I thought. Maybe if I thought of it the way I thought of any novel I had read, it would lose its grip on me. I hurried out, making sure I didn't look back at my bed and that diary burning under my pillow, the covers closed but the voices not silent.

When I arrived at school, my girlfriends practically attacked me with their questions about Kane's party. It was happening tonight. Suddenly, I felt like I was moving in a spotlight. Everyone was more interested in my opinion. What was I going to wear? What should they wear? What did I think of this blouse, this skirt, these shoes? What about lipstick? Eye shadow? How should they wear their hair? What would I suggest?

Girls who really couldn't care less about my opinions about their hair and clothes before were suddenly intent on hearing what I had to say.

"We don't know what kind of a party it is," Lana exclaimed when I didn't give them any specific answers. "Is he having it catered?"

"Catered?"

"Well, they're so rich. His parents would let him do that," Missy Meyer said. "He might even have people serving."

I just shrugged. My mind was still on the Dollanganger children and their being locked away in that mansion. Neither Cathy nor Christopher was going to go to any parties for years. For years, how Cathy wore her hair wasn't going to be important. For years, Christopher would not experience a girl flirting with him, nor would he be able to meet a girl and have a conversation with someone his own age. For years, they would never know what music was popular with their friends, what movie was exciting everyone in their class, what television show was being talked about at school, or even what was happening in the news that kids their age would be interested in. If they would complain that they were half alive, they wouldn't be wrong, I thought.

"I don't know any more about his party than you do," I told them.

"Well, you were with him yesterday after school," Lana said.

"You've been spending most of your time with him, haven't you?" Suzette asked. "So?"

I thought about it for a moment and laughed.

"What?"

"We never really talked about his party," I said, and went to my desk as class began.

Whenever Kane was close enough after his classes, he was waiting for me to walk me to my next class.

"The girls are driving me crazy asking me for details about your party," I told him.

"Let's have it be a surprise. I'll come for you around six thirty, okay?" he said the first time.

"Six thirty? So early?"

"We have a lot to do to prepare for the party. I'm

ordering in pizzas and salads," he told me. "You can help me warm things up. Our housekeeper has been given the night off."

"Sure," I said.

I had never been to Kane's house, but everyone talked about it. It was a refurbished antebellum built of whitewashed brick and timber that people half-jokingly called Hill's Tara, referring to the great house in *Gone with the Wind*. It was one of the largest estates in the area, about nine miles outside of Charlottesville.

"And I thought it would be nice to have some private time before it all starts. Not that we won't later," he added. "Tell your father I'll bring you home, too. It will be a good way to throw everyone else out."

"Is that your only reason?" I asked when we stopped at my next classroom.

He just gave me that grin, tossed his head to the side, and sauntered off to join the boys who were waiting for him down the hall. I watched them close around him as if they could draw his energy into them and glow like he did. When I turned to go into the classroom, I found I had the same sort of thing awaiting me, my girlfriends gathering around me, still asking questions about the party and obviously trying to be my best friends.

I knew all of this was coming at me because now it was even mōre obvious that Kane was very fond of me, and as far as most of the girls in high school were concerned, he was the most desirable boy. Who wouldn't want to be his girlfriend, at least for a little while?

Today there was something else going on, however. I think they could all sense that there was something different between us, and there was. This wasn't just another little romance. Even I had to admit that I was feeling that was true. Perhaps it was because of the time we had spent at the Foxworth lake yesterday. Maybe he had felt something special there, too. Throughout the day, every moment he could be, he was with me. We were behaving as if we were oblivious to everyone and everything around us. I imagined that the contrast between how nonchalant I was about him before and how I was acting this day raised eyebrows and started a chorus of whispers.

There was no reason for me to be surprised about that. Anyone, even our teachers, who usually didn't pay attention to such things, could see that we were looking at each other more intently. Those feelings, those moments gazing at each other so long that they could be called staring, were not easy to hide or prevent. Neither of us seemed to care if anyone knew about our deeper feelings for each other, anyway. Kane always seemed to me to be someone like that, but it was new for me. Suddenly, I wasn't as bashful or concerned about what other people were thinking of me.

When I thought about it, I wondered how Corrine and Christopher Sr. had hidden their passion for each other from her parents, at least in the beginning. Probably, they reached a point when they knew they couldn't any longer, and that was when they had decided to run off together. I couldn't help but imagine them sneaking around that mansion at night, clinging to each other in shadows, terrified they would be discovered, and hating that it had to be that way. It made them feel as dirty and as sinful as her parents would think they were, and who could live with that?

Kane and I had known each other for a long time. Were he and I always going to be this passionate about each other? Were my feelings for Kane and his feelings for me always this obvious to everyone else but me? My girlfriends were always telling me that he liked me more than he liked other girls he had dated, but I didn't dwell on it, especially during these last few days when I was reading Christopher's diary. Besides, I was always skeptical about Kane. To me, it still looked like he was shopping around, and I was reluctant to be easy, anyway. I thought my girlfriends knew that. Maybe those others he had disappointed just wanted me to be another victim caught in Kane Hill's web.

Or maybe it was always my fault. Maybe I was simply too afraid of being disappointed. Was I more like Uncle Tommy than I was like my father? Being deceived and betrayed after you had exposed yourself in a commitment could be devastating. You'd never trust any boy after that. Kane, despite what he had said and how he had behaved, especially at the lake, was so casual about everything he did that it was easy to have this feeling, this fear. Even now, it sneaked in under my growing affection for him. What if he began to date someone else the following week? If just like that, he turned away from me? How was I supposed to take it?

Too many of the girls I knew, especially in the junior and senior classes, were satisfied with what they called "hooking up." Committing themselves to one boy for a long period of time was for the insecure. It was more fun to circulate. "What's your goal, to be the king and queen at the prom or something? Please, give me a break." I overheard these conversations, and they weren't only coming from envious girlfriends. Many, if not most, believed it.

Maybe they were right to think that way. How did you know the right decisions to make when you were our age? How many of my girlfriends really had close enough relationships with their mothers to get some guidance, and how many even wanted it? Everyone seemed suspicious of her parents. Whose mother would ever suggest intimate relationships, much less condone them? But everyone was titillated with the prospect, including me, although that was my most secret thought.

Would Cathy have these thoughts before she left Foxworth? She'd have no experiences, no chances to develop even small relationships. Suddenly, she would find herself dropped into the world my girlfriends and I were navigating but without the benefit of growing into it, developing. It would be like taking a sixth-grader, having her in a coma for three years, and then pushing her into the teenage world.

According to what my father had told me about the Foxworth children, Uncle Tommy knew someone who had been a servant at the mansion and confirmed that Cathy was more than fifteen by the time they left.

She was just a little younger than I was. Three years without any contact with other girls, while her body was developing and her interest in boys and her own feelings should have had healthy room for exploration. How could any girl come out of that normal?

It was difficult to not get lost in these thoughts, even when my friends were chatting around me. I knew I looked preoccupied, but they all thought it was because I was so swept up in my first big love affair. They continued to press me on what I was wearing for the party, but I told them I wasn't sure.

"Nothing fancy," was all I would say. I really wasn't sure. I never was one to plan what to wear in advance. Sometimes I would decide only minutes before going somewhere.

I did go right home after school with the intention of figuring that out, but when I realized Kane was coming for me in less than two and a half hours, I decided I had to get into the diary for at least an hour and a half of that. I had nothing else I had to do but dress for the party. I scooped the book out from under my pillow and lay back on it to turn the page and begin.

One day dragged into another so seamlessly I lost track of time, but Cathy was always there to remind me how long we had been locked away. If there was one thing I hated, it was wasting time. Besides games we could play and invent, there were, fortunately, dozens and dozens of books to read. Momma, true to her word, brought us games and cards. I tried constantly to keep the twins occupied with whatever toys Momma could bring and things I found that might amuse them.

Our grandmother was there with our meals. Most of the time, she said nothing, but she soon began cross-examining us about the Bible. We were ordered to read it daily and memorize important quotes. She demanded that both Cathy and I repeat one, obviously to see if we were lying when we said we had read the Bible. Cathy surprised her with her quote from Genesis, one I had taken time explaining and illustrating why it was a good one to throw at our grandmother. Cathy did it with that smug smile I was beginning to love: "Wherefore have you rewarded evil for good?"

I looked quickly at Grandmother Olivia. Her eyes widened, and her face reddened a shade or two, but she sucked back her breath and spun on me. "Quote from Job," she ordered. I felt as self-satisfied as Cathy did, because the book of Job was my favorite story. I went on and on, until she shouted, "Enough!"

That turned out to be the first and last time she would question me. I could see how much it hurt her to admit to herself that I was intelligent enough to read and understand the Bible as well as, if not even better than, she could.

I hoped that maybe it would soften her treatment of Momma. Momma did look happier and more settled and comfortable when she arrived each evening, sometimes bringing us better things to eat, but never candy, which made the twins moan more. She rambled on about how she was slowly winning over her father. Then one day, she did bring us some melted ice cream and cake. I could see she was even happier. Her father had given her a car to use. She said this convinced her he would forgive her. Cathy wasn't impressed. We had been locked away for a little more than two weeks, but Momma made it clear that if he found out about us now, all would be lost. Reluctantly, Cathy retreated. I did my best to buoy her hopes, all our hopes.

We began a fully involved search of the large attic to pass time and amuse ourselves. Cory was fascinated by the piano but soon tired of its out-of-tune groans. I found five old Victrolas. One worked better than the others, but all we had were Enrico Caruso records, very scratched. Cory was intrigued with winding the Victrola and amused at the way the great singer sounded when it was made to go too fast or too slowly. I winked at Cathy. One of the twins was satisfied for a while. Carrie still hated the attic and went back downstairs to play with her dolls and other toys. She surprised us with her willingness to be alone, separate from Cory, but it also underscored how much she hated the attic.

Bored myself finally, I decided to amuse them all with my imitations of Grandmother Olivia barking her orders and rules. I even had the twins laughing like children again, but their attention spans were short. They wandered about, getting into trouble, cutting fingers, getting splinters. Cathy was good at mothering, and I made sure they didn't get infections. Sometimes they pouted and were defiant, holding their breath until their faces turned red. It made Cathy nervous, but I told her to ignore them.

"Just like Momma is ignoring us," she fired back, and did some pouting herself, flaring at me and asking, "How can she leave us all up here so long?"

I didn't feel like going through the explanation again and again, emphasizing how much this could mean for us. "Momma is doing all this to guarantee our future," was all I said.

Then weeks went by without Momma visiting us on Sundays. Inside, I was beginning to panic, but I did all I could to keep it to myself. Finally, she showed up wearing a beautiful and expensive-looking sailing outfit. I had been upstairs sifting through books I wanted to read and heard the shouting below. Cathy was tearing into her. When I descended, I saw how Momma was near tears. I had to help her. She looked desperate.

I raved about how beautiful she looked. "What a change since we came here," I emphasized, looking at Cathy. "You're succeeding. It's obvious."

"No!" Cathy screamed. "This has got to stop. I hate it up here. You have to tell your father about us."

Suddenly, Momma leaned forward, covering her face with her hands. I put my hand on her shoulder, but she shook her head, and when she looked up, I saw there was pure terror in her face. Cathy gathered the twins to her, and I sat beside them.

"What is it, Momma?" I asked.

She admitted she hadn't been completely honest with us. I thought she wasn't going to say why, but Cathy demanded it. "The letter I told you my mother wrote to me when I pleaded for help . . ."

"Yes?" Cathy asked. "Well, tell us. We can take it. After what we've been enduring, we can take anything."

"Cathy," I whispered.

She shook me off and glared at Momma.

"My father wrote a note at the bottom of her letter."

"So?"

"He said he was glad you father died."

"What?" I asked.

"He said evil and corrupt get their just rewards."

I was about to curse him out when Momma coldly added, "And that the only good thing about my marriage was that it hadn't created any devil issue."

"He means children," I told Cathy.

"I know that. I've been reading the Bible, haven't I?"

"He considered Daddy evil and corrupt solely because he married his half-niece?"

"What else could he consider? Your father was a wonderful, good man." Her face turned bitter with hot, angry rage. "Your grandfather could find something evil in an angel."

She ranted on about him, practically spitting every time she mentioned him. Then she softened and told us how her original plan was to bring us to him, hopeful that when he saw how brilliant I was and how talented and beautiful Cathy was, his horrible ideas about our being the devil's issue would disappear.

"But that was my dream, my fantasy. I don't know what I was thinking when I planned that."

"So you're not going to tell him about us?" Cathy asked. "Ever?"

She shook her head.

"Great, let's go," Cathy muttered.

"No, no. Don't worry," Momma said. "He's going to die soon." She pleaded with Cathy to be patient. The tears streamed down her face. "We're close," she kept saying. "So close."

I rose and embraced her. Looking at Cathy, I said, "Don't worry. You're not asking too much of us, not when we consider what we'll all gain."

Cathy looked away and shook her head, but Momma was pleased and stopped crying. The twins sat there, still stunned at the scene playing out before them. Momma hugged them and then tried to hug Cathy. She didn't hug back. She just stared at the floor, shaking her head. I walked Momma to the door.

"Don't worry," I whispered. "I'll keep them amused."

"You're so much like your father," Momma said. "So mature and so strong." She kissed me on the lips. I couldn't help but kiss her back, luxuriating in the soft sweetness of her lips. Then she left and locked the door behind her.

I turned and looked at Cathy.

She was staring at me in a way I had never seen her look at me. It was as if she had just discovered who I really was.

How strange Corrine was, I thought. What sort of way was that to kiss your own son? And a mother who wanted her own father dead and wanted her children practically to pray for it to happen? This was really bothering me now. Couldn't she find some other way to get them safe and secure? And once she realized what it was really going to be like for her children and her, why didn't she abandon her plan? How could she let them suffer so? I couldn't stop envisioning those poor gullible children, even Christopher, who was so blinded by his devotion to her, believing it wouldn't take much longer.

Even lower forms of animals had instinctive drives to protect their young. It was unnatural for a mother to endanger her own children. From what I had read so far, Corrine's parents were so fanatical and cruel it wouldn't exactly take a brain surgeon to be intelligent enough to see the writing on the wall. This was hopeless.

I sat there stewing over it so long that I was shocked when I looked up at the clock and saw it was nearly six, and I hadn't yet showered, brushed my hair, or even thought about what I would wear.

I jumped up as if springs had popped under me and then threw off my clothes as I charged into the bathroom. My friends had convinced me that because I was Kane's girlfriend, I was practically cohosting this party, and with all that was being done for it, it was going to be the blast of blasts. Despite my casual attitude about what I would wear, I knew I had to look special, act my part. This wasn't just some house party. Money and influence made families royalty in America, not birth and blood. The Hills were major contributors to the campaigns of the mayor, the congressman, both state senators, and the governor. If you bought a vehicle at one of the Hill dealerships and had a problem a politician could solve, Kane's father, Crosby Hill, would make a call for you.

There were no real castles in America handed down for centuries. There were, however, huge houses and estates that more than rivaled old castles because of their expensive construction materials, pools, tennis courts, landscaping, and technology. Kane's home was one of those nouveau castles to which people dreamed of being invited. For a few hours of one evening, I would be like the lady of Hill Hall.

My father hadn't done any work on the Hill house himself. He knew other builders who had, and he never drove us past it without making some comment about the house that was "practically built out of solid gold." He would go on and on about the high quality of the plumbing or the newest materials for roofing. Until now, I practically fell asleep listening, even though he spoke with passion. He was like an artist admiring the achievements of another. I smiled to myself about it, but I wasn't exactly fascinated with the house—at least, not until now.

I was afraid to ask him how the restored Foxworth Hall compared, but just from what I had seen of the property and the amount of rubble, I could see that Foxworth Hall had been much bigger and, of course, had much more acreage. Although Corrine's parents weren't popular people and were apparently more concerned with religion than their social status and political influence, I couldn't help believing they were quite important at one time or another. Perhaps Corrine dreamed of all this, saw herself as assuming a throne of some sort, once her parents were gone and she had inherited it all. Maybe she wasn't just selfish but coldly ambitious after all.

I really did try to put the diary out of my mind as I sped through my preparations. It wasn't easy. I couldn't help thinking that thirteen- and fifteen-year-olds did a great deal more socializing today than they did back when the Dollanganger children were incarcerated in that attic world, but kids back then still wanted to go to parties and had romantic thoughts. Although Christopher had not yet written about anyone romantically, he did mention the girl who liked to press her body against his. I felt sure he had looked at one girl or another and imagined some sort of romance. From what I imagined he looked like, I was confident that girls were interested in him.

Cathy was already dreaming of being as beautiful as her mother. What good would it do her to look pretty while she was shut up and away from any other girls and boys her age? Surely, Corrine, after having suffered so under her parents' iron rule, could appreciate what she was doing to her daughter especially.

I was desperately trying to drive these thoughts from my mind. They were spoiling my mood, ruining my excitement about the party and being with Kane. I practically ripped the black jeweled designer jeans that I had decided to wear off their hanger. I kept glancing at the diary, still open on my bed, mumbling my rage at Corrine, her parents, all of it. I was going to add some color with my blouse, but I was in a dark mood and decided to wear my three-quarter-sleeved cowl-neck blouse that clung tightly to my torso and hips. It had been a while since I had worn it, and it was a little snug, especially around my bosom. Normally, I didn't dress like this, but I didn't feel normal at the moment.

The only makeup I decided I had time to put on properly was my lipstick. I added a pair of my mother's amethyst dangle earrings, which had images of swans. Then, just before I reached for my black leather jacket, I decided to put on a string of pearls. I started out, stopped as if I heard a voice calling to me, and returned to close the diary and shove it under my pillow. I could smother the book, but the voices were stuck in my head.

Kane was already at my door ringing the buzzer as I started down the stairs.

"You're as prompt as a schoolteacher," I said, maybe too critically. I saw the way he winced. "Don't you know a girl has to be late?"

He smiled. "Don't you know how anxious a boy can be?"

"If I didn't, I know now," I said, closing the door behind me.

He looked from me to the house and then back at me. "Anything wrong?"

"No," I said, now beginning to feel bad. "I'm sorry. I didn't mean to sound so sharp."

"No problem. I have Band-Aids in the car," he joked, and reached for my hand. He stopped us half-way to his car and turned around to look at me. "Something has your blood up, but I have to say, it's pretty sexy."

Now I really did feel the blood rush to my face. Kane was the first boy who had ever said I was sexy. "Thanks. I think," I said, and we continued to his car.

After we got in and he started the engine, he turned to me with that winning soft half smile of his and asked, "Why did you say 'I think'? Don't you like being sexy?"

"I'm not sure what it means. Some of the girls are so obvious about it. Boys call them sexy, but I don't want to be that sort of girl."

"You're definitely not."

"What am I, then?"

"I told you. You're a surprise. At least, to me." He started to back out but then put his foot on the brake and turned back to me. "And maybe even to yourself."

"I heard from some other girls you've driven crazy that you like to speak in riddles."

He laughed and continued backing out, turning, and heading us away. "It's not a riddle. I'm having trouble explaining it, that's all. I feel like I'm at the grand opening, the revealing of a new model."

"Like a car? One of your father's new-model cars?"

"Use what you know, Mr. Stiegman says in English class."

"Check my tires," I quipped.

"I plan to. Later."

"All right. I'll bite. Why am I like a grand opening?"

"You're discovering who you are, and I'm with you at just the right moment," he said. "Is that okay?"

I was silent. He was right about me. Kane wasn't simply a good-looking, popular, rich, intelligent, and athletic boy. He was sensitive, too. And that was something I really had not expected. Could you really fall in love with someone when you were this young, and if you did, what would happen? You had so much further to go in your life, so many other people, boys, men you would meet. How was it possible to make any sort of real commitment to someone before you experienced any of that?

I did once read that you should fall in love many times, each time just a little more deeply. It was like drilling a well. Each affair brought you closer to understanding what it was going to be like when you were finally there. Was that all romantic gobbledygook?

As if he could read my thoughts, Kane glanced at me and said, "Relax. Let's just have a good time and not be so analytical."

"Said the spider to the fly."

He laughed hard for a moment and then shook his head when he looked at me again. "Kristin Masterwood, I think I'm going to fall in love with you, and you're going to break my heart. But I'm going to enjoy every moment," he added.

His words had the ring of honesty and for the first time, I wondered if I could trust him with what I was reading. My father would be very angry if I did, but something inside me was longing for another pair of eyes, another mind to help me understand and clearly see what really did happen in Foxworth Hall decades ago to four innocent children, two of whom were, like me, just discovering who they really were.

The moment I set eyes again on Kane's home, this time knowing I was going to go inside, another question about Christopher occurred to me. Was the impression the huge mansion made on him when they had first arrived, even at night and at a back entrance, at least part of the reason he was so trusting and hopeful?

To think that his mother's family, estranged as they had been, owned something so regal must have given him confidence in his mother's plans. Just as clothes, cars, and jewels could convince you of someone's importance, a mansion like Foxworth Hall had to have filled Christopher with a sense of real hope. Those people, his grandparents, could easily save them from disaster. It would be a drop in the bucket to them.

Seeing the Hill house from the road as Dad and I rode past it was one thing, but approaching it through the elaborate cast-iron gates and going up the winding driveway with its perfectly spaced maple trees lining the sides, even now nearly leafless but still impressive, overwhelmed me. It was easy to believe important things happened on this elaborate estate and that the people who owned it could easily change, influence, help, or hurt so many other people.

My eyes went everywhere, like the eyes of someone feasting on a world-famous place like the Taj Mahal in India or Buckingham Palace in London. Beneath the trees that lined the driveway was a bed of multicolored leaves not yet cleared away. Kane told me his mother liked the colors to linger as long as possible. His father wanted "the mess" cleared up, but he always waited for her to give him the word every year. The driveway lights were subtle and low, all solar-powered, which I knew was more expensive and something recently done. At the top, the driveway became circular and had an island of plants, trees, pottery, and stone at the center. And at the center of that was a statue of a lion with water flowing from its mouth.

"Where did you get that fountain?" I couldn't help asking immediately.

"My mother had it imported from Florence, Italy," he said.

No less impressive was the front entrance. Thanks to my father, I knew the giant pair of raised panel doors with raised molding on both sides was made of mahogany. There was leaded antique glass in the sidelights and transom. Four pillars on the redbrick front patio gave it the Tara look. Kane drove halfway around the circle and then off to the right to reach the very well-disguised six-car garage, one space reserved for his car. One was for his sister's car when she was home, and there was one for each of his mother's two cars and two for his father's current cars. Kane reminded me that his father had a Bentley dealership, too, and mainly drove the latest model.

When the door went up, I realized the six-car garage was probably wider from one side to the other than our entire house. We got out, and Kane opened the door to a small entryway and a hallway.

"The kitchen's on the left," he said. "This hallway leads to the downstairs hall and my father's home office, our dining room, living room, larger den, where we'll have our party, and smaller den. Off to the right is where Lourdes Rosario lives. She's been with us since I was two, I think. As I said, she's off tonight and tomorrow and visiting her cousin in Richmond."

"One woman cleans this whole house?" I asked, impressed with the crown moldings on the hallway walls and the care taken with the round corners, which were part of the finishing when it was constructed. Probably no other girl would be, but I was, after all, my father's daughter. The floors were a beige Spanish tile. Along the way were niches for art, small statues, and figurines that I recognized to be expensive Lladro and Herend porcelain.

"No, she brings in her three nieces twice a week," Kane said. "Dad has a groundskeeper who has a small crew. They're here five days a week, but everyone's off this weekend. I made sure we had plenty of paper plates and cups and plastic spoons, forks, and knives. There'll be little to clean up afterward."

"You hope," I said.

He led me into the kitchen.

"I don't remember anyone talking about you ever having a party here."

"I had a few small things but nothing like this," he said. "When I was little, they had birthday parties here, for my sister and me. Mostly relatives. We've got a lot of relatives," he added. "As Dad became more and more successful, more came out of the woodwork, as he says. How about you?"

"Just an uncle and an aunt. My uncle's coming to visit us on Monday. He's my father's younger brother."

"No leftover Foxworths?" he asked. He turned when I didn't respond. "I mean, none of them ever tried to contact your family?"

"No."

He shrugged. "Probably a good thing," he said. "If you consider the crazy story about the kids up in the attic coming out distorted or something."

The words were on the tip of my tongue. I wanted

to say that whatever the children eventually did in that attic and afterward wasn't solely their fault. I had the urge to defend them and tell him that I wouldn't mind them contacting me, but I kept silent. He'd surely want to know why I had that opinion, and it might lead me accidentally to mentioning the diary.

We began to take out the plates, cups, napkins, and plastic dinnerware to set up the counters where everyone would go to get food and drink later.

"How many have you invited?" I asked.

"About thirty, I think."

"You think?"

"I don't remember. We'll find out when the party starts."

When we were finished, he led me down the hallway to what he had called the larger den. It was more like a grand ballroom in an upscale hotel. He said his parents used it for their parties, some of which were fund-raisers for political candidates.

"Thirty people will get lost in here," I said. "Are those tables and chairs around the room always here?"

"No. Before he and his crew left for the day, I had Curtis put them out the way he does for parties. Curtis is the house manager and grounds manager. We'll get it all put away again before my parents return."

"There's a house manager?"

He just smiled.

"So from what you're saying, your parents really don't know about the party?"

"Oh, they know. It's their way of testing me, I'm sure," he said.

"Why did you decide to have the party? It can't be only because you're alone in this . . . palace," I said.

"Why, to impress *you*. Why else?" he said, smiling.

I looked at him skeptically, but he didn't break his smile. "You didn't need to throw a party to impress me, Kane."

"I know, but I like to hedge my bets," he joked, or maybe didn't. "Let me show you a little more of the house."

He took my hand and led me through the hallway to look at the formal living room, the dining room, and a smaller den with a pool table and walls lined with shelves and shelves of books.

"It rivals the school library," I said.

"Believe it or not, my father can tell when one is missing. Many of these books are first editions. My mother is into art; Dad is into antiques. There's too much to show you in one day, and besides, I don't want to share your attention with too much more. C'mon. We still have a good hour before our guests arrive."

"*Our* guests?"

"They're your guests now, too," he insisted.

He led me to the winding stairway, with its polished mahogany balustrade and dark brown carpeted steps. All the bedrooms were upstairs. His was off to the right, and his sister's was just down from his.

"This is embarrassing," he said the moment we stepped into his bedroom. "My mother designed it for a prince."

"No kidding," I said. "Though a prince might not have as nice a bedroom."

If I were to measure it against anything we had, I'd say his bedroom was as large as our living room and dining room combined. On the left was an entirely separate area for his computer desk, shelves, and some electronics, including speakers for his own music. The floors were done in a dark blue tile with area rugs. All of the lights were recessed. On the right was the doorway to his en suite bathroom. Through the open door, I could see a shower probably three times the size of mine with multiple shower heads. I imagined that the door down from the bathroom doorway was his closet.

His king-size dark maple bed had a headboard embossed with trees and birds, some in flight, some settled on branches.

"Quite a headboard."

"My mother had that custom-made. It's an illustration from a children's book I loved when I was about four. She said I always told her I wanted to sleep in the forest depicted in the book. Now I do. Over the top, wouldn't you say?"

"Everything about this house is over the top, Kane, but your father worked for it. I'm sure he's proud of what he's accomplished."

"You have a lot of compassion in you, Kristin, even for the rich."

"Why do the rich need our compassion?"

"I remember what you said when we were at the Foxworth lake."

"What did I say?"

"You asked if I thought money made people happy

when I said they should have been happy there because of how much they had."

"That was different. They didn't use their wealth
to help each other."

He cocked his head to one side and looked at me,
half joking, half serious. "Why do I get the feeling you
know a lot more about them then you let on?"

I didn't answer.

"I want to show you something," he said, and led
me deeper into his room. There were two large windows, one on each side of his bed. He took me to the
right window and opened the curtain wider. "We're
looking west," he said.

I gazed at the acres of trees, spotted here and there
with homes and a highway that snaked along and disappeared over a small rise. It had grown much darker,
so windows were lit in the homes and car headlights
looked like the eyes of robotic creatures slithering
through the darkness. "So? What am I looking at?"

"I don't remember it, of course, but we could see
Foxworth Hall from here before the last fire. The trees
weren't as grown up. There were many fewer houses
between it and here, and the mansion loomed above
everything. I was just five and a half when the place
burned down, so I don't have any memory of the
fire, but my sister does. She told me she came into my
room back then to watch it all from this window."

"Darlena would have been about eleven."

"I know. I understand it was practically an inferno.
They thought that the woods might catch fire back
then and maybe even spread over so many acres that

it would threaten other homes. She said the sky was lit up so brightly the stars disappeared."

"That would be impressive," I said.

"Probably as impressive as the first fire, maybe more because of the added trees and stuff."

I knew it was a strange feeling to have, but suddenly, Kane was more important to me because of what he was saying, what his sister remembered, and what could once be seen from his bedroom window.

"Next time she's home, I'll ask her to tell you what she remembers," he said. "She's got one of those photographic memories. She can recall the details of every doll she ever had and especially movie scenes, even the ones she saw at an early age. She's already been accepted into the NYU graduate school film-study program, you know."

"Oh. How exciting. I would enjoy talking to her, I'm sure."

"Didn't your father ever tell you about the last fire?"

"Not really. He just says it was big. Of course, we don't have this view."

"Right."

"However, I know that for our community, Foxworth Hall's second demise, with all its mystique, was something historic. It was like having witnessed a famous earthquake or a volcano erupt *again*, I guess."

"Exactly."

"What were you told about the first fire?" I asked him. "I mean, it must have come up from time to time. I'm sure your father knows a lot about it."

"Nothing firsthand. That was more than forty years ago. He talks more about the second fire. He said it seemed to burn forever. My mother said it was like the burning of Atlanta in *Gone with the Wind*. She's prone to exaggeration, but the fire department could do little to save it, just like the first time. No one died in that fire because the house had been abandoned, and as you know, the bank got stuck with the property. Once in a while, I look out here and try to imagine what the fires were like. I do remember overhearing my parents and some friends talking about the first fire one night and someone saying, 'Imagine if it had happened years before, when those poor children were locked in that attic.' It gave me nightmares when I was younger."

"It seems it gave lots of people nightmares and still does, even after all these years," I muttered.

"Right. But I used to worry about being up here. I couldn't exactly just jump out this window. Kinda high up. My father assured me we had the most sophisticated fire protection and warnings any home could have. You know . . ."

"Sprinkler system and smoke detectors," I said. I looked up at his ceiling and pointed to two nozzles.

"Exactly."

"How come you didn't mention all this when we went up to the Foxworth property, especially what it was like seeing the mansion burn a second time?"

"I didn't want you to think I had a weird interest in it like so many in this town do. I wasn't sure how you felt about it. I know you're sensitive about being asked questions and talking about being related, even though you're a distant relative."

"A very distant relative," I said.

"Are you upset about me telling you all this?"

"No," I said. "Actually, I appreciate it."

"Good. I didn't want to do anything to spoil the evening, but . . ."

"You didn't. Stop worrying about it."

He nodded and then widened his eyes. "Oh heck, I forgot to keep the gate open. We'll have them buzzing us like crazy."

He went to his phone and punched in a code. "Now we can relax," he said. "Come on. Let's organize the music for the night. We have a full media room that coordinates what is heard and seen throughout the house. The house has internal video security."

We started out. I paused in the doorway and looked back at the window from which his sister had witnessed the second fire at Foxworth. He paused, too. "How old is this place?" I asked.

"It wasn't here when the children were supposedly up there, if that's what you want to know," he replied. "If you believe the stories, they were there about 1957, '58. That's more than fifty years ago. That's probably why so much of it is confusing and distorted. Anyone around who was our age then is in his or her seventies now. Anyway, this house is only twenty years old, and it's been remodeled, expanded in some way, almost every year after it was first built. My father built it. There was no other house on the property. No one _lived_ here and witnessed the first fire from here, so there was no other property owner who told my father firsthand stuff. He and my mother know only the junk everyone else seems to know. And neither of them thinks about you inheriting Foxworth madness just because your mother was a distant cousin or something. Our children won't be weird," he added.

"Our children? Aren't you getting a little ahead of yourself? There's a proposal and a honeymoon in my story," I said.

He laughed, took my hand, and walked me back to the stairway. "My mother imagines she's Scarlett O'Hara going down those stairs some days. I've caught her fantasizing, and she was embarrassed and confessed that was exactly what she was doing as she descended the stairway. She's infatuated with that novel and movie. That's why our house was built to look a little like Tara. Everyone wants to step out of their life and be someone else, at least for a day. My mother would like to be someone else forever."

"Why? She has so much now."

"She never has enough," he said dryly.

"What about you? Do you want to be someone else, too?'

"Not lately, not now," he said. "I'm happy just being in my own shoes." He leaned in to kiss me.

We descended holding hands, and I couldn't help it, I felt like a princess walking with her prince. It wasn't hard to be like his mother and fantasize that I was someone very special to help people enjoy a very special party.

Most of those invited to Kane's party did treat it

like a very special invitation. Many of his close buddies in school, boys on teams with him, and some of
the girls in the senior class had been here for much
smaller events, as he had said, but always with his
parents at home, too. This was his first time without
even the housekeeper. However, Kane was very good
at protecting his home, declaring what was out of
bounds. He wanted everyone to be confined to what
I was freely calling the ballroom. The girls who were
my friends wanted to assist in bringing out the food
and drinks. Kane was firm about no alcohol or drugs,
and not only because his father had laid down the law.
Recently, Don Hudson, a senior, had a house party
that his parents were unaware of, and one of the boys,
Ryan Bynes, drank too much and got into an automobile accident five minutes after he left. An elderly
woman was seriously injured, and the police were at
Don's house less than a half hour later. His parents
needed a lawyer.

Once the novelty of being at the biggest estate in
the city wore off, many of the kids became bored and
were wandering about aimlessly. Tina Kennedy kept
annoying me with "So when's the real party going to
start?"

I heard some complaining that without booze
freely pouring or someone passing around "something," it was "like a chaperoned school party."
Neither the music nor the food was holding their
attention. An hour into it, some broke off to find
excitement somewhere else. Before eleven, the crowd
was dwindling. Those who were already paired off left

to be by themselves. I heard Steve Cooper suggest a group of them go up to Foxworth for kicks. I stepped in quickly.

"My father has been working on demolishing and removing what's left of the debris up there. It's fenced off now. There's lots of dangerous material lying around."

They all looked at me strangely.

"Whatever," Steve said.

"She oughtta know that it's dangerous up there," Tina said. Lana had already told me she was quite jealous of my being with Kane.

"What's that supposed to mean?" Kane asked, coming out of nowhere and practically pouncing on her. She backed off quickly.

"Nothing. Jeez," she said. "Let's go somewhere fun while the night's still young."

She and those with her were the only ones who left without thanking Kane.

"Hell hath no fury like a woman scorned," Kane muttered after them. "Don't even ask," he told me immediately. "I never even had interest in getting to first base with her."

Lana and Suzette remained behind to help with the cleanup. After they left and we were alone, Kane said Curtis would clear the room tomorrow before his parents returned.

"I guess we did all right," he added. "Nothing broken."

I saw that he was a little down. "It was a great party, Kane."

"Right. I don't know what some of my so-called friends expected. Dancing girls? I wasn't going to open my father's bar. I made that clear to everyone for days. You didn't see it, but asshole Barsto brought something he was passing around. I invited him to leave."

"Oh. I missed that."

"Probably the earliest end to a party this year."

"Not for us," I said, and he looked at me oddly for a moment and then smiled.

"What's your curfew?"

"My father never set one. He depends on me to be responsible. I know he'll be waiting up no matter what, so I don't want to push it, but another hour won't do any harm."

"In that case . . ."

He began shutting down lights and took my hand to lead me into the den, where there was the pool table, books, and another of what must be at least a dozen televisions. There was a very comfortable, soft leather settee. He poured us both some ginger ale, which was what we had been drinking all night, and sat beside me.

"I shouldn't have bothered with the party," he said. "All I wanted here was you."

"Not everyone was a dumbass, Kane. Most had a good time."

"I spent too much of my time being a host. I don't think we danced three times."

"You're right, it was two."

He sipped his soda and looked at me. "I think I figured out what's different about you, Kristin."

"And that is?"

"You're more mature. Not in a stuffy sort of way. You're more stable, secure. You're not arrogant about it, but you're a few hundred miles above your girl-friends, above just about every other girl in school, as a matter of fact. That used to intimidate me, but now I find it fascinating. I feel more mature being with you." He put down his drink. "Duh! I sound stupid, I know."

The first thing that came to my mind was that those were words I could imagine some girl saying to Christopher.

"Things happen that force you to be older than you'd like, Kane."

"Yes, I know. I know the reason. I'm sorry for that, but I'm not sorry that you are who you are. I think I can trust you, depend on you, be confident being with you, and I can't say that about any other girl in our school."

He took my glass from me and put it down, then kissed me with such passion that I could feel the tingle travel down my spine and wake the sexual energy in me, nudge it, opening me like a flower longing to blossom, a flower feasting on the sunshine.

His hands moved over my body gently. I lay back and then slowly began to slip under him. He was kissing my cheeks, my neck, before going back time after time to my lips, as if that kiss gave him the fuel, the energy, the permission to return to my neck and then my shoulders, as his hands smoothly lifted my blouse and his lips traced along my stomach and up and over my breasts.

"Kristin," he whispered. "I can't stop dreaming about you."

He fingered the clasp on my bra and lifted it slowly away from my breasts, touching my nipples with the tip of his tongue. I could feel myself sliding deeper and deeper down into the place where your resistance weakens. Was this it? Was this going to be my first time? His finger went to the buttons on my jeans. I didn't stop him, but I couldn't help the small sob, the tension that came into my body, and the way I simply froze.

He paused. "How far do you want to go?" he asked softly. I had the feeling that it was a question he didn't bother asking other girls he had been with. "I'm prepared," he added.

"Not that far. Not yet," I said.

He nodded, kissed me quickly on the lips, and then sat back and looked thoughtful.

"What?" I asked.

"What makes some girls so easy about that decision?"

"It's never a problem for boys?"

"It is if they don't think ahead and get both of them in trouble."

"Girls don't always get into trouble doing it, Kane."

"I know that, too, but the risk is much bigger, don't you think?"

"So you've answered your own question."

"Not really. That's why some girls might not want to do it if their boyfriends are unprepared, but that's all it answers."

"Maybe you should attend the girls' session of health class," I said.

"I'm not sure Mrs. Kirkwood would let me in."

"There are many answers, I guess. How you're brought up is one. Some girls think of it as some accomplishment, a step into maturity or something."

"You don't?"

"I think of it as more of a commitment. No, I don't want you to give me an engagement ring, but I don't want to just hook up or something. I know some girls who think being as casual about it as boys makes them equal or something."

He nodded. "I thought you'd have an intelligent answer. No," he said, holding his hands up and standing, "don't ask me to try again or ask you to stay over." We looked at each other, and then we both laughed at the obvious reverse psychology attempt. At least he wasn't as crude and immature as most of the boys I knew at school.

"I guess I'd better get going," I said. I straightened myself out, checked myself in the closest powder room, and joined him in the kitchen.

"Can I take you somewhere tomorrow night? To dinner, a movie?"

"I'll check my schedule."

He looked stunned.

"Just kidding, Kane. Yes, I'd like that."

He nodded. "I was right about you. You're different." He took my hand and led me out to the garage. He opened the car door for me and got in. We backed out and started down the long driveway.

Maybe I *was* different, I thought. Maybe that was why I was so fascinated with Christopher's diary. I thought too much. I analyzed everything and was always afraid my fantasizing would make me too vulnerable. I was not willing to forgive people, especially boys, their little faults, their small dishonesties. Was that good, or would I end up alone in some room as despondent as Christopher in the attic?

Dad was happy I didn't stay out too late. Despite how subtle he wanted to be about it, he stayed up waiting for me, most likely watching the clock and pretending to be so interested in what he was watching on television that he couldn't go to bed.

"Have a good time?" he asked as soon as I stepped into the living room. I was sure if I asked him what he was watching and what had just happened, he wouldn't know.

"Yes, very."

"Quite a house, eh?"

"That and then some," I said, which was another of his responses to questions like that.

He laughed. "Everyone behave?"

"Wouldn't be a party if everyone did, but actually, yes. Kane saw to that," I said.

"Good."

"Unfortunately, some thought not being raucous was boring," I added, "and they left early."

"Oh. But not you?"

"I had more reason to stay," I said, and he laughed.

"Oh? Care to elaborate a bit?"

"No," I said, and he laughed again. "I'm going up," I told him.

"Just want to see the end of this," he said, nodding at the television.

I gave him a kiss and left him pretending to know what he was watching.

I had told myself I would avoid reading the diary before I went to sleep tonight. I should have been too tired. I was tired, but I was also restless. Kane's telling me about his sister witnessing the second fire and some of the comments his parents had made about it and the first fire had stirred up so many different feelings that I felt my nerves were like sparklers.

I slipped my hand under my pillow and brought out the diary. Before I turned the page, I listened to my father's footsteps. He lumbered along to his bedroom, and the lights in the hallway dimmed.

Now it was just the Dollanganger children and me again.

It was clear now that we'd be locked up here until our grandfather died. Cathy was more despondent than ever. I had my work cut out for me: how to keep her spirits and the twins' spirits up, how to keep them all occupied. Cathy wasn't stupid. She would spot insincerity very quickly. But I had another ability that came in very handy now. I could will myself to believe in something. I wasn't like other people who fool themselves or lie to themselves. I knew how to dress up something I doubted so that I looked convinced about it, but I had something people who lie to themselves don't have. I knew what I was doing. I knew the truth, and I could retreat to it whenever I wanted to or had to. Maybe that sounds arrogant, but to me, it's just a statement of fact.

"He could live forever," Cathy moaned almost immediately. "We're doomed, Christopher. No one else knows we're up here. All of my friends are probably calling each other for news, and maybe some of them are asking their parents to call the police! I hope they do. I hope there's a nationwide search for us, and our pictures are put on post office walls. People locked up like this go mad and even shrink. I read it in a magazine."

"Stop the dramatics," I told her in our father's most assertive voice. Her eyes widened. "It's not going to be anywhere near that bad. Our grandfather is suffering from heart disease. That means his arteries are blocked with something called plaque. If—not if, I should say when—a piece of that breaks free, he'll have a heart attack and die on the spot. We're so far away from the city that by the time the ambulance arrives, he'll be long gone."

"He has a nurse around the clock. He's rich. Maybe he has an ambulance parked out front all the time."

"Nurses aren't doctors, and they can't possibly

have all the life-saving machinery hospitals have, Cathy, no matter how rich he is. The man is in critical condition. It's classic intensive care. He should be in a hospital. He obviously wants to die at home. He knows himself that he hasn't got long to go."

She looked at me askance.

"Think about it," I added even more strongly. "If Grandmother Olivia didn't believe it herself, she wouldn't have permitted us to come here in the first place. You see the way she treats Momma. She doesn't have much faith in Momma's ability to win back her father's love. His death is the only thing that makes sense. It's impending."

She squinted.

"Impending, imminent, can happen any time."

"In the meanwhile?"

"In the meanwhile . . ." I looked around. "Let's do some fun things. Why don't we stage a play? You love dramatics. You write it, and I'll act in it, and the twins will be our audience. We certainly have enough material for costumes." I held my breath. Would she buy into it?

"You always made fun of my interest in acting."

"I was teasing you. Brothers tease their sisters all the time. That's what it means to be a brother, but if anyone could succeed as an actress, it's you. You have a flair for it."

"Are you just saying that to shut me up?"

"No. I believe it. I'm always telling you to stop being dramatic. I just did."

She thought a moment. "All right. I want to do 'Gone with the Wind,'" she said without any hesitation.

"'Gone with the Wind'? The whole thing?"

It didn't surprise me. She had sat watching that with Momma more than once, and afterward, both she and Momma pretended they lived in the South and were Southern belles. Momma loved playing Scarlett O'Hara, and Cathy loved imitating her. Momma gave her a book about "Gone with the Wind," and she would often sit and thumb through it, sometimes reciting lines she had memorized. At the time, I thought it was all foolish, but I kept my opinion to myself. I was very glad now that I had.

"No, just some scenes, but you have to do exactly as I say. Of course, I'll be Scarlett O'Hara, and you'll have to play Rhett Butler."

"You're the writer and the director," I told her, looking as serious about it as I could, and she suddenly looked even less irritated. Her eyes widened with her thoughts. She took off immediately to sift through the old clothes and hats.

The twins didn't understand what we were doing at first, but just seeing Cathy so animated and interested captured their attention, and for a while, they weren't moaning and groaning. Even Carrie, who hated going up to the attic, followed Cathy around, trying to do something to help whatever it was she was planning.

Seeing how my idea had captured their

interest, I went ahead and built a mock stage,
creating curtains with ropes and blankets. Cathy
surprised me with her inventiveness. She used
some of the dress mannequins as characters,
finding costumes for them, giving them names, and
having Cory and Carrie help her set up her scene.
They thought it was fun to talk to the mannequins
and call them by the names Cathy had remembered
from the movie. Then she sat and scribbled lines
on a pad.

I had obviously unleashed some of her stifled
fantasies. Although I thought it was all quite
childish to continue, I had to get into it with
the same sort of energy, or they would all lose
interest. She found my Rhett Butler costume,
which I had to admit was creative: cream-colored
trousers (I had to roll up the legs), a brown
velvet jacket with pearl buttons, and a satin vest
with red roses all over it. The moment I put it all
on, I turned to her and, in my best Rhett Butler
imitation, pleaded, "Come quickly, Scarlett.
We've got to escape from Atlanta before Sherman
reaches here and sets the city ablaze!"

The twins' eyes were suddenly full of greater
excitement. This was make-believe like they had
never seen it, especially with me participating.

"There's going to be a fire?" Cory cried.

"It's only make-believe," Cathy reminded him,
but that didn't change their expressions of awe.

Cathy had found her costume, too. She wore
a cage under a skirt at least three sizes too large,

pantaloons with lace, large shoes, and a ruffled silk blouse. She found a great Scarlett O'Hara hat, too, and we were soon at it.

She threw herself into the scene she had created. It wasn't long, but I thought the way she used the mannequins was quite clever. Naturally, the twins didn't have the attention span for a long, overly dramatic scene that included Cathy's desperate pleas for love in front of a mannequin dressed to be Ashley Wilkes. Carrie was soon crying for lunch. She hated being in the attic, even for a show.

"These clothes stink, anyway," Cathy declared, the air going out of her balloon of excitement quickly.

She looked at me with disappointment, but I promised her we'd return. We stripped off the costumes and went to eat our lunch. All through it, Cory complained about not being in the garden outside. The dreariness of our surroundings was wearing on us all. It suddenly occurred to me that another way to divert their attention from our dire situation was for us to dress up the attic.

"Let's turn this ugly caterpillar into a butterfly," I declared. The twins looked astonished again. "We'll decorate it. We'll create our own garden the way God creates a real one."

They looked to Cathy.

"It's too filthy," she said.

"We'll clean it up. We can do it," I insisted.

That night when Momma finally appeared,

I told her about my plan. She was looking despondent when she came in, but suddenly, she looked at the four of us and considered the idea.

"Why not?" she declared. "I'll help. We'll do it. We'll show my mother how creative and clean we can be. She's always saying cleanliness is next to Godliness. Well, we'll show her we know exactly what that means."

Cathy looked as skeptical as ever, but Momma delighted us all by bringing up mops, pails, brooms, scrub brushes, and boxes and boxes of soap powder. She said her mother knew nothing about it. She had sneaked it all to us. That seemed to be the one thing that pleased Cathy about the idea the most. Deceiving our grandmother or doing something behind her back made it more precious and fun. That seemed to be even more true for Momma. And I have to admit, it was what made it fun for me, too.

However, to be honest, I was very surprised at Momma's enthusiasm. Suddenly, she was with us daily, scrubbing floors and washing everything in sight. She even brought insect repellent, and we cleared out gobs of dead spiders and ants. I had Cory believing that he and I were great hunters. Both twins now saw it all as a new game and argued about who was doing more and better. For a good week, we were suddenly a family again, people with a common cause and helping and loving one another constantly.

"You see," I told Cathy one night that week,

"Momma hasn't lost her love and concern for us. We've got to continue to help her fulfill her plan."

With reluctance, she nodded and agreed. The only discordant note came when Momma brought real flowers to the cleaned attic, including spiky amaryllis that she said would bloom by Christmas.

"Christmas! You're saying we'll still be here for sure?" Cathy cried.

Momma looked at me.

"She's not saying that," I said, even though it was obvious to me that she was.

"What are you saying?" Cathy demanded.

"When we leave, we'll take the plants with us for our Christmas celebration somewhere else. That's all," she replied.

Cathy was silent, but I could see it in her eyes. She didn't believe a word. Maybe she could pretend and do dramatic things like become Scarlett O'Hara for a while, but Cathy was hard on fantasies when she had some skepticism.

None of this was going to easy for me. I'd have to work even harder to get her and the twins to give Momma the chance and the time she needed. I needed Momma to help me with this as much as possible.

"Can you come back to see the twins before bedtime tonight?" I asked her.

"Oh, I've already made arrangements to go to a movie with an old girlfriend of mine. I want my father to believe I'm back to my life the way it was."

"What friend?" Cathy demanded.

"Her name is Elena. She has two unmarried brothers, one studying to be a lawyer. The other is a tennis pro," she said with surprising excitement.

"You're going on a date with one of them?" she asked.

I looked at Momma quickly. Was she?

She laughed, but I didn't feel confident about it. It was a forced laugh. She was going to lie to us again. It felt like another needle in my chest. Whenever I knew she was lying to us, I felt that way, but I had to do my best to hide it, or Cathy would go bonkers.

"Of course not," Momma said. "I'd rather go to sleep. I'm so tired from the work we've done. But it's better not to have people, especially someone like Elena, ask questions. She was always a busybody."

"Then why go out with her?" Cathy asked.

"I told you. We all have to make some sacrifices," she said. She gave us quick kisses and left.

"Sacrifices?" Cathy said the moment she left. "She calls going out to a movie with friends a sacrifice?"

"I suppose in a way, it is, if you don't like the friend that much and you're doing it just to keep your mother and father from becoming suspicious."

"If he's so sick, how does he even know or care?"

"People as rotten to the bone as he obviously is come alive for a few moments when they think something's not right. Why chance it?"

Cathy narrowed her eyes and shook her head at me before retreating to read a story to Cory and Carrie. The atmosphere around us was suddenly heavy, foreboding. Darkness seemed very attracted to this place, I thought.

And for the first time, really, I felt a darkness in my heart.

Cathy wasn't wrong to be suspicious. I knew Momma wasn't telling us the truth again, only this time, I didn't think it was for our benefit.

But I wouldn't show an iota of this fear to Cathy.

How ironic, I thought. Kane's mother was infatuated with *Gone with the Wind*, and Cathy had been, too. Was it because we were all in the South, or was it a universal fantasy, especially for a woman, to be on such a big stage with all its opulence and glamour? What was it Kane had said, everyone liked to play a part?

What part did I want to play?

I closed the diary and put it under my pillow. After I turned out my bedside lamp, I lay there staring up into the darkness. Was Christopher upset because his mother was lying and he knew it, or was it that he couldn't stomach the idea of her even hinting at another romance with another man so soon? To me, it sounded like the latter. I wasn't about to blame him for it.

I recalled how I had felt when we were reading *Hamlet* and the Player Queen said, "A second time I kill my husband dead when second husband kisses me in bed."

Did all men and women who had lost their spouses feel this great guilt if they remarried or even just seriously dated someone else? My father couldn't get himself to go out on a real date even after all these years, not even with Mrs. Osterhouse, at least as far as I knew. From the way Corrine had talked about Christopher Sr. when they had first met and secretly courted, it sounded like the greatest love of all time, a Romeo and Juliet story, because their love was so intense for each other that they'd risk and even willingly lose all family contacts. In Corrine's case, she was also willing to give up a great fortune. Now that she had lost her love, she wanted that fortune back. Was that something understandable or just plain hypocrisy? Where was the young woman who had been so in love and willing to live a much simpler, poorer life, or was the truth really that she never did live a simpler life, that she always lived beyond their means?

I turned over and forced myself to stop thinking about the Dollangangers by concentrating on Kane instead and dreaming of when I might just "cross the Rio Grande," which was the phrase Serena Mota used for losing your virginity.

I fell asleep quickly and woke to a surprise. My father had brought me breakfast in bed.

"What's this?" I asked.

"Every once in a while, you have to treat the women in your life like queens," he replied.

I sat up quickly. I couldn't recall another time when he had referred to me as a woman in his life. What had changed? My seriously dating someone? Was this that moment all fathers experience, that awareness that their little girls were starting to shift to edge their fathers further away, gently but firmly? Should I be sad or happy about it?

I couldn't help being happy about it, but I also couldn't help seeing things from his point of view. As long as he had me as his little girl, the gaping hole in his life didn't expand. There would soon be a time when he was really alone. At minimum, that would come when I went off to college, and then, if and when I did meet someone with whom I wanted to spend my life, he would drift even further back.

Into what?

Perhaps I shouldn't be so hard on Corrine, I thought. From what I understood between the lines of what Christopher had written about her, she was really not a very strong person. She craved pampering, comfort, and luxury. Yes, her husband had spoiled her, but maybe he felt guilty about sweeping her off her feet and stealing her away from her legacy. Maybe he felt a great responsibility to succeed in a big way and compensate for all she had lost, and in doing that, he had lost his own sense of balance, put them into vast debt, and left them vulnerable and helpless. Christopher Jr. seemed willing to give her the benefit of the doubt, to continue to think of her as someone who mainly wanted only to please and protect her children.

Cathy was more reluctant to do that, but thinking back to how she had reacted to Corrine's pregnancy, I was of the opinion that she was the most spoiled of all. I could be unfair. She was still a young girl but beginning that amazing metamorphosis into full femininity. A young girl couldn't open herself fully to an older brother, surely. I couldn't imagine myself doing that. I couldn't even discuss my womanly things with my father. She had no mother there most of the time, and when her mother was there, her attention was so divided, the twins needed so much, and Cathy had no place to go for her answers.

I didn't know for whom I should feel sorrier. I would never reveal it to my father. He would physically tear the diary out of my hands, but I was twisted up inside, my feelings crisscrossing, knotting up, and stealing away my attention from my own world, my own happiness.

"It looks terrific," I said, gazing down at the tray. He had made me his pancakes, served them with the delicious maple syrup we bought from the Wilsons, who tapped the trees on their two hundred acres and prepared the syrup to sell from their own garage on Sundays, and the blueberry and blackberry jam Mrs. Wheeler made.

"But you'll be eating breakfast alone," I told him.

He laughed and nodded at the clock. "I've been up nearly two hours, Kristin. It's Saturday, but I'm putting in a full day at the . . . job," he said. He was starting to avoid calling it the Foxworth estate. He wanted it buried and gone.

"Sorry. I didn't realize the time and . . ."

"Hey, you're entitled to sleep in once in a while."

"What about you?"

"Your mother tried to get me to do that, but I was always up ahead of her. I'll be up early the day I die." He started out.

"Oh. Kane was thinking of taking me to dinner tonight," I said.

He paused, looked at me hard for a moment, and then smiled. "Okay." I could see his mind spinning. He was debating whether to voice his next thought. He decided he would. "Don't go too fast. I know your mother would say that."

"And then she'd tell me she got a speeding ticket riding your smile," I replied.

His lips quivered, but his eyes brightened. "Wear your safety belt at all times," he concluded, and left.

That was the closest he would ever come to warning me not to "cross the Rio Grande" too soon. I couldn't imagine a harder thing for a father to tell his daughter. His face was probably still red with embarrassment when he got into his truck.

I laughed to myself and dug into my delicious breakfast.

Usually, I scheduled myself to do my homework calmly on weekends, taking long breaks and not finishing up until Sunday evening, but the diary was in charge of my life at the moment. I didn't want to rush anything, especially the math and my English essay,

but I couldn't help thinking that if I had my other responsibilities out of the way, I could read more of the
diary and get to the answers faster perhaps. Not that I
wanted to rush through it. It was both infuriating and
fascinating. Finishing it would be more like regretting
the last lick of a delicious ice cream cone.

I did the best I could on my math. Around ten
thirty, my girlfriends began to call. I was impatient
with them all, especially Suzette, who insisted on
knowing not only how long I had remained at
Kane's house after they had all left but how far I had
gone.

"Did he take you up to his bedroom? Don't say
he didn't," she followed. "Theresa Flowman said he
did the first time she was at his house and his parents
weren't home."

"Good for her." In my heart of hearts, I knew
Theresa was a liar. She, more than any of the girls,
fantasized aloud and tried hard to make what she said
sound like fact.

"So?"

"He showed me the house when I first arrived, and
his bedroom was part of the tour."

"The tour? That's it?"

"I've got to go. I promised to give the house a
complete once-over today, and I have homework and
a date with Kane."

"Where?"

"Dinner, probably. I'll call you tomorrow," I
added. "'Bye," I said, and hung up before she could
take another breath.

Lana called ten minutes later. I got rid of her quickly, but then Tina Kennedy called and really got me angry when she said Steve Cooper had told her I had slept over at Kane's house and did it like a pro. She claimed Kane had called Steve to brag.

"That's a stupid lie. You had better not spread it," I warned.

She laughed. "Everyone said you'd deny it. That's okay. Your secret's safe with me, as safe as those cousins of yours in the attic," she added, and I slammed my phone shut so hard that I thought I had broken it. It took me almost an hour to calm down. I was in no shape to return to my math.

Kane called an hour later and heard the tension in my voice. "Did your father think I kept you out too late?" he asked.

"No."

"What's wrong? You're forcing me to put antiseptic salve on my ear."

"Antiseptic?"

"I thought I'd impress you with my expanding vocabulary."

I laughed and told him about Tina's phone call.

"I haven't even spoken to Steve Cooper today," he said. "And the last thing I would tell him is something that was personal to us. I might as well post it on Facebook."

"I thought so," I said. Of course, I meant I hoped so.

"I think survival of the fittest applies more to women than to men."

He had me smiling. "We'll see," I said.

"I'd like to take you someplace special tonight."

"Where?"

"The River House. My parents practically own a table there."

I knew it was one of the most expensive restaurants in the city. "That *is* special. I don't know if I have the right clothes for it."

"Whatever you wear will be right," he said. "I'll pick you up at seven, okay?"

"Yes," I said. "Seven's fine."

What was my father going to say? I wondered. Would he be impressed or even more concerned, thinking I might get swept off my feet? It was one thing for your father to have confidence in you being responsible when it came to your schoolwork, the house, and driving but another when it came to romance.

After I hung up, I did think about what I would wear, and it suddenly occurred to me to do something I had never done. I would go up to the attic and look through my mother's clothes. I was just about her size now. Naturally, my mind went to Cathy sifting through the clothing in the Foxworth attic. Maybe, like her, I was preparing myself for a role in a play.

From the way Christopher had described the Foxworth attic, I imagined ours was a tenth of the size, if that, and ours had areas dedicated to wires and pipes. The need for a great deal of attic space wasn't there when our house was built, and few people I knew actually used their attics for anything more than storage. Because my mother's things were still up there, my father took care of the space. He wouldn't permit it to become "a reservation for insects or bats," nor would he permit it to be too dusty. Once a month, he went up (I would often go with him now) and do the two windows, vacuum the floors and stored furnishings, and be sure my mother's things were not "moth food." Everything was kept as neat and as organized as it had been in their bedroom.

I wondered why the Foxworths had kept all their ancestral things, pictures, clothes, old Victrolas, and the like. From the way Christopher had described the condition it was all in, including the insect-ridden books, it was clear they had no emotional ties to anything. Maybe in their fanatical religious way of thinking, it was sinful to throw away anything. Or maybe they were clinging to those dying memories, the way my father said most people did in the houses he refurbished.

I opened the large wardrobe and began sifting through my mother's dresses. Her more expensive ones were on the right. I had only very vague memories of her wearing any of them, but one stood out for me. I knew it was a classic black, something that seemed never to go out of style. It had an asymmetrical neckline and was sleeveless, with a pencil skirt. I stripped down to my bra and panties and put it on. My breasts were as large as hers had been, and my waist and hips were almost identical. It had a concealed zipper. I thought our shoe size would be dramatically different, but when I slipped on her peep-toe platforms, I found them to be comfortable.

Excited about the dress, I took it off, put my clothes back on, and went down to hang it out in the fall sunlight and cool crisp air to give it some freshness. It really didn't need anything else done to it. I pondered what jewelry I would wear, what purse I would take, and how I would wear my hair, and then I tried to return to my homework. That was nearly impossible to do. Having been up in my attic and thinking about it all, I felt an even greater desire to return to Christopher's world. I thought I would bring the diary downstairs, have some lunch, and read for a few hours in the living room.

When I sat at the kitchen table, I poured some lemonade, bit into my ham and cheese sandwich, and turned the page.

Momma was excited about my plan to dress up the attic, but I had no illusions about why. She saw it all as another way to occupy us all and distract us from the situation we were still wallowing in. Every time she came to see us after her secretarial school classes, she would bring more materials, crayons, paints, anything to encourage us to continue with "this major project." As always, she added the fact that what we were doing would impress our grandmother and go far toward not only helping her win back her parents' affections but also convincing her mother that we were not "the devil's spawn."

Oh, how Cathy hated it whenever she said

those words. How could our own mother let her mother call us those names and describe us as evil? What had we ever done that was sinful? "Especially Christopher," she would say. "He wouldn't even cheat on a school quiz!"

Momma would take on that mournful, sympathetic look and describe how it was more painful to her than it was to us. "It tears at my heart and the memory of your dear departed and wonderful father whenever she utters those ugly words. You should see the way she glares at me sometimes. It's enough to make anyone's heart shatter into pieces."

Cathy was skeptical. How come she was wearing beautiful new clothes? Who bought them? She had such a variety of shoes. How could they still hate her so much and yet spend so much on her?

"It's only because I'm applying myself," she told us. "My father respects hard work and ambition. Of course, I hate the schoolwork, but I tolerate it for us all."

"Do you have a good teacher? Are you at least fond of him?" I asked. There was something about the way she described those classes that made me think he might be flirting with her.

"Oh, I have this old biddy for a teacher," she declared. "Not that she thinks of herself as that. She has a bosom that enters the room two minutes before she does, and she's not shy about putting it into the faces of her male students, especially this one particular man. I think it annoys her that he looks more at me than at her, even with all her flaunting about. She's actually a bit messy about her looks. I could teach her a thing or two about makeup and hair, if she let me."

Cathy was surprised she was in classes with men. Why would men want to be secretaries? Momma described them as writers, journalists, who needed to master typing skills. From the way she described how some of them leaned on her for help, I wondered just how much she was concentrating on her own work. If there was one thing I knew would capture my mother's attention, it was a man's attention on her. I often wondered why that didn't make my father angry. It made me angry.

"Are you thinking of dating any of them?" I came right out and asked.

Cathy looked surprised for a moment and then nodded to herself.

"No, no, of course not." She described one of the men as so tiny and short that she could carry him out of the room. She went on and on about Daddy again, about how handsome and tall he was and how he was still so alive in her memory. She told me she spent most of her nights crying and thinking about him and how cruel he was to die so soon.

"He should have been more careful, and he should have provided a safety net of financing.

He should have been thinking about me," she moaned. All of us stared at her. She realized it and quickly added, "I mean about all of us."

"He couldn't help being killed," Cathy said angrily.

"No one really can," Momma said. "I'm not blaming him for that. I'm just . . . upset with what I've had to do. But don't worry. I have it under control. We'll be fine. We'll all be just fine."

None of us said anything. She put on that smile mask I hated to see her wearing and then left after kissing the twins, kissing me, and hugging Cathy, who kept her arms limp at her sides.

For a few moments, I couldn't think of anything encouraging to say after she left. Cathy looked at me.

"What?"

"Nothing, Christopher. I have nothing to say that you want to hear," she said, and turned back to dressing up the attic. Soon we were all back to it.

To make us even more excited about our decorating work, Momma began bringing books on arts and crafts. It was my job to run the work as if we were all in a kindergarten classroom, with me as the twins' teacher and Cathy as my assistant. At first, the twins began to rebel. They didn't like sitting for long at desks and getting instructions. Then, with all the added materials and Momma's suggestion that we do animals, too, they became more involved. I began to think we just might get through this, giving Momma the time she needed to master the secretarial skills and get a job after all. But as Cathy began questioning her more and more about her school progress, skepticism started to infiltrate my wall of hope and put holes into my optimism.

Something wasn't right, but I wasn't about to suggest it to Cathy. She was hanging by a thread the way it was. Besides not being able to be outside and at a school where she could mix with other students, have girlfriends, and flirt with boys, she had to be a surrogate mother to the twins and join with me to fulfill our mandatory tasks. Every Friday, we had to strip down the room and clean the bathroom at dawn and then drag or carry the sleepy twins up into the attic to wait and have our cold breakfast cereal while the maids under our grandmother's barking orders cleaned below.

Cathy wondered why they never realized we had been there. "Don't they sense us? They should smell us. They should have heard something. It's like we really don't exist anymore," she said. "We're all ghosts."

Actually, I thought that was an interesting idea. After all this time alone with my brother and sisters and not being able to pursue my own interests the way I used to, even when we were struggling after my father's death, I wasn't above some fantasizing.

None of this existed in the real world, I told myself. What if when we entered Foxworth that night, we had crossed into someone else's nightmare? We were invisible to anyone else. Our grandmother was a powerful witch who waved her hands over us and made us little more than ghosts of ourselves. She had life-and-death power over all of us, including Momma. We had fallen down a much darker tunnel than Alice in her Wonderland.

"What are you thinking so hard about?" Cathy asked me.

For a moment, I felt like I had been caught doing something I shouldn't. Then I smiled. "All the wonderful things we will have and do once we are out of here," I said.

She looked disappointed for a moment and then said something that hurt me more than she could ever realize. "If there was anything I believed for sure—for sure, Christopher—it was that you weren't a dreamer like me. Or more important, like Momma. I was depending on that. Now I really feel alone."

How sad for her, I thought, but Christopher's fantasy about becoming invisible was interesting, not because I was a science-fiction fan or anything. I didn't take him literally, but I could understand why children, especially children who were once the objects of so much attention, would feel like they were disappearing in their severely imposed isolation. All they could do was try to keep happy in their make-believe world, a decorated stuffy old attic filled with forgotten people and forgotten things. It wasn't hard to believe that they were beginning to feel like they could be forgotten, too. In a sense, they were living in a graveyard.

My deep thoughts were jarred at the sound of our doorbell. I knew it wasn't Uncle Tommy. He wasn't arriving until Monday. I leaned over, parted the curtain, and looked out to see Lana and Suzette. For a few moments, I thought I might let them believe I wasn't home. They pushed the door button again and again. They were knocking, too. I knew how they both could be like bulldogs when they were determined.

I rose, looked at the diary, and quickly hid it under a pile of magazines before I went to the front door. The phone was already ringing.

"Oh, I thought you might be home," Lana said. "We saw Kane with Ryan at the mall having lunch and wondered why he wasn't with you."

"I told you we're going out tonight," I said, sounding a little more testy than I had intended.

They both smiled. Why did my close friends suddenly look so immature and unimportant to me? Hanging out with them suddenly was a distraction, a waste of time. Nothing we could do together had any meaning. What did they know about real suffering? Children locked in an attic was just another Halloween story to them.

"Lana said she thought you might be getting a little snobby," Suzette said. I still hadn't stepped back to invite them in.

"Why?"

"You rushed me off the phone, for one thing," Lana said. "We always told each other everything and cared about each other's opinions. Suddenly, Kane Hill is off limits? There was never anything off limits between us."

"I didn't mean to give that impression. I had things to do."

Neither was smiling now. Neither believed me.

"Well, did you or didn't you stay over at Kane's house after the party?"

"I already told you. That's a stupid lie Tina Kennedy is spreading."

"Well, if you don't talk to us and tell us what really happened last night, how are we able to defend you?" Suzette asked, as if they were the ones being maligned.

"Come on in," I said with a deep sigh, "and stop pouting like children."

They looked at each other, laughed, and entered.

"I'm dying of thirst," Suzette said, crumbling the sheet of ice that had formed between us.

"And I'm starving. We didn't eat anything at the mall."

"Once we saw Kane was spending the day with Ryan instead of you, we thought we had better check this whole thing out," Suzette added, and hurried into the kitchen.

We were always like this at one another's houses, opening refrigerators, finding things to eat in the cabinets, looking through whatever magazines were on tables, inspecting one another's rooms, acting as if we all lived in whoever's house we were in at the time. We could often be more like sisters. We tried on one another's clothes, borrowed anything and everything from one another, and shared secrets and stories that might, at least in their case, not please their parents if they knew. Until now, nothing seemed too personal to share, especially our little romantic experiences.

I helped make sandwiches for them and then made myself a cup of tea to have with a biscuit just so I could sit and eat something with them.

"Well?" Lana asked after she bit into her sandwich. "Inquiring minds want to know."

"Sorry to disappoint you. It was PG-13 all the way," I said. "I wasn't there that long after you all left."

They both looked disappointed.

"With his reputation, I thought you surely would 'cross the Rio Grande,'" Suzette said.

"Maybe she will tonight," Lana added, sounding hopeful.

"You sound like that's all you think about," I said.

"You don't?" Suzette fired back. "All of a sudden, you're eight years old again."

"I think about it, but that's not all I think about."

"It's not all we think about, Kristin, but it wasn't that long ago that we all talked about it. How close did you come last night?" Lana asked—more like demanded.

She was right. The three of us did talk about it often. I wasn't sure why I was being so defensive. They stared at me, at my silence.

"I think we talked about it all the time because we weren't really serious about any of the boys. It was something abstract."

"Huh?" Lana said. "Return to English." She tugged on her earlobe.

"I guess what I'm trying to say is that when you like someone, I mean really like him, you feel different about discussing the intimate details, even with your best friends. Does that make any sense?"

They just looked at me.

"No," Lana finally declared. "It doesn't. We've shared things we wouldn't tell our own mothers. Nothing is sacred when you have a real friend, and I thought we were all real friends."

"We are! I don't know, maybe I'm just embarrassed about my feelings right now. Maybe I'm surprised at myself."

"That's too deep for me," Suzette said. She rose and began washing her dish and glass.

"He's going to hurt you, you know," Lana said. "Boys like Kane can ruin you if you're not careful."

"Stop it, Lana," Suzette said. "You don't know that. You sound jealous."

"I'm just trying to give her some advice. She doesn't have anyone else but us," she whined. She was trying to defend herself, but her remark was like a dart thrown into the center of my heart.

They had mothers to confide in if they needed to. I didn't. That was what she meant about my not having anyone else but them.

"I mean . . ."

"Oh, shut up," Suzette said. She turned back to me. "Where's he taking you for dinner?" she asked, anxious to get us all off the topic.

"The River House."

"Wow."

"He can afford it if anyone can," Lana said. "I've never been there. My father won't spend the money." Now she did sound a little jealous.

"What are you going to wear?" Suzette asked.

Her question brought relief. I stood up quickly.

"Something of my mother's. Come on up to my room. I just brought it inside from airing out. It's been in a closet for . . . a long time. I'll show you," I said, and we were back to being best friends.

They both thought I looked beautiful in the dress.

"Everyone says your mother was beautiful, too," Lana offered as a way of recovering for her remark in the kitchen.

Afterward, we sat around talking about different fashions, clothes other girls wore at school. They both went on about the boys they liked, but each admitted she didn't see herself getting too serious with any of them. At least, not the way I seemed to be getting serious with Kane. Our conversation ran on to upcoming parties and events, how we were all going to spend our Christmas holidays, and hopes for some sort of "real" New Year's Eve party.

At some moment during our chatter, I found myself drifting off and thinking about Christopher and Cathy and how these kinds of conversations and plans were things they could only imagine. If they really were up in that attic for more than three years, they missed the heart of their best young years, having boyfriends and girlfriends, going to parties, just hanging out, and having endless phone calls.

How could their own mother permit that to happen, permit them to miss these years, these experiences? How did she think they would turn out? Why did she let it go on and on so long? Didn't she realize that they would be socially immature the first day they returned to the world? It would be like coming up out of a coal mine and into the light of day. They would be blind for a while.

Suzette was the first to realize I was off somewhere else and suggested that she and Lana leave. "We can tell when someone is dreaming of what's to come."

"No, I . . ."

"You want to be fresh for your date," she said. "Do what my mother does. Lie down with pieces of cucumber over your eyes."

"Ugh," Lana said. "How smelly."

"You bathe or shower afterward, dummy," Suzette said, and we left my room.

"I think I need some help with the math homework," Lana told me when we were back in the living room. "Think you'll have some time tomorrow?"

"Sure. Call me in the morning, and we'll figure it out."

Suzette was always the nosiest of the three of us. She looked around the living room and then began to flip through the magazines. I started toward her, but she saw the diary.

"What's this?" she asked.

I scooped it up. "My diary," I said.

"You keep a diary?" Suzette looked at Lana, who shrugged.

"I used to," Lana said, "but after my brother found it and read it aloud, I burned it."

"So are we in it?" Suzette asked.

"You'll never know," I said. "A diary is personal."

"We know who's mainly in it by now, anyway," Lana said. "His name starts with K."

Suzette continued to look at me and the diary suspiciously.

"That looks pretty old," she said.

"It is. It belonged to my mother, but she never used it."

"Oh. Well, whatever floats your boat," she quipped, and they headed for the front door.

I followed but not too closely. I know I was clutching the diary so tightly that I made them suspicious, but I couldn't help it.

"Have a great time," Suzette said.

"Yeah. Whatever you do, do it for me, too," Lana added, and they walked out.

I stood in the doorway watching them get into Suzette's car. I waved, and they waved back. I could see they were talking a mile a minute as they drove off.

"Like I'd let anyone else touch you," I told the diary, and hurried upstairs to put it under my pillow. It was getting late, and I had a lot of preparing to do, but I couldn't stop thinking about our conversation. Had I done or said anything to give them a hint at what was really in this diary? Had they bought my story? They couldn't possibly imagine what I had. Could they? It would be like some sort of a betrayal if I let anyone else read it or even know about it. Christopher would hate me, I thought, which was a silly thought, of course. He didn't even know I existed.

Suddenly, that idea passed through my mind like lightning. What if he did know? What if I could meet him? What would I say? What would he say to me? Would he be terribly embarrassed that I had read his diary or terribly angry? I would give it back to him, of course, but he would know that I knew his deepest, most intimate thoughts, and the truth was, no matter how honest we wanted to be, none of us wanted anyone to know all our deepest, most intimate thoughts.

I literally had to shake myself to get back to what I was doing, but I put those images on a back burner. As Dad would say, "I'll be coming back to them . . . someday." I started rushing to get ready again.

My father came home only a little while before Kane was due to pick me up for dinner. I was already dressed, my hair and makeup done, when I heard him come into the house. I couldn't remember being more nervous about anything than I was when I stepped out of my room and started to descend the stairs. Dad was at the bottom looking up at me. The expression on his face stopped me cold. It was an expression I had never seen. He didn't look upset exactly, and he didn't exactly look pleased. I think it was more a look of shock and surprise.

"For a moment . . ." he began, and then stopped himself and brought up his smile. "That dress . . ."

"It's Mom's. I went through her things in the attic
and chose it. We're about the same size now. Is it all
right for me to wear it?"

"Sure," he said. "She'd want you to wear it. She'd
be proud of how you look. You look very beautiful,
Kristin, and very grown-up."

"Thank you, Dad," I said, and continued down.

He stepped back. "I like what you've done with
your hair, too. Reminds me a lot of her. I bought her
that dress for our tenth-anniversary dinner. I still remember how other people at the restaurant stopped
talking or doing what they were doing when we
walked in and they saw her. She hated being the center
of attention, but I got her laughing about it, claiming
they were really looking at me. Where did you say he
was taking you?"

"The River House."

"Right." He laughed.

"What?"

"I took your mother there for our *eleventh* anniversary. The food, especially the lobster fra diavolo,
is famous around here. And quite expensive. Your
mother wasn't going to order it, but I insisted. That's
the way she was."

"Then I'll order it," I said.

He continued to put away his things and went out
to greet Kane when he rang our doorbell.

"Don't scare him, Dad," I pleaded.

"*Moi?* I'm a pussycat," he said, but when he opened
the door, he would have stopped an army of ants with
his look. I could see Kane hesitate.

"Hi, Mr. Masterwood."

"They're calling for some possible cold rain tonight," Dad said instead of hello. "Mind your driving."

"Yes, sir. My father said the same thing just now when he heard I was going out."

"Your precious cargo," Dad continued, and stepped back to reveal me. I started to wrap my heavy wool black shawl over my shoulders when the two of them rushed forward to help. Dad realized Kane was intending to do the same thing and stopped.

"You look fantastic," Kane said.

"Thank you." I gave my father a stern look and saw his eyes begin to light his smile.

"You guys have a great time," he told Kane.

"Thank you, Mr. Masterwood."

We started out. Dad remained in the doorway watching Kane rush around to open the door for me. He waved to Dad, who nodded, and then he got into his car.

"Does your dad do that to all your dates who come to the house to pick you up?"

"Do what?"

"Intimidate them?"

"He's just being a dad," I said. "What do you think you'll be like when you're one?"

"The truth is, I can't imagine it."

"It's not that hard to imagine," I said, and he smiled and backed us out of the driveway very slowly, practically crawling away from the house.

"It wouldn't surprise me to see him follow us," he said, gazing into his rearview mirror.

I looked back. Would he? "I don't think so," I said. "He's probably alerted the police department instead."

"What?"

"Just kidding, Kane," I said.

He shook his head. "I think I've finally met my match in you," he said.

The smile on my face threatened to be permanent or at least last the rest of this evening.

"I hope you're hungry," he said.

"I starved myself all day just so you could spend a lot of money on me."

He laughed. "There are girls who would, but somehow, Kristin, I don't think you're one of them."

The River House was everything it was described as. The main dining room was luxurious, with mirrored walls and sconces that were made to look like torches flickering. There were at least thirty tables, all dressed with fresh flowers and soft white tablecloths. The place settings had gold trim, and all the silverware and napkins had the restaurant's icon, a seagull with the edge of one wing shaped into a fork.

I don't know if we made the sort of impression my father described when he and my mother had walked in here on their anniversary, but I did see that we drew the attention of most of the people at tables and some waiters and busboys. Kane was wearing a dark green dinner jacket and a light green tie. It brought out the green in his eyes. Because we were so young compared with the other couples there, I was sure we would attract some attention anyway. The waiter pulled out the seat for me and even unfolded my napkin for me to place on my lap.

"We'll have a bottle of Evian, please," Kane said. "Flat. Or do you like carbonated?" he asked me.

"No, flat's fine."

When the waiter left, I leaned toward him. Everyone around us seemed to be listening in.

"You really do look beautiful, Kristin. I was too frightened to look at you long with your father hovering."

"Stop making him sound so scary."

"He's not scary. Well, maybe a little. You're right, though. If I had a daughter who looked like you, I'd be armed when boys came around."

"You're going to make me conceited."

"You should be."

"You're not so bad yourself." I paused. "And that's no reflex response."

"A what?"

"You know, compliment for compliment."

"Oh. Well, thanks."

"Of course, all the girls think you are conceited," I added, and he smiled and gave me his Kane Hill shrug.

"Right now, the only girl's opinion that matters is yours."

The bottle of water was brought to us and the busboy poured it into our glasses. The waiter handed us menus, and my eyes went quickly to the lobster fra diavolo. It was fifty-five dollars. The least expensive entrée on the menu was thirty-eight, and that was a vegetarian dish.

"Don't worry about cost," Kane said. "I saved up all the loose change in the house."

"What?"

He laughed. "My father loves telling this story about himself and two of his friends struggling to pay for college, and one day one of them had the brilliant idea to search under the backseat of his father's car. They found enough change for the three of them to go to dinner. In those days, it was less than twenty dollars for the three. He tells me a story like that once a week, if not twice. I know he's making up half of them. He's terrified that I might take money for granted."

"Well, he's right to worry about it."

"I don't. One thing's for certain. I'll never take you for granted."

"I think that's a compliment."

He smiled, shrugged, and looked at the menu. "The fra diavolo is to die for," he said.

It was truly one of the most special nights out I had ever had. My father and I went to restaurants, and I had gone to them with friends, but it was usually fast-food types, and the experience wasn't unusual. My father had taken me out to eat, but it was different going to an especially good restaurant with my father. He was as attentive to me as he could be, and he was more relaxed and talked freely about his youth, his family, and my mother when we were out together, but this was so different, and not only because it was a very expensive, high-end place. I did feel more grown-up sitting there with Kane.

Because of his father's wealth and position in the community and his mother's upbringing especially, he had been schooled in dinner etiquette as a prince might be. He wasn't pedantic or condescending, but he instructed me about the extra silverware, the proper way to do this and that, never making any of it sound stupid or silly, the way I was sure my friends and most of the other boys would. Despite his casualness, he seemed to harbor a respect for all things elegant.

It was at that moment, when he was talking about how he was trained to sit and dine properly, that I compared him to Christopher. I had made a real discovery this evening. Yes, I thought, Kane wasn't just another pretty face. He really was more mature than his friends. Maybe, just maybe, he was someone who could be trusted.

"You look like you're drifting away," he said at one point.

"No, I hear you. You make me think about other things."

"Like?"

"Things I've read," I said.

"That's all I get?"

"For now," I said. "A girl can't give away all her secrets too quickly."

He nodded without smiling. "You'll be like opening a box inside a box inside a box," he said.

"You might get exhausted with the effort."

Now he smiled. "Please," he said. "Exhaust me."

What if my girlfriends could listen in on all he and I said to each other? Would they believe it? Would they grimace and shake their heads, mumbling that we couldn't be for real? Would they think we were being phony to impress each other? Would they get so bored with us that they'd plug in their headphones and drift off with the latest hit song?

They couldn't appreciate us.

And they certainly couldn't appreciate Christopher's diary.

After the meal we had, I didn't think I could eat any dessert, but Kane insisted we have the baked Alaska.

"They're famous for it here."

"I'm beginning to think they're famous for everything here," I said, but agreed we should have it.

It was so good I stuffed myself.

"I think you'll have to carry me out of here," I said.

"Okay."

"Don't even think of it," I warned.

He was capable of breaking out into some outrageous act at any time. After he paid the bill, which I didn't see but imagined to be the cost of at least a week's worth of food for my father and me, he came around before the waiter could and pulled out my chair for me. Then he took my hand, smiled, and nodded at some of the people staring at us. He led us out to give the ticket for his car to the valet.

"This was such a wonderful night, Kane. Thank you. I feel like the senior prom will be a letdown after this."

"Not if I can take you," he said. "Okay," he added after we were in his car and driving off. "I'll confess. I was out to impress, even overwhelm, you tonight."

"You succeeded."

He laughed at my honesty. "I don't think any other girl I would take here would have that reaction. Most of them would have looked and been uncomfortable in there."

"Would take? How many have you taken?" I asked.

He shrugged. "A few." He turned to me. "Always a disaster. Well," he said, eager to change the subject, "looks like the rain your father feared came and went. Look at the clearing night sky, the stars."

We were both silent for a while. I think it was one of those quiet pauses when two people ponder which road to take, which decision to make, or which suggestion to offer that would not endanger an early and fragile relationship. He already knew I wasn't someone he could rush along, but I was also conscious of the possibility that he would think I was too conservative or, worse, just a tantalizing tease.

"Why don't I call you late in the morning tomorrow, and if the weather isn't bad, we try a picnic?"

"A picnic?"

"Fall is hanging in there. Did you see the weather report for tomorrow? They're calling it a day of Indian summer. Winter is taking its time," he said. "My father told me he's not seen a fall like this since he was my age. He should have been a weatherman. He gives us a weather report like clockwork every morning."

"A picnic?" I smiled. "I'd like that. Where would we go?"

"How about we go back to that lake?"

"What lake? You mean the Foxworth lake?"

"Yes. It was different, maybe because it's so ignored. It looks interesting. We can find a nice spot there, I'm sure."

"I don't know. My father's still doing removal. Some of it has been fenced off and . . ."

"Not the lake. You've got influence," he said. "I'll pick up some sandwiches, drinks, fruit."

"Oh, I can prepare a picnic," I said. "It doesn't seem like a picnic if everything is bought."

He laughed. "Okay. I'll bring the blanket, then, and my new iPod and Bluetooth speaker."

"You're sure about the weather?"

"I'll call you around ten. We'll know for sure by then, and I'll pick you up around eleven thirty. Otherwise, maybe we'll go to a movie or something."

"I still have some homework. I'd like to be back by three."

"Yes, Madam Valedictorian," he kidded.

We talked for a few minutes in his car in my driveway. I thanked him for dinner again, but he insisted on thanking me, telling me I had made the dinner worth it, not the restaurant.

We kissed, a long kiss but a soft, warm kiss that was full of promise, and then he walked me to my door, kissed me again, and whispered, "Good night. Dream of me, please. I know I will dream of you."

I watched him walk back to his car. He paused, gave me that tantalizing smile, and slipped in behind the wheel gracefully.

I opened the door and entered. There was my

father waiting up in the living room, doing his usual pretending to be too interested in something on television to go up to bed.

"Well?" he said, turning to me. "Was it still everything it's cracked up to be?"

"More. At least, to me."

"Really?" He looked thoughtful. "Well, I'm glad for you, then, Kristin. You deserve good things."

"So do you, Dad. Oh," I said, "it's not raining. It was just a short shower, apparently, and the sky's clearing. Kane wants to take me on a picnic tomorrow."

"Crazy weather. I heard it was going to be about ten degrees above normal tomorrow. Picnic in early November, but I guess you could enjoy it. Where are you going?"

"We thought we'd go to the Foxworth lake, if that's all right with you."

"The Foxworth lake? Kind of overgrown."

"It's interesting. Kane thinks so. I guess I do, too. All right?"

"Just stay away from the building site and the wreckage. I have it all fenced off, but there's still a lot to do around it."

"Okay," I said, kissing him good night, and I hurried up the stairs to prepare for bed.

The thought of returning to Foxworth, however, brought me back to Christopher's diary seconds after I had brushed my teeth and slipped under the blanket.

Dared I think it?

It was almost as if I was going to where my family had been, my lost family, almost as if they were drawing me to them with this diary and with what else they had left behind, especially all the secrets.

Maybe, because I didn't have many intellectually challenging things to do or adults to talk to, I began to think more and more about our grandmother. What had turned her into the monster we saw? Was it simply being married to a very hard, fanatically religious man? What was her youth like? How did she come to marry such a man? Or was she the one who influenced him?

A number of times, both Cathy and I caught her peering in at us. She would open the door slightly and spy on us as if she had expected to catch us doing one of the unholy things she had forbidden. Then I thought maybe she was really curious about us now, not thinking that we would do evil but wondering how we could be such attractive and intelligent children and yet be born of what she called a sinful act. I even wondered if she didn't believe we would change form or something, become other creatures once the door was closed. Rarely did we see her spy on us when we were in the attic.

One day, Momma told us why her mother wasn't keen on going up the narrow stairway to the attic. She said she was claustrophobic ever since she had been locked in a closet when she was a young girl. That was apparently a form of punishment her parents had used on her. Locking us up wasn't all that unfamiliar to her, then.

Whenever she confronted us, she was obsessed with questions about our sexuality. It had become almost a religious chant for her. Did we touch our private parts? Did we look at each other naked? Did boys and girls use the bathroom together? She asked the questions like a police interrogator, asking quickly in the hopes of catching us lying or maybe one of the twins blurting out something sinful that we were covering up.

"I bet her husband never sees her naked," I told Cathy. "Not that he would want to."

"Don't they share a bedroom?"

"I don't know, but even if they do, she probably has her underwear glued on."

Cathy's eyes brightened. At last, we had something to ridicule. "No, they're nailed on," she said.

"How did they have children?" I pondered.

"Blindfolded," she suggested.

I thought that was clever. The twins thought we had gone mad. They had no idea what was making us laugh so hard.

One time, while I was painting and needed water, Cathy went down the stairs and ran into her. When she came back, she described how angry our grandmother was about her doing my bidding. She warned her about being so obedient and following my commands. Cathy said she told her that I knew what was evil more than she did, because the male of the species was born knowing evil, and I would only lead her to damnation.

"Ha," I said. "So much for her Bible study.
Adam wasn't the one who listened to the devil
in Paradise. It was Eve. She obviously never
read Shakespeare's 'Macbeth,' either. It was
Lady Macbeth who got him to kill the king. Our
grandmother has it completely opposite to the
truth. Women are a bigger influence on men than
men are on women. Look at how much Momma
got Daddy to do!"

"You tell her all that, not me," Cathy said.

"If she says that to me, I will."

Cathy nodded, but I thought I saw her look at
me a little differently. Did she think it was so? Did
she expect something evil would come from me?
How easy it was to plant a suspicion, I thought.
Perhaps our great-grandmother had done that to
Grandmother Olivia, and now she was passing it
down to us.

I put the diary down and thought about the ideas
Cathy's grandmother was putting into her head about
Christopher and men in general. She struck me as
being too young to really understand, and yet from
the way Christopher described her, I thought she was
at that point where she was more aware of her own
budding sexuality. How difficult that surely was for
a girl her age, being so confined and rarely having her
mother available to speak with her privately.

Even though Christopher had made it clear that
neither he nor Cathy was ever ashamed of their nudity
because their mother wasn't ashamed of hers, there

had to come a point when they would feel differently. Would Christopher reveal that? Would Cathy say something to embarrass him or make him feel guilty?

Lana, Suzette, and I did reveal very intimate things about ourselves to one another. It made the three of us feel better about ourselves, our own bodies, and our feelings to know that we all had similar thoughts and experiences. We didn't mature simultaneously, but changes began to happen to each of us at about the same time. Lana was the last of the three to have her first period, but both Suzette and I had described it enough for her to know exactly what to expect. Between Suzette's mother and Lana's, Lana's was apparently the more prudish and reluctant to answer questions and discuss things. Lana said she would often say, "You'll learn about it in school." I told them most of the things my aunt Barbara had told me. We often compared notes and revealed sexual fantasies, laughing about them most of the time. The point was, we had some self-confidence about ourselves. We were never afraid of what was happening. We never felt we were dangling out there on some kind of wild roller coaster of emotions.

How would it have been to be in an attic with my older brother, my much younger brother and sister, a mother who was practically never around, and a grandmother who wanted me to believe that my own body was a vessel of sin? Nobody who wasn't there with those children, especially Cathy, and no one who didn't have this diary would have any idea what exactly her mother had done to her by shutting her up in an attic just when she was about to fly into her femininity.

There were different kinds of tears in my eyes when I picked up the diary again, tears of compassion and pity and tears of rage, so many I didn't think I could read another word, but I sucked in my breath, wiped my eyes, and turned the page. From the first few lines, it looked like maybe there was some hope.

Later in the afternoon, we all looked up with surprise when Grandmother Olivia came into the room. Except for her spying on us, she rarely appeared any time other than breakfast, lunch, or dinner. None of us complained about not seeing her, but I couldn't help wondering if we weren't always on her mind one way or another. I think she felt confident that she had hidden us away well, but even if one of her servants suspected something, I doubted that he or she would ever dare question her about it. She appeared to have control of everything and everyone associated with this mansion.

Of course, that made me ask myself many questions, questions I would never voice aloud in front of Cathy. If Grandmother Olivia had so much power, why didn't she simply tell her husband we were here and that this was the way it would be? How could a sick old man put up much opposition? She seemed well and strong. He surely depended on her for every morsel he ate and everything that had to be done legally for the Foxworth family.

Maybe that was all true, I told myself, but maybe she wanted to see us suffer, punish Momma, and test us to see if we were as evil as she suspected. How long would it take to satisfy her? Why wasn't all the time that had passed already enough? What else did she want from us, from Momma? Was this her way of ensuring that we would be doomed after all? What children in our predicament wouldn't have broken one or more of her precious rules by now? Was she always out there on the other side of that door waiting to pounce? She couldn't hate us, she didn't know us, but she surely hated the idea of us.

I really believed all this, which was why I was taken aback when she entered the room this time. She was carrying a clay pot of yellow chrysanthemums, real yellow chrysanthemums! She walked right over to Cathy and put the pot in her hands. Cathy's mouth fell open. The twins were fascinated. I took a step forward, debating whether to say thank you, or ask her why she was giving them to us.

"Here are some real flowers for your fake garden," she declared.

Cathy looked at me, helpless for a moment. I mouthed "Thank you," and she began to thank her.

Our grandmother stared at her as she fumbled one statement of gratitude after another.

Was she studying her, seeing if Cathy had the

capacity to be grateful for something, had any
manners? Was this whole thing an experiment,
another test? I was just as surprised as Cathy was
that Grandmother Olivia had even taken note of
what we were doing in the attic.

She turned to look at me, and for a second, I
thought there was some sign of human kindness in
her. It was as if love had come up into her throat
like a burp, and she had to get it out, maybe
because she didn't want it to be there. Maybe she
hated herself for having even an iota of feeling for
us. She marched out without saying another word.
A silence fell. We were waiting for a second shoe
to drop or something, but nothing happened.

The twins closed in on the flowers. It had been
so long since they had seen anything from nature
that was real, alive, and beautiful, something that
would make them feel they were in the world
again. Carrie wanted to hold the pot. Cathy
handed it to her gently, and the twins hovered over
it as if it were a pet.

"We'll put it on the east windowsill so it will
get morning sunshine," I said.

"What the hell is this?" Cathy asked, suddenly
realizing what had happened. "Is she changing?
Did something Momma do change her mind about
us? Did she decide she likes us or something?"

"I don't know," I said. "Let's wait to see what
else she does."

"Maybe we won't be stuck here much longer,"
Cathy said. Her whole demeanor changed. Her

face brightened. I could see she was off and running with her plans for when we were let out into the world again.

"The first thing I will do is get to a phone and call my friends. They probably thought we were kidnapped by aliens or something. And I want a big fat chocolate ice cream cone before I eat anything else. I want to go to Momma's beauty salon and have my hair washed and styled. I want to go shopping and get some new shoes, new dresses and blouses. I want—"

"Cathy," I said sharply. The twins were beginning to listen. I nodded at them. "You'll have them crying again."

She looked at them and then at the door. "She'd better not be teasing us," she threatened. "She'd better not."

That idea hadn't even occurred to me, but what if Cathy was right? Was she cruel enough to do that? She seemed cruel enough to do most anything. Did Momma know about these flowers? Was she holding out a promise just to see if we would lunge and claw and maybe prove to be the evil children she claimed we were?

"Let's not think about it right now," I said. "Let's just take it a day at a time."

"A day! Why don't you say it the way it is, a week at a time, a month?"

"All right, calm down," I said. "Please."

She bit her lower lip and went off to care for the flowers.

Despite my feeling the same conflicting emotions Cathy had obviously felt and my need to learn more and discover what this gift of flowers was all about, I had trouble keeping my eyes open. It wasn't simply reading too much. I could read tons of history and science, especially compared with how much I had read of the diary, and not be as sleepy. It wasn't the reading so much as the emotional involvement.

As I read, I felt myself getting tenser. It was draining. Subtly, in so many small ways, I had entered Foxworth and lived alongside Christopher, Cathy, and the twins. I felt like I was there, invisible, right beside them, seeing and feeling what they were seeing and feeling. All of it, but mainly having to care for their younger brother and sister, who were more fragile and confused, was simply too heavy a burden to bear. Christopher wasn't giving in to it, but I could sense his fatigue.

All teenagers wanted to rush our lives, become old enough to do more and be more independent. We wanted adult responsibilities. We were always envying older girls who seemed to have far more control of their own lives, even the ones who hadn't gone to college but were still living at home. They had no curfews, no rules beyond the rules they set for themselves, and certainly fewer lectures and chastisements to tolerate.

Who among us wanted to be younger? Who wanted to be told when to take a bath or a shower, when to eat and sleep, and where we could and couldn't go? Who wanted all our decisions made for us and just to be content looking forward to birthdays and holidays? Who complained about not being able to pretend with dolls? No, none of us longed to be younger.

In a real way, Christopher and Cathy had been dragged back years when they were locked away in Foxworth. Everything they did and had was strictly controlled. Even the little independence they had begun to enjoy before coming to Foxworth was washed away. They had to eat, bathe, and sleep when they were told to, and they were submitted to more scrutiny than even when they were Carrie and Cory's age. It was hard for Cathy because she was on the verge of becoming a young lady, and it was hard for Christopher because he was already light-years older than most boys and had really serious ambitions.

On the other hand, while they were being handled and treated as if they were infants, Christopher and Cathy were forced to be more like parents than siblings to the twins. They had to care for them as their parents would, and they bore the responsibility for their health and happiness. In a way, they were being pulled in two different directions. It had to have been exhausting. What would I have done?

Just thinking about it made me even more tired. My eyes closed like two window shutters being slammed shut. I fell asleep with the diary in my hand and didn't wake up until I heard my father knocking on the door.

"Come in," I called, and quickly put the diary under the blanket as I sat up.

"You okay?"

"Yes, I just . . ."

"Read too much?" he asked, standing with his arms crossed over his chest, looking down at me and nodding.

"Probably," I said.

"I have a meeting with the architect and the new owner today. It will carry over into lunch."

"Okay. Oh, I'm doing the picnic with Kane at the Foxworth lake," I said, reminding myself as much as him.

"Well, the weatherman was right for a change. You've got the weather for it," he said. "You be careful. Don't go near the site."

"We won't."

"Remember, your uncle Tommy's coming tomorrow. Don't make any other plans. He's only here for one night."

"I won't. I can't wait to see him."

"Good. Maybe it'll take your mind off some other things for a while." He looked at me, at my blanket, at where my left hand was, as if he could see the diary through it. Then he nodded and walked out.

It occurred to me that perhaps this wasn't only about my reading the diary. Perhaps my father worried more about me than my friends' fathers worried about them, because he and I were the only ones in this immediate family now. Their fathers had someone else with whom to share the burden of worry. Just like Christopher had a greater weight placed on him, my father had that, too, when my mother died. And yet my father never was oppressive and controlling. He wasn't obsessive about caring for me. I truly believed he trusted me more than the fathers of my friends trusted them.

My mother's death hadn't created any conflict between my father and me. It had made us more dependent on each other. I didn't want to have to be older, more careful. Like Cathy, I wanted to enjoy being young, but because of how loving my father was, I couldn't be rebellious and angry, careless and wasteful. I was even careful about being moody. I knew how sensitive my father was to my every expression of deep thought or any sharpness in my voice. I kept as much of it as I could submerged under a smile, but sometimes I felt like I might explode. Many times I witnessed my girlfriends whining or throwing a tantrum in front of their fathers and mothers. I couldn't imagine doing that to my father.

None of my girlfriends did grocery shopping for their families. Only Lana ever mentioned cooking anything, and that was only under some duress. They weren't spoiled so much as not relied on for anything really important. Oh, they had to take care of their things, keep their rooms clean and organized, and not let friends come over and mess up any part of their homes. They all had driver's licenses, and most had either their own cars or their parents' cars at their disposal. No one seemed to want for anything, and they all had whatever money was necessary for whatever they wanted to do.

I think the biggest difference between them and me now was that despite their possessions and privileges, they were still thought of as children. I was, too, of course, but it was different. My father and I had developed a more mature relationship. We truly respected each other.

The real reason for that, I believe, was that he showed me how vulnerable he was. I saw his pain. He was honest about it. We were equals that way, and because of that, our love for each other had grown stronger. I was confident that he was as terrified of losing me as I was of losing him. It was odd to think it, but what made us *less* lonely was knowing how lonely we both were and how much lonelier we could become.

I took the diary out from under the blanket and wondered if Christopher and Cathy would grow stronger or weaker together. Would their love for each other protect them all, or would their unhappiness eventually drive them apart? Christopher was smart enough to understand the dangers, but was Cathy? Did he want her to understand how vulnerable and tragic they had become? Probably not, but how long could he conceal it? And what would he do when the time came when he couldn't lie to himself and to her anymore?

Dad was right, I thought, as I rose to get dressed. I had to take a holiday from all this. I was on an emotional merry-go-round. My head was spinning with thoughts and questions. Besides, I had to enjoy my day with Kane and my time with Uncle Tommy. I couldn't do that if I didn't give them my full attention. Dad was wise enough to suggest that, and yet, even after I had put the diary out of sight, I knew it wouldn't leave me.

Not for a moment. It wasn't that easy.

I hurried downstairs to breakfast and to prepare the picnic lunch. Afterward, I spent much more time than I dreamed I would deciding what to wear. I could look at my summer wardrobe, because it was going to be warmer than usual again, but I was always in a quandary about which color complimented me best. I couldn't depend on my father's opinion. In his eyes, every color looked good on me, and no matter how I wore my hair, it was perfect, too. I'd had limited experience with my mother, of course, but I was certain she would be more critical and helpful if she were alive.

There really wasn't anyone who could substitute for her. I never trusted my girlfriends' opinions about my clothes and my hair. Jealousy had a way of rearing its ugly head, even among dearly close friends. I had to confess to a little of it, too, that green-eyed envy. I would never admit it, especially if a boy made the accusation, but I did believe it was natural to our sex to be at least a little jealous of one another. Even sisters might not be wholly truthful, particularly if they were close in age. That brought sibling rivalry in to add to our natural competition. You really couldn't depend on saleswomen in department stores or boutique shops, either. They had another motivation for compliments and criticism: selling something more expensive to get a bigger commission.

I wondered if my girlfriends, who often complained about their mothers for one reason or another, knew how lucky they were to have someone with honest eyes to help them look and feel their best.

Everyone takes so much for granted, I thought, until you lose some of it. Again, I imagined myself as Cathy. She was as motherless as I was, and as she grew older in that attic, she would have only her brother to tell her things and advise her, and he couldn't be completely honest. He couldn't tell her how much she was missing or how much better she would look and feel if they were free. He had to keep her calm so the twins would stay calm.

Despite my plan to be otherwise, I was so deep in thought about all this that I almost didn't hear Kane at the front door, knocking and pushing the bell. I seemed to come up from under inky, dark water and rushed to greet him, apologizing so profusely he stood there with a dumb smile on his face.

"I want to be a part of whatever had you in such deep thought," he said when I was finished.

Would you? I wondered, and I went about getting everything together for our picnic.

"Did you really have a good time last night?" Kane asked when we were on our way to the lake at Foxworth.

"Oh, very much."

"Me, too."

I saw the way he kept looking at me. "What?"

"You seem . . . distant. You wanted to do this today, right?"

"Oh, yes, Kane. I'm sorry if I seem distant."

"Everything okay? I mean, I don't mean to be nosy, but . . ."

"Everything's fine. In fact, I'm excited. My uncle

Tommy's coming to visit us. He's my father's younger brother and lives in California. He'll be here only one night, but I'm so looking forward to it."

"That's nice. Tell me about him," he said, and I did. "Whoa. I hope you have that kind of enthusiasm if anyone asks you to tell them about me," he commented when I had finished.

"We'll see. You're a story that's just being started," I said, and he laughed.

Ahead of us loomed the trees that lined the Foxworth property. They seemed to be sentinels standing guard over the memories. Could my father really rip down all the destruction and rebuild an entirely new house, driving the ghosts away? I knew it was going to be a great deal more than what he called "putting lipstick on a pig." Whatever the design, the house would surely be totally different from Foxworth Hall. It would probably be something modern. And then there would be changes in the landscaping. Dad had already mentioned some things like a swimming pool, maybe a tennis court, and a much bigger driveway. No one who was old enough to remember the original Foxworth mansion or even the second one would think of it if they came to the new house.

"Any hints about what's going to be replacing Foxworth?" Kane asked, as if he could read my thoughts.

"My father's meeting with the architect and the owner today."

"I bet it will be spectacular."

"Yes," I said. "I hope it will."

We parked and gathered up our picnic stuff. He had a blanket. I couldn't help looking back at the cleaned-up foundation as I walked alongside Kane into the woods and to the lake. I was sure the Foxworth children had never been able to take this walk.

Dad was right. It was a beautiful day for a picnic, with just a slightly cool breeze coming off the water. The sky was a deep blue, making the puffy clouds look whiter. There seemed to be no wind at all up there to move them along. They looked pasted against the light blue background. Maybe they were asleep, I thought, and smiled to myself, recalling how I used to assign meanings to their different shapes. Some looked like animals, some like mountains and hills. Once I thought a dark cloud looked like a witch. Sometimes I would give one a name and be excited if I saw the same shape again. It was as if it was coming back just for me.

"Why are you smiling?" Kane asked.

"I was just thinking of something I used to do when I was little. I would give clouds names, identify them as things."

"I do that once in a while, even now," he said.

I smirked.

"I do," he insisted. "Even Kane Hill gets bored sometimes."

"I wasn't bored. I was imaginative," I said. "When you're young and alone, your imagination has no boundaries."

He looked at me oddly for a moment.

"What?"

"What I like about you is every time I'm with you, it's like unwrapping a surprise gift," he said. "How about over there?" He pointed to an open area not more than a dozen feet from the edge of the lake. "Looks flat enough."

"Okay."

He spread out the blanket, smoothed it down, and helped lay out our picnic lunch. "I have a confession to make," he said.

"What?"

"I've never been on a picnic. I've been on a safari in Africa, but that was like having a hotel moving around with us, and the tents were pretty elaborate. All the food was prepared for us, but we saw some incredible things and took great pictures."

"I haven't been on a picnic since . . . since I was very young."

He nodded and poured us both some apple juice out of the thermos. Then he took off his jacket, folded it, and laid it down for me to use as a pillow.

"Thanks," I said, and lay back.

"I didn't tell any of my friends I was doing this."

"Embarrassed?"

"No. Just want to start having some secrets," he said with that impish little smile of his.

"You can rest your head on me, if you want. I'm soft in some places."

"I'd say you're soft in all places," he said, shifting quickly to do it. We both stared up at the sky silently. I felt his hand reach for mine, and when he grasped it, I grasped his, too. "Can you feel it?" he asked.

"What?"

"The earth moving?"

I laughed and then thought about it. Was I imagining it? "I think I can. I never felt it or even thought about it until now."

"When you're with someone you really want to be with, like I am with you right now, everything you've seen before, every color, every shape, anything, really, looks different. Looks . . ."

"Looks what?"

"Brand new," he said.

I smiled and sat up again so I could lean toward him and run my fingers through his hair. He closed his eyes. "What happened?" I asked him.

He opened his eyes and looked at me quizzically. "Happened?"

"You and I have known each other a long time, but suddenly this."

He started to shrug and then stopped. "You changed," he said.

"What? I changed? Why? How?"

"Or I should say I changed."

"To what? From what?"

"From being frivolous to being . . . older, more serious. And when that happened to me, I wasn't just drawn to you by your good looks. You seemed to be there already. It was like you would understand," he said. I waited for him to say more, but he just shook his head. "I guess I'm not making any sense."

"You are. And I'm glad," I said.

He sat up, turned, and kissed me, softly but long. I

lay back, and he sprawled beside me. We kissed again. His lips were on my hair, my eyes, my cheeks, down to my neck.

I was kissing him, too, each kiss a little longer, a little more demanding.

"Kristin," he whispered. I was sure he could see the yes in my eyes, the yes that was echoing through every part of me.

Was I ready? Was it my time? I wondered. Could I feel this special with any other boy? Should I "cross the Rio Grande"? The resistance that was in me, which came from fear and from an uncertainty about what was right and what was wrong when you were with someone for whom you felt deep affection, was weakening. Perhaps he sensed that. He was moving quickly, finding his way under my clothes, touching me as if he were pushing invisible buttons on my body, softening it, molding it. My breathing quickened. I felt captured, but willingly. It was going to happen. I knew it, and I didn't resist, which only drove him to be more intense.

"I want you," he said. "So much."

Were those the magic words, the keys to the kingdom?

"Don't you want me, too?"

The yes in my body reached my lips, but just before I was going to utter it, I imagined I saw a teenage boy standing just a few feet away, looking down at us with an almost scientific detachment.

Christopher, I thought, would look at us this way, and my body tightened when the boy didn't avert his glance or even smile.

"I want to. I do, but I'm not ready yet," I whispered. "Please understand."

He paused, and I supposed the way I was looking past us caught his interest and attention. He turned fearfully, wondering if someone was there, perhaps even my father. I could feel the passion recede like an outgoing tide. He sat back, brushed back his hair, and took a breath. "I don't know if I can keep myself from being any different when I'm with you, Kristin," he said.

"That's not a bad thing," I whispered. "If we give it time."

He nodded and smiled. "Well, no harm done," he said, working on as quick a recovery as he could make. "It's made me ravenous in another way. I'm starving." He turned on his iPod and Bluetooth speaker. He looked in the direction I had been looking again. "Did you see something that frightened you?"

"No," I said quickly, sat up, and began to unwrap our sandwiches.

"Thought you might have seen one of those famous Dollanganger ghosts," he joked.

I looked at him. "What if I did? Would you want us to leave?"

"Not if you weren't afraid," he replied. "Whatever you wanted to do, I would do," he added.

Would he? Did passion and affection bring trust along? I wondered. Was I willing to risk it to find out? He saw how deeply I was thinking.

"What?"

I looked up at him. Not yet, I told myself. It wasn't just me.

It was Christopher, too, that I was risking.

I shook my head and handed him his sandwich. He narrowed his eyes for a moment and then smiled and looked out at the water.

This was still a special place, I thought, maybe especially for me.

After we ate, we walked around the lake and talked, both of us revealing more and more of ourselves. Once in a while, we stopped and kissed. As we came around to our blanket, he asked me again if my family knew what really had happened here when the children were imprisoned.

"No, I don't think so," I said. "At least, not yet."

He smiled quizzically but seemed to understand, to know not to ask any other questions about Foxworth.

Afterward, we drove for a while aimlessly. It was as if we both wanted to prolong the day. At my house, I saw that my father wasn't home yet, but I didn't invite Kane in.

Someone else was waiting upstairs in my room. I even imagined him looking out from between the curtains. He knew where I had been.

I thought I might be able to get in a dozen pages before my father came home.

For a while, I thought we no longer could keep track of time. Days floated into each other as if the clock had become gigantic, and seconds and minutes were so small they were no longer noticed. The leaves were changing to the yellows, browns, and reds that told us fall was here. It seemed to happen overnight. Never before had that had such a stunning effect on the four of us, more so on Cathy than on the twins and me.

"We've been here two months!" she whispered, mostly to herself, as we stood by the window. "Two months!"

I could feel the tension building in her and knew that if I didn't do something, say something, immediately, she might burst into hysterical screaming. I had to keep her busy, I thought, get her distracted.

Suddenly, she laughed. Cory and Carrie looked at her, confused, and then at me. What was so funny?

"What?" I asked.

"I used to think being in history class was boring, but I would sure like to be there being bored now." She fixed her eyes on me. They looked like they were ready to launch darts.

"I understand," I said. "What we have to do is stop wasting time."

"Stop wasting time? What do you think we've been doing? What do you call all this?" she cried, raising her voice a little more. She was on the verge, I thought. I had to think.

"I meant we should be preparing ourselves for when we get out of here."

"Get out of here?"

"Sure. Look, tomorrow I'm adding a barre to the area we've decorated. You'll start practicing your ballet again. Daily," I insisted.

"I will not. I'll look like a fool if I practice without a costume, dancing in an attic."

"'Look like a fool'? To whom? That's stupid."

"Stupid. I'm stupid? Of course I'm stupid. You're the one who was born with all the brains in this family. You're the genius."

"Cathy?"

"No!" she screamed, and ran out of the attic and down the stairs.

The twins were shocked, and Carrie started to cry.

"Cathy sick?" Cory said.

"No, no. No one's sick," I told them. "C'mon, let's go cheer her up."

I held out my hands, and they took them and followed me. I saw how frightened they were. We were so close to breaking, shattering like frozen Dresden dolls, I thought. Downstairs, Cathy was facedown on the bed, sobbing.

"Let's give her something to make her happy again," Cory said. She heard him but didn't stop her sobs. Cory poked her, and she turned to look at him. "Here, Cathy," he said, and handed her his Peter Rabbit storybook. "You don't have to read it to me," he added.

She stopped sobbing. Carrie handed her

crayons to her. Cathy took them and looked at me. I sat on the bed and watched her sew up the rips in her heart. She wiped away her tears and embraced our brother and sister.

"I'm okay," she said. "I'll be all right. Thank you, Cory. Thank you, Carrie."

She kissed them and smiled, and they turned to occupy themselves with other toys and books. I waited for a moment and then reached for her, and she took my hand.

"It's going to be all right," I said. "I promise."

She nodded. She was quiet again, but she didn't believe me, and despite all I could do to convince myself, I wasn't confident about it, either.

I heard my father enter the house, and I closed the diary and shoved it under my pillow. When I looked at myself in the mirror, I saw that I had been crying. How odd, I thought. I didn't even realize it. It was almost like . . . almost like anything Cathy did now, any feeling she had, I did and felt, too. I felt possessed.

When I heard my father's footsteps on the stairs, I rushed into the bathroom and washed my face. He knocked on my open bedroom door.

"Hey," he said when I stepped out of the bathroom. "How was your picnic?"

"It was fun, and you were right. It was a perfect day for it. Is the new owner going to do something about the lake, clean it up, fix the dock? It's so beautiful, but it could be even more beautiful."

"All of the above," my father said. "This is going to be the biggest project I've ever done. We'll be doubling the help. I'll have an architect's rendition to show you in about two weeks. I'll get cleaned up and then think about dinner. You don't have a date, do you?"

"No, you have my full attention," I said.

He tilted his head. "Oh?"

"It's fine, Dad. We had a good time. I told him I wanted to get all my homework done tonight so I can spend more time with Uncle Tommy and you."

He nodded. "It's pretty soon to be telling him what he can and can't do, isn't it?"

"It's never too soon to tell a man what he can and can't do," I said, and he looked like he was having the best laugh of the day, even the week.

As always, I set the table and helped with anything he let me do when he made a dinner for us. I thought he was going to grill me about my growing relationship with Kane, but he didn't ask a single question. Instead, he talked about his new project. I could see that this one excited him more than anything else he had done, and not simply because it was the most expensive and largest residence he had ever worked on. He liked the owner and the architect. While we ate, he described the new mansion in detail, pointing out what he thought was brilliant about the design.

"They were very educated about the views up there," he said. "They want to create some water effects, too. You know, little ponds and fountains and a Pebble Tec pool with a hot tub. I love the suggestion for the outside tile, and oh, the landscaping they're planning, fantastic. It creates this almost magical approach to the property. Not simply straight in but curved, with hedges and interesting lighting. There'll be nothing like it around here." He leaned toward me. "Kane's father is going to be quite jealous."

"More like his mother might be, from what I understand."

"Yeah, sure," he said. Ever since my mother died, he seemed always to try to avoid referring to the mothers of kids my age.

"You're like a little boy with a new Lego set," I told him. "I guess it's true."

"What's true?"

"Men turn everything into toys."

He stared at me for a moment and then smiled. "Your mother used to accuse me of that," he said. "I guess as long as I have you, I'll have her."

"Then you always will," I said.

"Right. Like you're not going off to college, where you'll meet your Prince Charming and move to some other state or continent."

He was joking, but I sensed that this was a real fear for him. Was that true for the fathers of all daughters, or was it especially true for mine? I couldn't imagine not missing him as much as he would miss me, although he was convinced that whoever I fell in love with would replace him.

I had read through the part of the diary about Christopher Sr.'s death so quickly that I really didn't digest how traumatic it must have been for Cathy. Reading between the lines Christopher Jr. wrote, it seemed to me she obviously was fonder of her father than of her mother. It was natural for her to be angry at the world because of her father's death alone, but afterward, to be imprisoned in the home of grandparents who didn't want her, who didn't even want her to exist, had to sharpen her rage. Christopher hadn't said it yet, but I was sure that deep in his heart of hearts, he was terribly disappointed in their mother for being so oblivious to their economic condition after the death of their father and for putting them where they were now.

I cleaned up the dinner dishes and pots and pans and then went up to do my homework. Every once in a while, I paused and looked at the diary. Was I rushing my work so I could get back to it? If my grades suffered because of the diary, my father would have another reason to criticize me for reading it, I thought, and I tried hard to concentrate on my math, science, and history assignments. By the time I finished, it was late. My father had already stopped by to say good night.

Nevertheless, after I prepared for bed, I slipped the diary out from under the pillow, promising myself I would read only a few pages. There was another way I was getting to be like the Dollanganger children, I thought. I was lying to myself when I told myself I could limit what I read, even for an hour, as long as I was in the same room with this diary. It had become a magical door through which I passed to enter the Foxworth attic.

Cathy had no idea I had done it, but one afternoon soon after, when Momma was about to leave, I slipped her a note: "Momma, you have to do me a great favor. You have to get Cathy her ballet costumes, the leotards, toe shoes, and matching tutus. Quickly."

She read the note and looked at me. She understood what I meant, how close Cathy was to breaking and how difficult that would make our continuing to cooperate with her efforts to win back her father's approval. The next time she came, she had the box. She had cleverly slipped in a card with the words "From Christopher" on it.

I was right about the change it would bring. I put up the barre, and Cathy went at her ballet practice, reviving all she had been taught. The twins would sit and watch her for hours, fascinated with her exercises. I had to admit that I had never realized just how graceful and beautiful Cathy was until I saw her dancing in the attic. How ironic. It took this dreadful situation to get me really to look at her and think of her as being on the verge of some greatness. She was blossoming right before my eyes.

Once she caught me watching her as intently as the twins were, and she suddenly turned and floated across the floor. That's the way it seemed. She wanted me to dance with her. I thought I would escape by saying I was interested only in the waltz, but she found the right records and had me out there. I protested about my own clumsiness, but I had become a project for her. She would teach me every dance she could, even rock and roll.

"It's not me," I told her. "I can't be someone I'm not."

I saw how disappointed she was, but I couldn't, even up here. I distracted her by suggesting that we work on our attic garden and change the leaves we had created to fall leaves. The twins were into it, and we spent hours changing the season as if we had become nature itself and just as powerful. Poof, there was yellow and brown and red, just like right outside the mansion.

For a while, I had managed to keep them all content again. The whining and complaints were fewer and fewer. I knew that as long as Cathy was with me, helping, managing the twins, we could last until Momma succeeded. But I also knew that Cathy craved relationships. She needed friends far more than I did. She was naturally full of questions and plans, dreams and fantasies. Ordinarily, I would ignore all that. I hated pretending, but it was clear she desperately needed it. So for hours at a time, I would lie beside her on our crummy mattress and talk about our futures. Somehow the conversation always ended up on the topic of who would be the right man for her and the right woman for me.

It was clear from these conversations that Cathy did not respect our mother anymore. She accused of her being stupid and selfish, and I had to defend her continually. I could see that no matter what I said, Cathy held on to her feelings. She was still raging inside, her anger only taking a short nap and ready to leap up at a moment's notice.

Even though we were in a sort of limbo, which I feared because I could see the twins losing interest in so many things like even getting outside, I realized we were slipping into a darker and darker place. The withering of the real flowers frightened me, because I dreamed of us withering, too. Cathy sensed it. It was more her idea than mine for us to drag one of the old mattresses to the eastern windows so we could bathe in some sunlight. "Don't all living things need it?" she asked. I didn't want to mention those creatures that lived in total darkness, because she would say that was exactly what we were becoming. Instead, I dragged the mattress there.

Cathy asked me if it wouldn't be better for us to lie naked in the sunlight, "so more of our bodies benefit." We were never afraid of being naked in front of each other, but we were older now, changes coming faster than even I anticipated. I didn't want to get into all that, so I agreed, and we all got naked.

I tried not to look at the changes in Cathy's body, her thickening pubic hair, her budding breasts, the curve in her buttocks and the smoothness of her legs, some of the muscularity and shape coming from her dedicated ballet practice. She was looking at me now, too, but I resisted bringing my hands down to cover myself. I was afraid of that part of me acting on its own.

Suddenly, the twins were asking me questions about our sexual differences. Never was Cathy more interested in my clumsy attempts to make it all seem inconsequential. She wanted to know more about the male sexual experience, and I tried to change the subject, but I could see this was only the beginning.

Momma, I thought, please get us out of here soon.

I had more trouble than ever trying to fall asleep after reading this. The interest Cathy had in sex mirrored my own. I was closer than ever to realizing it fully with Kane. I would be lying if I said I hadn't fantasized about it repeatedly during the last few weeks, especially now.

In a dream, I saw myself lying in the Foxworth attic, but instead of being naked next to Christopher, I was lying beside Kane. In this dream, we had decided to do that and see how long we could resist touching each other. We were both closing our eyes, but I was sure his heart was pounding as hard and fast as mine. Every once in a while, one of us would open our eyes and look at the other. Finally, we did so at the same time. He smiled.

"Kristin," he whispered, and began by reaching for my hand. I gave him mine, and we held each other for a long moment. He turned toward me, and I turned toward him. He edged closer, and we kissed, only our lips touching. We both pulled back. "I'm dying inside," he whispered.

"Don't die," I said, and he smiled and moved closer now, his legs against mine, his stomach touching mine, his lips grazing softly over my face, my neck, and my breasts. I could feel his growing excitement building between my legs, legs that were relaxing too quickly. The woman inside me was pushing to be fulfilled. I was growing more helpless, but it was a helplessness I welcomed. "Oh, Kane, we've got to be careful," I said.

"I know. I'm ready," he said. He was prepared. My last reason to resist dropped away. I was welcoming him, drawing him into me. We were sealing our lips together, clinging to each other as if we were afraid we would fall off the earth.

I think I actually cried out in my sleep. I awoke with my heart pounding and listened for a moment, anticipating my father coming to see what was wrong. A door opened and closed, but then the house was silent. I probably had imagined it, I told myself, and relaxed again. I was almost afraid to close my eyes. My body was like a bow pulled back, ready to be released. It was a struggle, but somehow sleep finally seeped in, slipping under my lids and soaking me in a repose so deep it took more than a splash or two of sunlight coming through my windows to waken me.

Since I had the day off from school because of teacher meetings, my father didn't come to the door, but I knew he was up already, working on breakfast downstairs. I could hear him moving about. I thought a moment, remembered that Uncle Tommy was coming today, and got up quickly to dress and get downstairs.

"I think when girls get older, they sleep longer in the morning," my father said as he scrambled eggs. No one made them tastier. He turned to me. "Is that because they have longer dreams or what?"

"It's 'or what,'" I said, and he laughed.

I looked at the table. There were three settings.

"Who else is coming to breakfast?"

"Tommy called. He should be here any moment. He surprised us. He flew in last night, stayed at the airport hotel, and got up early. I think he just wants a good breakfast for a change," my father said.

"You were always a cook, weren't you, Dad?"

"My father couldn't get over it. He was an old-fashioned guy. I did all the manly things he expected me to do, worked with him, fixed things around the house, joined different sports teams, whatever he had done at my age, but I did enjoy being in the kitchen with my mother. She had a lot of little tricks passed down to her, and I never forgot them. You're really going to be eating your grandmother's eggs today," he said.

The doorbell sounded. I practically flew to answer it.

"I must be at the wrong house," Uncle Tommy said when I opened the door. "The Kristin Masterwood I remember was an ugly duckling." He laughed and scooped me up in his arms.

"Hi, Uncle Tommy!" I cried after he kissed my cheek and I kissed his.

He stepped back and shook his head. Then he looked at me and shook his head again.

"What?"

"I'm surprised there isn't a line of boys waiting at this door."

"Stop blowin' her up," Dad said behind me. "This isn't one of your Hollywood gigs."

They hugged, and Uncle Tommy nodded at me. "I'm not exaggerating much, Burt, and something tells me she's got your levelheadedness when it comes to her ego." He stepped back and looked at him. "You, on the other hand, haven't changed much." He turned back to me. "I always thought your father was a tough old geezer, despite being only three years older than me."

"You haven't changed much, either, Dandy Man, although I see some strands of gray sneaking in."

Uncle Tommy had a wavy head of dark brown hair, neatly styled. I would never say he was better-looking than my father, but he did have an impish twinkle in his hazel eyes that probably titillated most of the women he pursued. He was slimmer and an inch or so taller. My father always said Uncle Tommy took after their mother more, which was lucky for him. He was always a stylish dresser, always coordinating his shirts, pants, shoes, and socks as though he expected to be photographed, even when he first got up in the morning. Today he just wore a light blue sweater and a white shirt with a pair of dark blue slacks and black loafers.

Suddenly, like a magician, he produced a small box in pink gift wrap.

"Found this on the plane last night," he said, handing it to me, "and thought it might be something you'd like."

"What?" I took it gingerly. "Found it?"

"Where's your bag?" Dad asked him.

"In the car. I'll get it later. I'm starving. You know how that food on the plane can be."

"Never ate it," Dad said.

He was watching me tear off the gift wrap and open the small box. There was a gold necklace in it with a pendant that had a ruby at the center and tiny rubies surrounding it.

"I remembered you liked rubies," my uncle said. "I hope."

"It's beautiful, Uncle Tommy. Thank you," I said, and hugged him.

I looked at Dad. We both knew I liked rubies because they were my mother's favorite. I was fighting back tears of happiness. They both could see it.

"When do we eat?" Uncle Tommy asked.

"Right now. Go on and wash up," Dad ordered. He was always the big brother.

Uncle Tommy laughed and headed to the bathroom. I followed my father into the kitchen. He paused to watch me struggle to get the necklace on.

"Here," he said, and took control, mumbling under his breath. "Found it on a plane. Once a story-teller, always a storyteller."

I retreated to the hallway and glanced at myself in the wall mirror near the front door. Then I hurried back to the kitchen when Uncle Tommy entered.

"Thank you so much, Uncle Tommy. It's beautiful."

"Now it is. It's on you," he said, and sat down at the table. "So tell me everything. How's school? How many boyfriends do you have? How much of a nag is my brother?"

"Not as much as I'm gonna be now that you're here," Dad said, and they both laughed.

I helped serve the toast, eggs, and bacon and poured Uncle Tommy his cup of coffee.

"Ma's recipe, for sure," Uncle Tommy said when he took his first forkful of eggs. "She was cooking for me right up to her last day on this earth," he told me.

"And who's cooking for you now?" Dad asked. "Certainly not you."

"I have some . . . domestic help," he replied, and gave an impish smile.

"I bet."

It was the best breakfast we'd had for a very long time, not because I didn't enjoy having breakfast with just my father but because I could sit back and be an audience as they reminisced about their parents, growing up together, and things they had done that had brought my grandparents both joy and consternation.

"Don't ever let your father convince you that he was an angel just because he was older than me," Uncle Tommy said.

"With you in the house, even Jack the Ripper would look like an angel," Dad said, and began to tell more stories about pranks Uncle Tommy had committed and how many times he had had to save him from getting into real trouble.

They were both into it so much that neither noticed me clearing the table and washing the dishes. I smiled to myself. It was rare that I felt so much attachment to my family. I noticed how they both tiptoed around any references to my mother, but it was impossible not to talk about her.

"I think I miss her more than you do," Uncle Tommy told my father. "She was the one who could make me feel guilty about being irresponsible."

"She could," Dad confirmed. "And you were and probably still are."

They were quiet a moment, and then Uncle Tommy said what my father often said after he took a long look at me. "She's getting to look more and more like her, Burt."

"I know."

"What a lucky break. She could have ended up with your mug."

"She could have," Dad said. "Get your bag, and get settled in the guest room," he told him. "I'll take you for a ride and show you the site of my newest project."

I looked up sharply. He was going to take Uncle Tommy to Foxworth?

"Yeah, you mentioned something about that on the phone. Sounds really big."

"It is."

"Okay. The princess is coming along, isn't she?" he asked, looking at me. I looked at Dad.

"No way you or I could stop her," Dad said. He looked around and saw what I had done in the kitchen while they had been talking. "Nice job," he said. "I just have a call to make, Tommy."

"Great. I'll unpack what I need and be ready."

He went out to his car and returned with his bag. Then he followed me up to go to the guest room.

"How's he been?" he asked when we were far enough away for my father not to hear.

"He keeps very busy," I said. "He's all right. I wish he would relax more, get out more, but . . ."

"But he's who he is. And you? Happy?"

"Yes, Uncle Tommy, and more so because you're visiting," I told him.

He hugged me, and I went to my room to change my shoes and put on something a little warmer. It was more overcast today, and the breeze coming out of the north suggested that our short Indian summer was, as my father would say, having heart failure. I was down and ready before both of them, which I knew didn't surprise my father.

We all squeezed into Black Beauty.

"I can't believe you still have this truck, Burt. I was going to call you because something like it was needed on a movie set. If it was a horse," he told me, "your father would have had it out to stud with a female truck to create another."

"Very funny. The only thing you've kept is your goofy sense of humor."

"Selling big right now."

"Which is why I never go to the movies," Dad countered.

I didn't think I could be more comfortable than

sitting between them, I thought, and wished we could all be together more, but my father never wanted to make the trip to California. He kidded Uncle Tommy by telling him it was like leaving the country.

They teased each other all the way up to Foxworth, and then Dad began to explain the project and why it was going to be the biggest construction job he had ever had. When we pulled up to the cleared-out area, I watched Uncle Tommy's reaction.

"Wow. You'd never know what it had been," he said. He turned to me. "I was here once or twice when you were a little girl, a very little girl."

We got out of the truck, and I followed Dad and Uncle Tommy as we walked around the site, with Dad pausing to describe what was going to be built. Of course, he spoke in much greater detail than Uncle Tommy needed in order to understand what was going to replace the second Foxworth mansion, but Uncle Tommy didn't complain. He kept his soft, loving smile, glancing at me with that twinkle in his eyes occasionally. The truth was, I was listening harder to my father's descriptions than my uncle was. One thing I picked up on was that there was not going to be an attic. There would be the usually necessary crawl spaces for utilities but nothing like what had been there before.

"There are other, smaller buildings for storage facilities and equipment," Dad continued, and then he began to lay out the general plan for the landscaping, pool, tennis court, and gardens.

"One of your Hollywood rich guys is going to hear about this and come out to see it and make an offer on it, for sure, not that the new owner is going to want to sell. Even if they make him an offer he can't refuse."

Uncle Tommy laughed and then leaned in to me to whisper, "I never saw him as excited about anything."

Afterward, Dad drove us around to show Uncle Tommy some of the other changes in the immediate area. Again, he had a high note of pride in his voice. I didn't think I had realized before just how much my father loved where we lived. Once in a while, as we rode along and he bragged to Uncle Tommy about things, he would mention my mother and how surprised and pleased she would be. He had to show Uncle Tommy my school and then, of course, his office building.

I knew that despite how much fun he made of what Uncle Tommy did and where he lived, Dad was proud of him, too, and wanted to show him off. We went to Charley's Diner, where he knew some of his buddies would be, and he introduced Uncle Tommy to those who had never met him.

"I gotta tell you," Uncle Tommy said when we finally got into a booth to order lunch, "there really are many countries in this country. Your father's not wrong. However, I think I'll stay where I am."

"You couldn't be approved for citizenship here, anyway," Dad told him, and they went on to talk about their grandparents and stories they'd been told.

When we returned home, Uncle Tommy had to make a few phone calls. I went to my room and put some finishing touches on my homework, read a few chapters of history, and then relaxed. Uncle Tommy was taking us out to dinner. I thought he would just go down to watch some television with my father, but instead, he knocked on my bedroom door.

"Hey," he said. "Busy?"

I put down my history book. "No, just tinkering," I said.

He came in and looked around my room. "I thought teenagers were supposed to be messy."

"Not with a father who was in the navy," I said, and he laughed.

"Don't let him fool you. He was like that before he entered the navy." He sat at the foot of my bed. "So my brother says you've been reading some sort of diary discovered at the Foxworth foundation."

"Christopher's diary, yes."

"Christopher? One of the children who was locked up in the house for years?"

"Yes. What's Dad been telling you about it?"

"He's worried you're getting too involved in some very messy things, terrible things done to children who were betrayed by people who should have loved and protected them. I told him you were too smart to be harmed by such stories and that worse things were being made and shown on the screen these days, but he's feeling like . . . well, things are tougher, because there's only him, and he's always worried he's not doing what a parent should do."

"It's not going to hurt me to read someone's diary, Uncle Tommy, even someone who was imprisoned with his brother and sisters. I want to understand what happened, and not only because they were distant cousins of my mother and me."

He nodded. "I can't blame you for being curious."

I didn't want to tell him that it had gone way beyond curiosity. Then he would worry along with my father.

"It was always a fascinating tale for people here," he added.

"You once spoke with someone who knew more about what really happened there, didn't you?"

"Someone who wanted to pitch it to Hollywood. He said he knew the truth, but you have to remember that it was third-hand information. I don't doubt there were some pretty nutty people living in that original mansion, cruel, in fact, but what actually did happen has been so distorted and exaggerated it's beyond reality, probably. What's the diary like?"

"I think it's honest. I'm only about halfway through it. It's like taking bitter medicine sometimes. But I can handle it," I added firmly.

He nodded. "I'm sure it is."

"What do you really know?"

"Really know? I wouldn't say I really know anything. As I said, I was told some things by . . ."

"Someone who was friendly with a servant. Dad told me that."

"Oh, he did. Well, what we can be sure of was that the kids were kept up there for years," he added. "That's true. Whether someone deliberately was poisoning them or they just happened to ingest some rat poison is unknown. The only thing I can tell you is that this servant came to believe that their grandmother had told their grandfather that they were there, and he had insisted on their being kept locked away. This servant did not like their mother at all and believed she went along with everything knowing those kids would not be freed so easily. But that's just this man's opinion about it. I guess the point is, what difference does it make now, Kristin? Actually, don't you have better things to read?"

"No," I said firmly. "I need to read this to the end."

He nodded. "Okay. But don't ask him any more questions about it. He feels like he . . ."

"Would be betraying my mother, who never wanted to talk about it?"

"Exactly."

I looked away. "Somehow I believe she would want me to read it, but it would probably have been our secret."

He stood up, smiling. "Maybe. Everyone has a few. Look, if you get confused or too deep into it and need to talk to someone, call me. Will you?"

"Sure," I said.

"Who knows? Maybe there *is* a movie in it." He held up his hands instantly. "Just kidding. Although kidnapping people and holding them hostage for some reason is always a Hollywood possibility."

"I'm sure Christopher didn't write his diary for that purpose," I said. "Do you know if he's still alive or where he would be today?"

"No," he said quickly.

"Could you find out for me? Ask a detective to locate him?"

"I live in the make-believe world, Kristin. The only detectives I know are Philip Marlowe and Sam Spade. Get a crush on some boy, and forget about all that," he advised. "That's what I do whenever I confront something unpleasant. I fall in love . . . for five minutes," he added, and laughed. Then he hugged me. "Let's have a great dinner and work on getting your father to let you come see me in Hollywood."

"That," I said, "frightens him the most."

He laughed and kissed me again and went out.

I stood there in silence for a moment, and then I whispered, "Don't worry, Christopher, I won't leave you." Almost the way someone would swear on a Bible, I had to touch the diary after saying that, and then I went to shower and dress for dinner.

Nothing was mentioned about Foxworth or the diary after that. Uncle Tommy worked on getting my father to let me go to Hollywood during one of my school vacations. I could see how hard it was for Dad to be apart from me for even a short time. He had been just like this when I had gone to visit Aunt Barbara. I dreaded how terribly traumatic it would be for both of us when it came time for me to leave for college.

Reluctantly, though, he promised to think about it. He even vaguely suggested that he might go, too. The rest of the evening was given over to their memories and talking about Aunt Barbara. Plans were vaguely made for a real get-together in the near future, maybe to celebrate Aunt Barbara's next birthday. Dad said he would relent and go to New York for that, and Uncle Tommy often traveled to New York on business.

I had driven us to the restaurant and drove us home. Both of them had had a bit to drink, and I thought they were funny, especially my father, who was fighting not to appear even slightly drunk. He didn't have to tell me—I knew he was like this only because he was with his brother and they had not seen each other for so long. The love they had for each other was palpable. At times, it brought tears to my eyes. I could only imagine my mother sitting there beside me, smiling.

Breakfast was quick the following morning. I had to get to school, and Uncle Tommy was off to make a flight. All three of us refused to say good-bye. It was reduced to a simple "See you soon."

Kisses and hugs, Uncle Tommy's whispers of how proud of me he was, and his offer always to be there for me followed me out to my car and traveled with me all the way to school. I tried to keep my tears buried under my eyelids, but some escaped. I sat in my car in the parking lot to catch my breath and get my eyes to look less bloodshot. Kane saw me and lifted his hands to ask why I was just sitting there. I got out and went to him quickly.

"What?" he said.

"Nothing. Just hold my hand for as long as you can."

"Ask me something hard to do," he said, and we walked into the school.

I did my best to concentrate on my work and participate in conversations with Kane and my girlfriends, but anyone probably could see that I was preoccupied.

I knew that the mood in our home would be darker when I returned from school, but my father did everything he could to push it away. He made his special meat loaf for us and talked incessantly about the job. It was smart. Get busy, I thought. Get so busy you don't realize why you were even sad for a while. And then push back into hope and dreams as soon as you can.

I did.

And I didn't even read any more of Christopher's diary until the following night, when my father had gone to bed and I had done all my homework, spoken to Kane, and gotten under my blanket. Then I reached back for the diary and whispered, "I'm still here, Christopher. Still listening."

Fall came rushing down around us, a cold season unlike any I could remember, perhaps because we were trapped in such a cold place. Without a stove or even an electric heater in the attic, we could sometimes see our own breath. Momma was afraid of bringing an electric heater, afraid of fires, and there was no way to have a stove without a chimney. Her solution was to bring us heavy underwear.

It was getting more difficult to find new ways to amuse the twins. I came up with hide-and-

seek, and that became our main distraction. The
attic actually provided many hiding places. The
twins loved the game, but one day, Carrie became
bored and despondent. She could be very moody,
and she just decided to go back down to the
small bedroom. When all of us were in it, it was
claustrophobic. We needed the attic.

After she left, we called to Cory. We wanted
to end the game, but he didn't come out, and we
couldn't find him. At first, I thought it was funny.
My little brother had outsmarted us. But gradually,
I began to get more frightened. He wasn't capable
of holding out this long. He wouldn't stay in the
game without Carrie, anyway. I came up with a
frightening possibility. He must have gone into
one of the trunks and the lid got stuck.

I called for Carrie, and she came back up to
the attic. In a frenzy, we began opening trunks,
and I finally found him locked in one. He was
blue from lack of oxygen and ice-cold. My heart
pounded with the possibility that he would die
right there and then. I remembered what to do
and got him into a warm bath quickly. Gradually,
he became more and more conscious. I felt like I
was resurrecting him. Once he realized what had
happened, he began to cry for Momma, just the
way any child would. Cathy looked at me. Now
I was the one who was desperate. I couldn't get
Momma for him.

And then my sister suddenly, instantly matured
in my eyes. "I'll be your momma," she told Cory.

He clung to her, accepted her, as she sang "Rock-a-bye Baby" to him just the way Momma used to sing it. I saw the calmness return to his face. As I watched them, I felt a great longing inside me, something I had not felt for a long time, a longing for family, for love, and for protection.

I sat in the rocker, and the others joined me. I held them close. Cathy rested her head against my shoulder, and the twins clung to each other and to me.

"We'll be fine," I whispered. "Our time will come." I recited from Ecclesiastes: "There is a time for everything and a season for every activity under the heavens."

"For us, too?" Cathy asked.

"Yes. We'll put in our sacrifice. We'll get through this, and then we'll live and enjoy a bountiful life, full of all the things we dreamed of having."

I rocked on.

The twins were asleep.

Cathy closed her eyes, and before she dozed off, she whispered, "But we have to wait for an old man to die. We have to wish for it."

Of course, she was right. It seemed wrong, but as I caught the reflection of the four of us clinging to one another, I thought it wasn't wrong to want someone as dark and hateful as him to die.

I put the diary away and went to sleep wishing that the old man would die soon, too. It was really the first time I had wished anyone any harm. It frightened me a little. Was my reading of the diary turning me into someone I didn't want to be? Were my father's fears justified?

I knew I was becoming as moody as Cathy in the diary. I couldn't help it. Every time there was a lull in classwork or I was alone, even for a minute or so, the vision of those children shivering, clinging to one another, withering away like the flowers they were given, would return. I felt so frustrated for them.

Of course, my friends had no idea that I had a black cloud hovering over me. The problem for me was the contrast between feeling the pain in the diary and seeing my lucky classmates giggling over the silliest things, arguing over trifles, and growing impatient with me because I didn't laugh at the things they thought were funny and I didn't have the same excitement about the fun they were expecting on weekends.

No one was more tuned in to my growing depression than Kane. Even so, for days, he tried to ignore it, telling jokes, and then one day, he surprised me with a ring to match the ruby necklace Uncle Tommy had bought me. I had told him how Uncle Tommy had presented it.

"Found this on the sidewalk," he said when we had a few moments together at lunch.

"Oh, Kane." He watched me as I unwrapped it.

I couldn't help it. As soon as I saw what it was, I started to cry, and I cried so hard I had to jump up and run to the bathroom. Lana and Suzette came after me.

I was sitting on the toilet in a stall and sobbing as I looked at the ring in my palm.

"What's going on?" Lana asked. She tapped on the door. "Kane is in shock. He thinks he did something terrible."

I bit on my lower lip and tried to swallow back my tears before I dabbed my face with tissues and opened the stall door. The two of them stood back as if they thought I might explode or something.

"What happened?" Suzette asked.

Of course, I would never tell them why I was crying. I wasn't completely sure of the reason myself, but I opened my palm and showed them the ring.

"That's beautiful," Lana said. "Why did you get so hysterical?"

"My uncle Tommy bought me this," I said, lifting the necklace. "It was my mother's favorite jewel. Kane bought the ring to match."

They both stared at me.

"So?" Suzette finally said, after looking at Lana.

"It's hard to explain. I don't have very much family," I added.

That seemed to satisfy them. They both moved forward to hug me, and for a few moments, the three of us just stood there clinging to one another.

Maybe we were all shut away in some sort of attic, I thought. Maybe we were all terribly alone at times.

"Thanks," I told them. "I'd better get back and thank him."

"He might have committed suicide by now," Lana joked.

"I doubt it," Suzette said. "He's not the type. He'd just say, 'Next,' and move on to someone else."

"How do you know?" I asked her. "I wouldn't bet on it."

Their eyes widened.

"You didn't cross the Rio Grande?" Lana asked. "Did you?"

"Only my hairdresser knows," I said.

"What?" Suzette asked.

I laughed. "My dad has this book about old commercials and advertisements, and that was a line in one selling hair color, but it got to mean more, if you get my drift."

"Drift? Did you sleep with him or didn't you?" Suzette demanded.

"Figure it out," I said, and started to leave.

They both were stunned, I was sure. They caught up before I reached the cafeteria.

"You'd better tell us," Lana warned. "We're your best friends."

I just smiled at them and hurried to join Kane, who still did look shocked.

"Sorry," I said, sitting beside him. "Help me put it on." He slipped the ring onto my finger. "Thank you. It's beautiful, Kane." And then I kissed him, but not quickly and not like you would kiss a relative. I could hear the conversations around us pause.

He smiled.

Neither of us said anything else. We ate and talked to our friends. For me, it was like coming up out of the cold, dark, deep water for a little while. But it wasn't long before I was thinking about poor Cathy. She probably never got to experience this sincere feeling. Even after she got out of that attic.

Later that day, just before dinner, I showed my father what Kane had given me. I could see how surprised he was, and impressed.

"First ring I gave your mother was out of a Cracker Jack box. It was a joke, but she kept it a long time. Might still be in a drawer."

"It's what it says, not what it is," I told him, and his eyes widened.

"Your mother wouldn't have said it any differently."

I looked away quickly. No tears, not tonight, I told myself.

Dad was working very late every day now, so I prepared our dinners. Twice during the week, however, he had to have dinner with the owner and the architect. He wanted me to come along, but I told him I had to do my homework and not to worry, because I didn't mind eating alone. The second night, however, I asked him if I could invite Kane.

"Sure," he said. "Used to be that you could win a man over through his stomach, but it looks like you've done it already."

"Never hurts to be sure," I told him.

He laughed, but I could feel the hesitation in the laugh and in his voice. I imagined that it seemed to him like Kane and I were moving too quickly in our relationship, and although he probably wouldn't ask, he had to be wondering just how far had we gone.

These days, if you were with the same boy for two dates, it was assumed you had had sex. I wasn't going to tell anyone, especially my girlfriends, but I was impressed at how Kane wasn't demanding. At first, I had told myself that he really respected me, but lately, I was telling myself he had deeper feelings for me than he had ever had for other girls he had dated, and that was the real reason for his patience. Nevertheless, a part of me remained suspicious. I couldn't help feeling that Kane was much more sophisticated than I was when it came to sex. He was very bright and very perceptive, but then I reminded myself that he wasn't conniving, devious, or sly. At least, he wasn't to me.·

He came over right after school and watched me prepare a vegetarian lasagna. He sat in the kitchen, entranced, as if I were doing an amazing chemistry experiment.

"I don't think — in fact, I know my mother can't do what you're doing," he said.

"I'm sure she could if she wanted to."

"I'm not."

"Maybe I should have said if she had to."

"Maybe."

I paused and looked at him sitting there with admiration so clear in his face. He smiled softly, his eyes warm and loving. "My girlfriends think you're going to break my heart," I said.

"Hand me that knife."

"Why?"

"I'll sign a pledge in blood."

I couldn't help but laugh. He rose and came over to kiss me and then brushed back my hair.

"I really like you, Kristin. I've never liked any girl this much. I want to say 'love,' but I'm afraid you'll doubt me."

"Say it anyway," I told him.

He widened his smile. "Kristin Masterwood, I, Kane Hill, declare that I love you. When I'm away from you, I think so hard about you I forget what I'm doing. I don't hear anyone talking to me. When I close my eyes, I see you. You're with me when I'm asleep, and you're the first thing I think about when I wake up. If I could skip everything between now and the day I could marry you and care for you, I would do it."

We kissed.

"Let me finish making dinner," I said softly. His words had taken away my breath. I could barely do more than whisper. Every part of my body he had touched was tingling with anticipation of his lips and fingers caressing me lovingly again. He nodded and stepped back.

"I'll go up to your room and start some homework and leave you alone so you won't be distracted. I'm gonna be very hungry."

"You'd better be," I said.

He walked out slowly, paused in the doorway to smile again, and then went up to my room.

I didn't know when I had felt more content, more happy. I made sure to follow my father's recipe exactly, measuring his ingredients carefully, and then put the lasagna in the oven. After that, I worked on the salad and got out some bread to heat. We had some of my favorite frozen yogurt. I planned to put some fresh fruit on it and surround it with ginger snaps for dessert.

Confident that we'd have a great dinner together, I finished setting the table and then went upstairs to join Kane and maybe start some of my own homework, but when I stepped through my bedroom doorway, I stopped as if I had walked into a glass wall.

Kane was lying on my bed.

And in his hands was Christopher's diary.

Epilogue

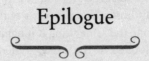

"I was bored with my history assignment. It actually made me tired, so I leaned back on your bed and thought your pillow was really hard."

I didn't speak. All I could do was stare. Every muscle in my body felt locked. It made him nervous. He fumbled with the diary.

"So I moved the pillow and saw this. At first, I thought it was your diary, and I swear I didn't open it, but then I realized how old it was and was naturally very curious. You look so upset, Kristin. I didn't mean to . . ."

"How much have you read, Kane?"

"Just the first page. What is this? I mean, who is this? Was he your mother's old boyfriend or something?" he asked, and put the diary down.

I picked it up. "No," I said. My mind reeled as I tried to think of different things I could say. Should I make up something? Would he see right away that

I wasn't telling the truth? I sat at the foot of the bed, still stunned.

He sat up. "I'm sorry, Kristin," he said.

I shook my head. "It's not your fault. I probably would have done the same thing if it happened in your bedroom." I looked at the diary. "There were many times when I almost told you about this, but I had promised my father I wouldn't tell anyone about it."

"Why?"

"It's complicated. It has to do with our family, but . . . actually, he doesn't like that I'm reading it, either."

"Oh. Well, I promise. I'll never mention it."

I looked at him. Should I believe him? Didn't everything boil down finally to trust? What kind of relationship could we have if we didn't trust each other? "There would be no way you could hurt me worse than if you did that, Kane."

"I understand. I'll never do anything to hurt you, Kristin." He smiled. "I'm still willing to write it in blood. Why exactly is your father so adamant about it?"

"Okay," I said, deciding I would trust him. "When my father was first inspecting the foundation at Foxworth, I went along, and he and one of his employees found a locked box. They thought they had found something valuable, like jewelry or even money, but when it was opened, this was in it."

"Foxworth? You mean, that diary belonged to someone who lived there?"

"Someone who didn't want to live there. This is Christopher Dollanganger's diary, his story about what happened in the attic."

Kane's face lit up with surprise and excitement. "I never believed most of it. I thought it was all just exaggerated and distorted."

"The basic story is true. Four children were locked in the house and spent years mainly in the attic. Christopher was the oldest. I've read up to here slowly," I said, indicating my bookmark. "It's not easy to take."

"Is that why your father doesn't want you to read it?"

"Yes. He's afraid it will have a bad effect on me. They are, as you know and I'm often reminded, distant relatives of mine."

Kane smiled. "I don't see how it could harm you. It's just someone's diary."

"It's more than that. There's no way for you or anyone else to understand until you read it."

"I see. From the little I did read, it looks like it's well written. He must have been a pretty smart kid."

"Very intelligent."

"I'd like to read it, too," Kane said. "With you, I mean. I would have to catch up to where you are, of course."

"Really?"

"Sure. It's obvious that it's important to you, and what's important to you is important to me, but I guess I'm also very curious about it."

"I don't know."

"It's better to have another opinion about it all, Kristin, and from the way it sounds, your father's not going to read it."

"Hardly."

"So?"

"We'd have to read it here. I wouldn't let this out of my house."

"Tell me something hard to do," he replied. "I'll tell you what. Once I catch up to where you are, I'll read it aloud to you. It's written by a boy, so I'll pretend to be him."

"You'd want to do that?"

"Absolutely. It'll be more . . . interesting for both of us. What is it they always tell us in literature class, you've got to identify with the character, care about him or her, to really enjoy or get into the story?"

"Yes."

He reached for the diary. "So. Let's do it the right way," he said.

I gave it to him, and he stared at it and then looked at me.

"We're going to do this secretly, I imagine."

"Absolutely," I said. "My father would be very upset with me otherwise."

"Then I have another idea."

The way he was looking at me actually gave me a chill for a moment. "What?" I whispered.

"We'll read it only when you're home alone.

Mostly after school but also on weekends while your father's at work on his new project."

"Yes, of course, but . . ."

He looked up at the ceiling and nodded to himself.

"What?" I asked.

"And to get into it, really get into it, we'll read it up in your attic," he said.

I didn't say yes to that immediately. The idea was both exciting and frightening to me. Kane was right. It would get us both into the story and the situation quickly and dramatically, but did I want to be in it that deeply? I was already finding myself identifying so closely with both Christopher and Cathy that I feared what he feared, cried when she cried, and felt the claustrophobia they both felt. My attic wasn't as large by any means, but it was still closed in and full of memories. Just like the Dollanganger children had to keep what they were doing secret from all but their grandmother and their mother, we would have to keep what we were doing secret from my father.

I had never kept anything as serious as this secret from my father. What secrets had I kept? What I had bought him for his birthday and Christmas? He knew everything I did at school and everything that happened to me there. He knew every one of my friends. Oh, I didn't talk about what girls talked about, and I didn't give him a blow-by-blow description of my dates, especially with Kane, but these weren't secrets so much as what gave me my independence and my femininity. He didn't expect to know or hear any of that.

What was more important, perhaps, was that I had never really disobeyed him. I had already done so by telling Kane what the diary was and how I had come to have it. Somehow, in the end, I had to believe in my heart that my father would understand.

"My attic is nothing like the one they were in. I mean, it's probably not even a tenth of the size."

He shrugged. "It's like being on a movie set. Movie sets are only suggestions of what places are really like, but you get the sense of it."

It was a weird idea, but I thought Christopher would approve of it. He'd want me to fully grasp what they had experienced.

I nodded slowly. "Okay. We'll start tomorrow after school. Right now, I want to get back to our dinner," I said.

"You need help?"

"No, I've done everything. Just like a man to ask afterward," I added, and he laughed.

"Okay. I'll start catching up. Call me when you want me to come down," he said.

I had to smile. He was into this almost as much as I was. "Put it back under the pillow when I call you."

"Yes, Mommy," he said.

I felt the blood rise in my face. Cathy Dollanganger had just stepped into her mother's shoes firmly and perhaps forever.

I nodded and started to leave the room. I looked

back. He was sprawled on my bed, and as crazy as it might seem, I didn't see him.

I saw Christopher Dollanganger.

Waiting.

For me to join him in the attic.

Read on for a sneak peek at what happens next in

Christopher's Diary: Echoes of Dollanganger

By V.C. Andrews®

Available in February 2015 from Pocket Books

Becoming Christopher and Cathy

The shorter days of approaching winter darkened every corner of my attic earlier and earlier every afternoon. Usually, when you think of yourself ascending, whether it's hiking up a mountain, flying in an airplane, or walking to the top floor of your house, you imagine moving into brighter light. But as my boyfriend Kane Hill and I walked up the attic stairway for the first time together, I could almost feel the shadows growing and opening like Venus flytraps to welcome us.

The stairs creaked the way they always had, but it sounded more like a warning this time, each squeak a groan of frantic admonition. Our attic didn't have an unpleasant odor, but it did have the scent of old things that hadn't seen the light of day for years: furniture, lamps, and trunks stuffed with old clothing too out of fashion to care about or throw out when the previous owners left. They were still good enough for someone else to use. All of it had been accumulated by those my father called "pack rats," but he also admitted to being one himself. Our garage was neat but jammed with his older tools and boxes of sample building materials, my first tricycle, various hoses, and plumbing fittings he might find use for someday.

The attic floor was a dark brown hardwood that had worn well and, according to my father, was as solid as the day it had been laid. He looked in on it once in a while, but I would go up regularly to dust a bit, get rid of spiderwebs, and clean the two small windows, spotted with small flies and other tiny bugs who thought they had died outside. I felt I had to maintain the attic mostly because my father kept my mother's things in an old wardrobe there, a hardwood with a walnut veneer that had embossed cherubs on the doors, another antique. Even after nearly nine years, my father couldn't get himself to throw out or give away any of her things: shoes and slippers, purses, dresses, blouses, nightgowns, coats, and sweaters.

Just like in the Foxworth attic Christopher had described in his diary, there were other larger items that previous occupants had left, including brass and pewter tables and standing lamps, a dark oak magazine rack with some old copies of *Life* and *Time*, some black and silver metal trunks that had once worn their travel labels proudly, bragging about Paris, London, and Madrid, and other pieces of furniture that had lost their places in the living room and the bedrooms when the decor had been changed.

Despite being thought useless and relegated to this vault, to my father they were almost a part of the house now. He said that their having been there so long gave them squatters' rights. It really didn't matter whether they had been there long or whether they would find another home, fulfill another purpose. Memories, no matter whose they were, were sacred to him. Things weren't ever simply things. Old toys were once cherished by the children who owned them, and family heirlooms possessed history, whether or not you knew exactly what that history was. It didn't surprise me that a man who built and restored homes had such respect for what was in them. I just hadn't paid much attention to any of it until now.

I was still not convinced that what Kane Hill had suggested the day he discovered Christopher's diary under my pillow was a good idea. At first, I suspected that he might be playing with me, humoring me, when he had said he would read it aloud to me, pretending to be Christopher Dollanganger, the oldest of the four children who had been incarcerated in Foxworth Hall more than fifty years ago. I didn't want to diminish the diary's historical importance for Charlottesville or in any way make fun of it. He had assured me that he wouldn't do that.

And then he had added, "To get into it, really get into it, we'll read it up in your attic."

The Foxworth attic was where the four Dollanganger children spent most of their time for years, there and in a small bedroom below. According to what I knew and how Christopher had described it, the attic was a long, rambling loft that they had turned into their imaginary world because of how long they had been shut away from the real one. The idea of reading Christopher's thoughts and descriptions aloud in a similar environment both fascinated and frightened me. We would no longer be simply observers. In a sense, by playing the roles of Christopher and Cathy, we would empathize, and not just sympathize, with them.

As soon as he had said it, Kane saw the indecision in my face, however, and went on to explain that it would be like acting on a movie set. Movie sets in studios were suggestions of what really was or had been, weren't they?

"This is no different, Kristin," Kane said.

I pointed out that my attic was so much smaller than the one in Foxworth, but he insisted that it was an attic, a place where we could better pretend to be imprisoned and therefore better understand what Christopher and Cathy had experienced.

He thought we'd get a more realistic sense of it. "It will be like reading *Moby Dick* while you're on a ship on the ocean. This way, you'll appreciate what happens to the older sister more, and I'll appreciate Christopher's words more, I'm sure."

Of course, I had found myself empathizing with Cathy often when I read Christopher's diary, anyway, but not to the extent he was suggesting. It was more like putting on her clothes and stepping into her shoes. In moments, I would lose myself completely and for a while become her. Maybe I did have to be in an attic for that. However, what frightened me about pretending to be her in front of someone else was the possibility that I would be exposing my own vulnerabilities, my own fears and fantasies. Everyone knew the Dollanganger children were distant cousins of mine.

What if I was more like her than I imagined?